breathe

my

name

breathe my name

R. A. NELSON

razor
bill

Breathe My Name

RAZORBILL

Published by the Penguin Group
Penguin Young Readers Group
345 Hudson Street, New York, New York 10014, U.S.A.
Penguin Group (USA) Inc., 375 Hudson Street, New York, New York 10014, U.S.A.
Penguin Group (Canada), 90 Eglinton Avenue East, Suite 700, Toronto,
Ontario, Canada M4P 2Y3 (a division of Pearson Penguin Canada Inc.)
Penguin Books Ltd, 80 Strand, London WC2R 0RL, England
Penguin Ireland, 25 St Stephen's Green, Dublin 2, Ireland
(a division of Penguin Books Ltd)
Penguin Group (Australia), 250 Camberwell Road, Camberwell,
Victoria 3124, Australia (a division of Pearson Australia Group Pty Ltd)
Penguin Books India Pvt Ltd, 11 Community Centre, Panchsheel Park,
New Delhi – 110 017, India
Penguin Group (NZ), 67 Apollo Drive, Mairangi Bay, Auckland 1311,
New Zealand (a division of Pearson New Zealand Ltd)
Penguin Books (South Africa) (Pty) Ltd, 24 Sturdee Avenue, Rosebank,
Johannesburg 2196, South Africa

Penguin Books Ltd, Registered Offices: 80 Strand, London WC2R 0RL, England

10 9 8 7 6 5 4 3 2 1

LIBRARY OF CONGRESS HAS CATALOGED THE HARDCOVER EDITION AS FOLLOWS:

Nelson, R. A.
   Breathe my name / R.A. Nelson.
      p. cm.
   Summary: Since her adoption, seventeen-year-old Frances has lived a quiet suburban life, but soon after she begins falling for the new boy at school, she receives a summons from her birth mother, who has just been released after serving eleven years for smothering Frances's younger sisters.

   ISBN 978-1-59514-094-4
   [1. Mothers and daughters--Fiction. 2. High schools--Fiction. 3. Schools--Fiction. 4. Family life--Alabama--Fiction. 5. Mental illness--Fiction. 6. Murder--Fiction. 7. Adoption--Fiction. 8. Alabama--Fiction.] I. Title.

   PZ7.N43586Bre 2007
   [Fic]--dc22

                                             2007003272
Razorbill paperback ISBN: 978-1-59514-186-6

Printed in the United States of America

breathe
my
name

when I lived in fireless

Today the blackbirds are watching us from the power line. I don't like them watching me. Momma says blackbirds are not really birds; they are people who have died and come back as birds. They want to see what happens to us after they are gone.

"In Fireless, every creature knows all about you, even birds," Momma says. "Even spiders."

Fireless is the country where we live. Every day Momma teaches us something new about it. Today she is carrying a blue Mason jar from the kitchen. I take her other hand, and we walk past the well pump, Tan and Ninny and Momma and me. A little cloud of gnats is floating over the pail Momma hung up that she said is just for pretend. I wish the water in the pail wasn't pretend water. But I can get some at the creek.

The grass in the yard is long. Daddy mows it, but Daddy has been away a long time. He said he will be back in time for my birthday. I'm going to be seven years old. I wonder what he will bring me.

It's hard to walk through the long grass. The grass holds the ground so tightly—I know this grass—you can't dig in it unless you're really big and strong like Momma. I have tried. All you can do is cut it with the shovel into little grassy fingernails.

I can hear last year's pig corn rattling in the field. But we don't go that way. We turn and walk up the drive to where the pin oak trees run beside the creek. The creek bank is not very steep, but we walk slowly down to the water so Ninny won't fall. Momma lets go of my hand and takes her big shoes off and puts them on the bank. She rolls her jeans up and steps out into the water.

"I'm the queen," she says, holding her long arms up. "The Queen of Fireless." The jar is very blue in the sun. Momma puts her arms down and looks at me. "You are my maidservant, Shine. All that we survey are our subjects. Even the crawdads. Come and see them."

Shine is my name in Fireless. Tan and Ninny are Fireless names too. Tan and me help Ninny take her shoes off; then we take our shoes off and go into the water too. The water is very cold. But it feels good. Momma bends down in the creek and dips her big knees in the water, kneeling to where her face is just as high as my face.

"Let me show you how to catch crawdads, Shine," she says. She pushes the Mason jar under the water, letting it fill, *blub blub blub.* "You put the jar behind them. Then you *scare* them." She reaches out with her big hand, fingers spread, fingernails shiny in the wet sunshine, and the crawdads scoot backwards, right into the jar.

Tan laughs so hard, she just about pees herself. "See?" Momma says, holding up the jar with the crawdads. "Everything knows about fear."

And it's true. I've seen spiders, the smallest spider you can see, little bitty red ones smaller than a freckle—they run like crazy if you put your finger down next to them. Their fear is as big as any fear in the whole world.

When she talks about Fireless, I watch Momma's eyes. That is the way you tell if it's going to be okay. If her eyes change, that's when I get afraid. I hope it's going to be okay today. I keep looking at her eyes as she crawls around in the creek with the jar. Momma is good at scaring things.

one

Eleven years later, somewhere out in the dark, a siren starts wailing. I wish they knew what this does to me. The sound of ambulances always reminds me there are monsters loose on the earth. They come past our house a lot, especially at night.

Somebody incredibly old must live on our street. So old they nearly die about once every couple of weeks, and the ambulance comes screaming in at the last minute and saves them over and over again. It's like the whole world is set up to save that one person and keep saving them over and over, even though they have already lived their whole life. It almost doesn't seem fair. Not after she did what she did.

In the night, in my imagination, there is no light where she is. Momma moves on the tips of her big fingers, scrabbling along on a dirty concrete floor like a spider. She is a spider. That's what she has become.

Maybe that's what she always was. Only none of us knew, because she kept it hidden. And through everything, all the times she was kissing us or playing games with us or being the queen of our pretend kingdom, really she was a spider underneath everything, just itching to break free. And every night the stiff little spidery hairs were coming to the surface, and she had to be careful to pluck them off each morning so that no one would suspect she was really a spider. Toward the end she began to smell different too. That was her spider smell coming out.

But still none of us knew. We didn't know a person could be a spider. We didn't know that in the middle of the night she would crawl out of her bed and get down on her fingers and toes and climb up the wall and scuttle across the ceiling just to keep in practice, because she knew she would be transformed into a spider again soon. Now she gets to have her wish. She can be a spider all the time.

The clock on my dresser ticks. The street is quiet for now. And that is when it comes to me—the phone is going to ring. Someone is going to call in the dead middle of the night, the phone screeching and shrieking, instantly terrifying everyone. I will pick it up and it will be *her*.

The house is so quiet, the knowledge that the phone is about to ring is shocking, unbearable. As the minutes ooze by, I become more and more certain she is going to call. I can't believe the phone is not ringing. The space around my head is like a balloon being filled with more and more air; something will prick it soon, the phone will jangle like a scream and burst everything around me.

The longer this goes on, the longer the swelling goes on and on and on, the longer the ringing of the phone doesn't happen, the more horrifying it becomes. She's locked away; she can't get to me. But how huge the sound will be when she finally calls—I just might die right then. I just might. There are some things in this world that can't be survived.

If they happen, a hole is poked into another world, the next world, and you get sucked through.

But nothing happens. The phone never rings. But its not-ringing, its bloated almost-screaming, ages me a hundred years by morning.

two

I shake my head to make the nightmares sink to the bottom of my brain. Light is already pouring in through my dormer windows. I've got my usual Monday morning stomachache. Mom says I should eat something, but I'm too sleepy to eat. It feels as if my forehead is rolling down over my eyes. Dad calls up the stairs.

"Hey, Button, you ready?"

That's what he calls me, Button. As in, *cute as a*. It's pretty sickening. I've always been really tiny for my age. I'm a junior in high school, but I'm four foot eleven and weigh precisely one hundred and three pounds. Dad started calling me Button back when it was appropriate, say around first grade. I've asked him to stop at least seventy thousand times since then, but by now it's a Tourette's kind of thing.

"Almost," I call.

"Be still, Frances," Mom says.

Even though graduation is a year away, today is the day for senior class photos, and she's determined to make me irresistible. She gathers a batch of my straight hair in her lacquered nails, tugging painfully. We're sitting in front of my vanity mirror with the faux-aged silvering. In spite of my sleepiness, I like sitting here, looking at myself. When I'm sitting down, you can't tell I'm the smallest person in every class I've ever been in. Sitting here, I could be anyone. If I smile just right, I'm even kind of pretty. My brown hair is parted in the middle, curling slightly at the ends. My eyes are large and amber. My best friend Ann Mirette says I have a heart-shaped face. And Mom—

"Your neck is so beautiful, Frances," she says. "You shouldn't hide it."

—is always telling me I'm beautiful. This is important to her. I'm her oldest, and her only girl. Her one opportunity to make good on all those childhood dreams of fussing over a daughter.

"Sit up straight."

She tugs harder, trying to maneuver two plastic combs into place. When you're short and have hardly any boobs, this is the way people treat you: as if you are perpetually twelve years old. They don't mean anything bad by it. It's unconscious, protective. Especially in a case like mine.

"I'm tired," I say, trying not to slump.

"Didn't you get any sleep?"

"I guess. It's just—" I stop, not sure of what to say. We never talk about monsters in this house.

Mom pulls my hair even tighter as if to give shape to my sluggish brain. "I keep telling you, eat some breakfast. You go too long without food. Hypoglycemia runs in our family. Your uncle Phil—well—"

She stops, catching herself. I've been her daughter so long, she sometimes forgets there was ever a time when I wasn't. We don't talk much about family history. Especially things like genetics. Traits that might be passed down from one generation to the next. I scramble to change the subject.

"Oh—I almost forgot. I have to come up with a quote for the yearbook. Some deathless words to remember me by."

Mom jabs the plastic comb into a wad of my hair until it embeds itself in my scalp.

"Ouch! Not so hard, please."

"I've got one," she says, a bobby pin in her teeth.

"One what?"

"A quote. It's perfect for you. It's from Franz Kafka."

"Who?"

"Kafka. The writer who wrote the book about a man who turned into a giant, disgusting roach."

"A beetle," I say, remembering. "*The Metamorphosis*. It was a beetle, not a roach, Mom."

"Six of one, half a dozen of another. Anyway, here's the quote: 'From a certain point onward, there is no turning back. That is the point that must be reached.'"

"Wow." I twist my neck to see her face. Mom is forty-five years old, but I'm always amazed at how smooth her skin is. Her hair is blond and parted at the side. Her eyes are the color of cornflowers. "That's actually pretty decent," I say. "Where did you get it?"

"My Little Zen Calendar." She smiles and pats my shoulder. "Done."

"Thanks, Mom."

"See how gorgeous you are? Let's go show your father. Wait. Your strap is showing. Let me fix that."

"Did anybody ever tell you I turned eighteen?"

"What?"

My voice is pretty small, too. But I don't like to speak loudly. It feels as if I'm announcing something earth-shattering to the world when I have nothing important to say. Or maybe I'm just afraid the wrong person might be listening.

"I said thanks," I say.

"My pleasure. Now go eat an apple or something. You're too thin. You want some toast, honey? A bagel?"

As we come downstairs, sunlight through the Palladian window blasts me in the face, and I realize today is the first day of spring. It's gorgeous outside. But this kind of day always makes me uneasy. There are moments that stick in my mind that I can never disconnect from things like the weather, a certain type of light, or the smell of kerosene.

"Whoa. Look at you."

Dad meets us in the foyer, suit coat slung over his arm. He's a big man with a football neck; gladiator features; thinning, steel-colored hair. He played noseguard for Bear Bryant at Alabama, and it shows. His eyes are a hard blue-gray, and he can crack walnuts just by flexing his arm. But if you look closely, you can see the laugh lines. Dad doesn't laugh often, but when he does, I remember how much I love him.

"You got everything you need?" he says.

"Yeah." That's another thing Dad's been doing since forever. As if I can't keep up with my own things.

"'Bye, girl," he says to Mom, pecking her sloppily on the cheek, and we head outside into the beauty.

Dad drives me to school every day, which I know is pretty embarrassing. I've had my license nearly two years, but they barely let me use it at all. The interior of the Navigator smells of vanilla and dings like money when he inserts the keys. Every week Mom puts new potpourri in a little cloth bag that hangs from the rearview mirror. It swings back and forth as we start down Springwater Street.

At the corner I watch the elementary school bus grinding its gears up the hill. It's full of messy-looking heads. I glance away, waiting for it to pass. Mom and Dad never let me ride in it when I was a kid.

"You're so small, honey," Mom used to say, patting my hair consolingly. "You'd be swallowed up in there."

The high school is less than five minutes away. We live in what used to be a sleepy little cotton town—before Interstate 65 came through—halfway between Birmingham and Huntsville. Dad's a big wheel with a dog food company here. We have a lifetime supply of dog chow, and we don't own a dog.

The name of our town is Bethel. Lots of Alabama towns are named after places in the Bible. Everybody here believes in God, or they're good at faking it. I'm still working on that one myself.

"Some people claim Jesus drives a Chevy," Dad says, chuckling. "Just don't tell us Ford people."

I'm pretending to listen but really just watching the sky. This morning the clouds to the east are scalloped like pink sand dunes. I can almost see the ocean up there.

We pass the Bethel Ready-Lock storage units, with their orange roofs and corrugated walls. It doesn't look like a scary place. But after last night—I can't help glancing at unit number thirty-six, the last one on the last row. I tell myself I don't care about the box that's locked up in unit number thirty-six. I don't care what's inside the box. I don't care that my parents won't let me find out until I'm twenty-one. Then the Ready-Lock is gone, and I can start breathing again.

Bethel High School was built of bricks the size of shoe boxes and has been around since the first stockbroker took a swan dive to the sidewalk in the Great Depression. A big cornerstone next to the main entrance says so. We swing wide of the parking lot so Dad can drop me around back by the lunchroom.

"The meanest, craziest guys always perch on the front steps," he says. "Like hyenas waiting for somebody weak to fall. You'd be a snack to them, Button."

I roll my eyes but don't let him see it.

"'Bye, Dad."

"'Bye, sweetheart."

I lean across the seat and let him kiss me on the cheek, trying to keep from inhaling his cologne.

When I straighten up, I see a man watching me from a shiny black Volkswagen Bug. His window is rolled down, and there's something really odd-looking about him—even from here I don't like his chilly gray eyes, his lightning-colored hair. I hold his icy stare a few seconds, then have to look away. I feel his cold eyes on me all the way to the door.

three

Hardly anybody uses this entrance. Just a trickle of introverted kids. Then it happens: somebody is actually holding the door open for me. I only look at him for an instant—it's a tall guy I've never seen before. Long and lean, wearing a striped pullover shirt and Levi's. I don't get a good look at his face.

"Thanks," I say, realizing I'm the only one who can possibly hear it. But it's too late—it would be humiliating to turn and say it louder now. He lets the door slap shut and falls in step behind me. Probably thinks I'm the rudest person on earth.

I can feel him trailing along as we make our way across the cafeteria. The chairs are still stacked. Steam is rising from the kitchen along with a smell of wet noisiness. I walk; he follows. Breathing.

His attention has to be focused on my body—I don't mean sexually, I mean that he *has* to look at me: there's nothing else to look at. The thought is like tiny acupuncture needles prickling the back of my neck. I hear his heavy footsteps but don't want to turn around. I'm conscious of my legs moving a little faster. I wish for once I had overruled my dad and come in the front door.

"Hey," he says.

I'm not sure what to say, so I just keep walking.

"Could I ask you about something?" the guy says.

I'm a little surprised. His voice is low and honey smooth, but without a hint of deep-fried Alabama redneck. Unusual for BHS. I stop and turn around and nearly gasp. The guy's at least a foot taller than me. Cute, in a retro kind of way—square jaw; small, interesting eyes; protruding Adam's apple; close-cropped, almost military-looking hair. His lips are full and turned up at the corners; I bet he smiles a lot.

"Hi," I say.

"What's it like here?" he says, shifting to his other foot. "This is my first day."

"Really?" I say. "It's okay, nothing special." I gesture at the greenish pipes in the ceiling. "Pretty old."

"You should see the place I came from in Metairie."

"Metairie?"

"Down in New Orleans. Talk about messed up—brown water in the drinking fountains, asbestos leaking out of the ceiling—completely *friable*. That's when asbestos is dangerous, when it's floating in the air. I guess that's what *friable* means—the asbestos is loose, *free*, burbling around our heads. Guess they'll have to fix it now or tear the school down."

"Really?"

I'm bowled over by the way he talks. It's all one amazing, drawling exhale of breath. Oh God—I touch the plastic barrettes in my hair—he probably thinks I primp like this every day.

"Yeah. It was pretty messed up by the hurricane," he says.

"Hey, what I really need is to find the office so I can get my classes."

He grins and the world feels as if it is cracking open from the force of his smile. I can't help it—I stare into his eyes—golden brown, sharp, intelligent.

"So what do you think?" he says.

"What do I think?" I say stupidly.

"Can you help me out? Show me around? I'm John Mullinix, by the way."

He gives me his hand, and I shake it in a kind of dream-like state. His fingers are warm, swallowing mine up.

"Frances," I say, looking into his eyes again.

"Excuse me?"

I make my voice louder against my will. "Frances. I'm Frances Robinson." I always hate saying my name. Frances is your grandmother. Frances is a dog. We start moving again, heading for the big double doors that lead to the main hallway.

"Nice to meet you," Mullinix says. "Just moved up here a few days ago from Louisiana. I'm a senior. I need help."

"You're a *senior*?"

"Yep."

"You moved to another school with only two months of classes left."

"Two? Hot damn. Down in Louisiana we go into June. Y'all are lucky. That means I must be lucky. I'm a very lucky guy." In his luscious accent, he draws the last word out: *guyyyyyyy*.

"We started in August," I say.

"What?"

I'm being too quiet again. Mullinix probably thinks I'm a freshman.

"August," I say. "We started August ninth. They move it back a little more every year. I think it's their sneaky way of transitioning us into a year-round program."

Why am I telling him these things? This strange new person who is about to graduate high school, who I'll never see again? A sea of arms and legs is suddenly pouring by, and I realize with a little shock we're standing in the middle of the hallway, surrounded by other kids.

I glance at Mullinix. He looks comfortable in a way I never am. Happy to be inside the skin he's wearing. You can even see it somehow in the cut of his chin. His eyes . . .

"Um, the office," I say, remembering. "You go straight that way, take the first left, then the next right, and it's—I don't know—about halfway down on the right. You'll see the name by the door."

"Let's see, first right, then left—"

"You've got it backwards."

"Hey, I'm not too good with directions. Put me down in the woods, I'm fine."

"Here, I'm sorry, just let me show you." I start walking again. "It's actually a pretty easy school to figure out."

"Great, thanks."

I take him the whole way, weaving through all the kids, conscious especially of the girls who are gawking at us, until we're standing outside the office door.

"Ms. Peavy, she does all the scheduling," I say. "She's kind of . . . big, and has superthick black hair. She's really nice.

She'll help you. Anyhow, it was nice meeting you."

"What do you have first period?"

"Period? Oh, you mean first block. That's how we do it here. Chemistry with Mr. Leakey. Yuck."

"Bad guy?"

"Not really. I'm just not all that great at science. Anyway, I need to get going."

This is not true, but for some reason I'm nervous standing here talking to him. Mullinix surprises me by taking my hand again, leaving it tingling, and watching me go. I get the feeling he wants to watch me the whole way up the hall before he goes into the office.

"Hey, call me Nix," he says, his hand cupped to his mouth to amplify the sound. "Everybody does."

I smile and wave. *Nix*, I think. "Okay," I say. Just before I turn the corner, I look back, but he's already gone.

four

I'm sitting in chemistry, still thinking about Nix, when the bell rings, shattering the blissful spell. I sigh so hard, my lips actually flutter. Why would he notice somebody like me?

I'm looking at Amanda Carter, how big and perky she is in that sweater. Word is, Amanda's newly expanded chest was an early graduation present. Her dad owns the local Chevy dealership (praise Jesus) and two chicken restaurants. At the moment, she's dangling her glands in front of Jamal Tinsley, the power forward on the Bethel basketball team. Jamal has a head like a lion; dark, springy hair gathered into a massive ponytail; and a rubber bracelet that says LEBRON.

There are thirty-one kids in this class, and I'm the only one who doesn't have a lab partner. But that was by design. Back in August I let everybody settle into pairs until I was the only one left. But my brilliant plan backfired. Now I get Mr. Leakey leaning over me, eyes on the gap in my shirt, man breath on my neck. I don't really think he's a pervert—he's just clunky and clumsy and makes me have to pay attention to all his social hang-ups.

Like today. Normally, Freaky Leakey is one notch above comatose, but this morning he's jumpy, agitated.

"Bet he missed stroking off in the shower this morning," Jamal says, and Amanda explodes into giggles.

Now I realize someone has just come in and is standing behind Mr. Leakey. I can't believe it. My heart comes up in my throat—it's the new guy, Mullinix. Freaky waits for the morning rumble to subside.

"Class," he says. He's got a bubble in his throat. He coughs into his hairy hand and tries again. "Class, we have a new student today who just moved up here from Louisiana. He's a senior, and his name is John Mullinix."

Freaky steps to one side and throws his arm up mechanically as if showing off a new car. Nix is grinning. Instead of sprinting for the first empty chair, he stands there looking at us. His grin is so spectacular, it's almost clinical. He reaches up and pushes back a nonexistent lock of hair.

"Thanks, Mr. Leakey," he says at last. Several of the girls gasp appreciatively. I wonder, *Has he seen me?* I pull my legs under me and sit up on my knees. *Over here.* Nix continues looking at us, comfortable, assured. He might as well be teaching the class. "It's good to be here," he says. "Before we get started, I want to make an announcement."

"What's he doing?" Amanda whispers to Jamal. Some of the other girls are giggling now.

"Because I'm the new guy," Mullinix goes on in his syrupy voice, "I don't have many friends yet. I just wanted to let y'all know there *are* openings available."

My heart squeezes down to the size of an unpopped kernel of corn. I slip my legs out and shrink back to Munchkin Land. The class is positively vibrating with embarrassment.

Nix doesn't seem to notice. He scans the room like a talk show host.

"Now, I know you're probably asking yourselves, 'What's in it for me?' Here's my answer: I'm very low maintenance. I've got my own ride out in the parking lot. I'm not all that great at sports, so I won't show you up. Best of all, my mom is French Creole, which means she can cook like nobody's business."

"Somebody put the bitch out of his misery," Jamal says under his breath.

Even Freaky Leakey is suffering. The expression on his face says *botched autopsy*. He can't speak. Rigor mortis of the tongue.

"One more thing," Nix says. "I don't like the name John. Too common. Too dull. Call me Nix. Everybody back in Metairie does. Or did."

I'm sure of it now—this is quite possibly the most gruesome flameout in the history of public education. Mullinix the Creole is dead, doomed, gone, lost. All in a matter of seconds.

Freaky does his best to recover. He looks around the room anxiously. You can see it in his large, drying eyes—the gigantic series of mistakes that led to him becoming a teacher.

"All right, John, er, Nix, I believe that's enough. Now let's find a place to put you."

I almost say the words out loud. *Oh my God.*

This is the moment after the engines cut out on a jetliner. I'm still in the air, still in one piece, but the outcome is mathematically obvious.

"There you go, Frances," Freaky says, as if he has just performed the most noble act of human kindness imaginable. "Now you don't have to put up with me anymore as a lab partner."

Nix beams. "And we have a winnah. What'd I tell you guys, a friend already." Then he puts his hands up, expression suddenly downcast, eyes *über*-apologetic. "Don't worry, don't worry, there are still plenty of slots left."

He makes his way back to the seat next to mine. The mushroom cloud over his head follows until it's over my head too. It takes every remaining particle of strength I have left not to leave the room screaming. I try not to look as he wraps his long legs around the black stool.

"Nice to meet you *again*," he says, about thirteen times too loud. Several people snicker. He sticks out his hand for me to shake. I take it, not knowing what else to do. "Thanks for all the help. Ms. Peavy was great. She fixed it up where I could pick my classes—and I thought, hey, Frances, chemistry, Mr. Leakey. *Perfect*."

"Um," I say.

"Good deal," Nix says. "Damn, this is going to be great. The thing about quiet people, they're generally smart as hell. Me, I'm always running my mouth. I probably get it from my mom. I bet it's a genetic thing."

I nod. What else can I do? I'm dying in parts; he's killing me piece by piece and doesn't even know it.

"What a dickhead," somebody whispers nearby.

Nix doesn't seem to hear. The clock ticks another second. Freaky Leakey is standing openmouthed in front of the class.

Finally—thank God—he starts going over our experiment for the day.

"Okay," Nix says. "Barking hydrogen. We did this back in tenth grade down in Metairie. Except our stuff wasn't near as nice as what you got here. Shiny black counters. Stools. We had to stand up the whole time."

"Um—so you just moved up here because of the hurricane? Did you—did your house get flooded out?"

"Nope. That wasn't it, really. It got flooded, but it was more because—well, we needed to come up this way for my brother."

"You have a brother? Is he in school?"

"Not anymore."

I wait for him to explain, but Nix pulls out test tubes and jams a length of black rubber hose into a beaker. I notice his right hand has a pale scar shaped like a painter's easel. The scar is shinier than the skin around it as it rolls over the bones in his hand. He catches me looking.

"That?" He holds his hand up as if I had asked for a peek. "Ever see the movie *Fight Club*?"

"No. I don't think so."

"You'd remember it if you did," Nix says. "This guy starts a fistfighting club where guys get together to basically kick the shit out of each other—excuse me. Anyhow, they're bigtime into pain. My old lab partner down in Metairie was a huge fan. He got a little creative one day with some hydrochloric acid. What a guy."

I don't know what to say about this. There is nothing I can say. We start barking.

houses of mud

Today in Fireless, it's raining. Momma promised us a big day, and now we're sad, Tan, Ninny, and me, standing at the window in the living room, watching the raindrops bend the grass. Momma is doing something in the kitchen, setting out pizza pans, banging them on the counter.

"When is the rain going to stop?" Tan says without turning around.

Momma doesn't say anything. There's a prickly feeling in the air, something that always seems to come with the rain. Momma has a pink dress on, and she's barefoot. She comes into the living room, making the floor squeak, walking on her big toes like a dancer. I like the way her dress spins when she turns. I check her eyes—they are very large today.

Momma smiles and throws the front door open. We can hear the rain hitting out there, a rushing, rattly, rustly sound. Ninny runs out on the porch and we can see the rain jumping, making dots on the cement steps. Now Momma runs outside too.

Momma is dancing on the thin grass in the rain, with us watching from the porch. She puts her arms out and her head back, mouth open, and dances in a circle, letting her hands spin. There is grass and mud on her toes.

"Come on," she yells. "Come out. This is the best time in Fireless. When they make their tinkling music."

"Pee-pee?" Ninny says, looking at Tan and pulling on her shirtsleeve.

"I don't want to come out in the fairy pee-pee," Tan shouts, starting to giggle.

But Momma is still dancing. Her feet are brown, and her legs are muddy. "Shine," she says to me. "You show them. You can do it. Don't be afraid. Come out, come out with me and dance."

I don't say anything, but I'm running out into the yard. The rain is cold, but not too cold. I put out my arms and spin, looking up. I can see single drops, thousands of them, falling from way, way up. Looking up is terrifying. The world has a ceiling, and it is dripping, but dripping from so high a place, it makes me nearly fall down trying to believe it. It is scary that there are places that high. I follow the high, high drops all the way to my face. But I have to close my eyelids, because I'm getting hit in the eyes.

"Dance. Dance," Momma says, taking my hand. "Dancing is the most important thing we do in Fireless," she says. "Dancing makes the world fresh. You can smell it after you dance in the rain. Aftonia, Queen of Dreams, commands you to dance, Princess Shine."

Tan and Ninny run over to us now, and we are all hugging in the rain and spinning. We stomp and dance and laugh, watching the ceiling the world has, feeling it reach down and touch our eyes.

"Now, *stop*," Momma yells. And she makes us all drop

our hands, pulling Ninny's hands down because she's stuck like that, reaching up; she can't put them down by herself. "This is just right," Momma says. "Here. Look what we have made."

She stoops in the clay mud, her legs shiny wet, the grass drowned, and scoops up two handfuls of clay from the yard.

"It's just the right amount of wetness," she says. "Tan, run and get the pail by the well pump." And Tan runs, and we can see her lugging the metal pail back. The pail is gray, but it has little patches of rust that look like countries.

"Hurry. Empty it."

Tan dumps out the pail on our feet, and we all scream and giggle, the water's so cold. Then we are down scooping the wet clay ourselves, dumping handfuls in the pail in flops. It's so sticky, it's hard to get it off our fingers, but we keep digging in the sloshy hole our dancing has made.

"Now go, go, go," Momma says, and we run with the mud inside to the kitchen table. It feels strange to be in this dry place now; we have been so wild and happy outside. We are getting the floor all wet and horrible, but Momma doesn't care. She makes us dump the mud from the pail onto the cookie sheets and pizza pans, and we start building things. We build houses out of the clay with pointed roofs. We build a castle with walls like big square teeth. We work very fast because the clay is starting to get dry. Ninny spends most of her time squeezing balls of clay, feeling it spurt between her fingers.

"Who farted?" Tan says, screaming and giggling when Ninny squeezes the clay.

"Now, into the oven," Momma says. And we shove the pans inside the oven, two racks of pans, a whole clay village. The kitchen is smeary with mud.

"How long do we wait?" I say.

"Not long," Momma says. "When they are done, the clay will be full of the fairy music. The music will be in the walls of the clay houses forever and ever."

She sets the timer and we sit down to wait, dripping and happy. While we're waiting, she is singing, and we try to sing with her, but we don't know the words.

five

Coach Jameson, who is built exactly like a balding, undersize, myopic bear, is counting heads in AP English. Ann Mirette is not here yet. I dig out a book and start reading furiously. Today it's *Watership Down*. I've read this book at least six times. If you've never read it, I won't try to explain it, because the whole thing with the psychic rabbit just makes it sound stupid. It's not.

But my eyes are running over the same paragraph again and again—this is not like me; I could read in a burning gunpowder factory. But I can't stop thinking about the crazy new guy, Nix. I'm afraid for him. I'm afraid for *me*. I'm not sure how a *Friend* with a capital *F* fits in at this school.

"He's hot, isn't he?" Ann Mirette says, slamming down next to me.

"Who?"

I look up and gasp. She's wearing glasses that make her eyes look shockingly enormous. I refuse to ask what she's doing with them; Ann Mirette has the sharpest eyes of anybody I know. I've always thought it's kind of funny that we're best friends. Ann Mirette's a big girl. Not fat, but tall, sturdy, strong. She's one of the best athletes in school and has the most amazing hair I've ever seen. Like billows on a crimson ocean.

"Come on, Frances. The cute new weird guy. I heard all

about him from Sabrina. That's why I'm late."

"You're always late." Ann Mirette bats cleanup for Coach Jameson in softball, so the Bear cuts her a lot of slack.

"True," she says. "So give it up, what's he like?"

"Cute, yeah. But he's kind of a head case."

"I heard! They say he's a crazy Cajun or something—"

"Creole, actually. Not that I know what the difference is."

"—*and* he's liable to say *anything*. Completely unconscious. Okay, tell me all about him. What did you talk about? What did you find out?"

"Nothing really. He's a senior."

"A *senior*. Who moves to Bethel freaking Alabama the last two months of their senior year? Was it because of the hurricane? Is he a refugee? Does he need somewhere to *stay*?" She grins, showing her crowded teeth.

"It has something to do with his brother. That's all I know, really. Freaky Leakey kept hovering around us since Nix is new."

"Nix. Damn. I love that. More."

"He's embarrassing. He wouldn't shut up. Everybody was watching us the whole time."

Ann Mirette puts her chin on the heel of her hand, pretending to pout. The glasses make her look like a depressed mad scientist. "What good are you?" She touches my black-and-pink shirt. "I like your hair, but what's up with this? You dress like an emo these days."

"I didn't pick it out, Mom did."

"That's your problem. No sense of your own style."

Ann Mirette, meanwhile, is wearing jump boots and a

light green work uniform with the words ARCADIA ARCHERY
stenciled on the back. Her family owns the range. She has
archery trophies three feet tall in her bedroom.

"I can't believe you wore that on senior pic day," I say,
giggling a little.

"What the hell," Ann Mirette says. "Give their shrunken
hearts a little jab. Yeeeeeowwwww."

Mom is always saying Ann Mirette has Social Issues. They
advertise a pill on TV that might help smooth her out. "But
who wants kidney failure, sexual dysfunction, or apocalyptic
diarrhea?" Ann Mirette likes to say.

Jameson the Bear grunts to let us know he's finally found
his lesson plan. This semester we're doing AP English poets.
Byron, Keats, Yeats, etc. He picks up his workbook and starts
reading in a growly voice more suited to a halftime pep talk.

"*Sailing to Byzantium*. 'That is no country for old men.
The young in one another's arms, birds in the trees / Those
dying generations . . .'"

"Snore," Ann Mirette says, head clunking over. "Wake
me up when I'm dead."

Later, we sit on a bench next to the track. The massive
pin oaks in their little grass islands have budded. I can smell
honeysuckle and exhaust. The parking lot is awash with kids
streaming out to their cars.

"There he is," I say.

We watch Nix coming up the walk. His cropped hair is
lustrous in the sun. I wonder if I should get mine cut.

"Oh my goodness," Ann Mirette says. "Sabrina's right—a
stone-cold keeper. He's beautiful."

"I like the way he walks," I say.

And I do. It's an unself-conscious walk, weight on the balls of his feet like an athlete, moving confidently through the crowd of kids. I watch his long legs and realize, okay, he *is* beautiful. Not so much in appearance, but beautifully himself. That's it. He's so okay with who he is inside, he doesn't mind taking you in with him.

"I love his hair," Ann Mirette says. "It's kinda—army-navy surplus. And that chin—mercy. Love it. *Love* it."

"He's not completely drop-dead, but—"

Ann Mirette jerks my arm around. "What're you talking about? He's a total gummy bear. Nix. What a twisted name. Oh no—" She laughs delightedly.

"Oh my God."

Nix pulls out a key ring and opens the door of a red Toyota van, circa George Bush Sr. It's a dusty anachronistic bucket of dents and dings. But it's not just the age, it's the multicolored spots, some as big as my hand, pasted all over the rear windows.

"Now that's just *sick*," Ann Mirette says, still laughing. "How damaged do you have to be to put spots on your car on purpose? Shit. Beautiful."

I feel myself blushing. "Maybe—God, I told you. There's something wrong with him."

"Oh, he's messed up all right. A rolling freak show. And only completely *perfect*. You are so damn lucky. If you don't go after him, I will." She bumps me so hard with her shoulder, I nearly fall over.

six

My brain is tired when I get home. I sink into the couch and do absolutely nothing but think about Nix until my middle brother, Terry, comes in. Terry is fourteen and terminally pissed off for no reason. He can move his fingers like lightning on a Nintendo DS. For everything else, he moves as if he's underwater. His hair could have been soaked in bacon grease—Terry's in that oozy drowning-in-puberty phase. And Mom wonders why I won't go near the boys' bathroom.

"This place smells like butt," he says.

I close my eyes. "Please. Go away."

"Why does this place smell like butt?"

"Leave me alone."

"Suck a duck."

"Mom," I yell, but I know she's not home yet. Terry trudges away, and immediately the den starts screaming. I hate cartoons. I can't even watch them anymore. I don't like this time of day. I feel like I should be doing something, but I don't feel like doing anything.

Jimmy, my youngest brother, who is twelve, tears in wearing half his soccer clothes. Jimmy has no sense of personal space. He jams himself into mine. He never stops moving. Perpetual motion. He spends the great majority of his life looking for things like shin guards. He obviously has not had a shower in at least seventy-two hours.

"I'm hungry," Jimmy says, voice squeaking at the joints. "What's for supper? I have to eat right now or somebody's gonna die. I think we should do Taco Bell. Tell Mom."

"I won't tell her anything. I don't know what she wants to do."

"Taco Bell."

"We just had Taco Bell."

"Zesty Chicken Bowl. With armpit sauce."

"Go away."

"But I need help," Jimmy says.

"Ask Dad," I say, groaning. I just don't feel like it right now. I don't know what's wrong. Ann Mirette says sometimes I anticipate bad things when they aren't really there.

"But you're good at math," Jimmy says.

"I suck at math," I say, closing my eyes again. "Ask Dad."

"But it's old stuff."

"He's an old person."

"No. I mean it's stuff I was supposed to turn in already," he says. "He'll know."

I open my eyes and Jimmy is scratching at a skateboard scab the size of a quarter.

"God," I say.

I'm such a pushover. I let him pull everything out of his bag and hand me the papers. Five minutes later I realize I'm doing his work while he messes with ringtones on his cell phone.

"How was your day?" Mom says when she comes in. She

pretends to sell real estate. I really think she just likes to see the inside of other people's houses.

"It was okay," I say. "There's a new guy I have for a lab partner in chem. He came up from New Orleans. He's a senior— can you believe that? Moving to a new school two months before graduation? Oh, Wiggles and the Thumb are starving."

I can tell she's distracted. "Honey, do any of your friends drive a black Volkswagen? One of those little Beetles?"

"No, why?"

"Coming home from lunch I saw one turning around in the drive. Now, I don't mind if they come around, darling, but I would prefer it be when we are at home."

"Mom, Ann Mirette drives a Hyundai. Wait—a Beetle?"

"Yes."

I remember the man at school, the man with white hair and chilly eyes. What would he be doing here? Surely it was somebody else. Mom sets down some white plastic Baggies on the counter. "It's so hot for March, honey. Let's see— cucumber, cucumber, cucumber—"

I put the math down and help her put away the perishables. "Here it is. Did you sell anything?"

"No. But I had three showings. All of the same house. I knew this was going to happen."

"The one with the swimming pool?"

"Yes, darling. I told them not to list it at that price and say it includes a pool. The pool is beautiful, but the house is a complete wreck. I think dogs lived in there. I'm sure of it."

"Lots of people have dogs."

"No, I mean the owners *were* dogs. You wouldn't believe

it. Completely filthy. It should be bulldozed. But I know what's going to happen. We'll show it a hundred times and no one will buy. The upstairs rooms are seven feet tall. And the kitchen! Purple tile. *Purple.*"

"What's for supper?"

"Did you say New Orleans?"

"Yeah," I say, surprised. "His name is John Mull—"

Mom slumps. "Oh, pooh, I forgot the milk. And I was going to have mac and cheese with ham steaks. Maybe we could make this a pizza night."

"Okay."

"Pepperoni?"

I sigh. "Please get something different. We have it all the time, Mom."

"All right. Pepperoni with sausage."

I groan. "How about some vegetables?"

"Terry won't eat it. We'll get some of both." She has her hand on the phone, is speed-dialing the number.

"The new guy is really strange," I say.

"Who?"

"Nix, the one from New Orleans. I'm afraid he's going to drive me insane."

"That's nice. Yes. Yes." She's speaking into the phone. "Do you still have that five-five-five special? Three for five dollars? You don't. No! I mean, five dollars apiece?"

This is how it goes at our house. We could be anybody just about anywhere. This is the family I feel okay talking about. The other one, eleven years ago . . .

I wonder what Nix is eating tonight.

when momma goes hard

"Is Fireless real?" I say.

Momma is stitching yellow flowers on a shirt. I like to watch the flowers get bigger and bigger. She puts the shirt down.

"Of course it's real, Shine. Anything is real if you make yourself believe it." She bites the thread. I don't like the sound her teeth make.

"Tan said it isn't real, Momma," I say. "She said I was stupid for believing it."

Momma looks out the window. Tan is in the yard doing something with dandelions. I look. Tan picks up a dandelion, sniffs it, then throws it up in the air and runs around in a circle very fast. She does it again—I can see what she's doing. She's trying to make a whole circle before the dandelion hits the ground. Momma is looking at her. Momma's face goes hard, like the bark of a tree.

"Tan doesn't feel Fireless the way we do," she says. She touches herself on the heart, then touches me on the heart. Except when she touches me on the heart she leaves her finger there. I can feel the point of her long fingernail. It's starting to hurt. Why won't she take it away? I lean back and she pushes more. I don't think Momma knows she is pushing.

Her eyes are excited and big. When is Daddy going to be home? I don't like Momma's eyes this way.

She takes her finger away from my heart. Her eyes are starting to come back. She has been somewhere very far away inside. But she's coming back now. I'm rubbing my chest, the place where she put her finger.

"But is it *really* real?" I say. "Not just pretend real, but like in real life, Momma?"

Momma doesn't say anything. She stands and puts her hands on the window and gets very close to it. I can see a place on the glass where her breathing makes smoke on the window. Tan, outside the window, throws another dandelion up in the air and runs around. She doesn't make it. She throws another one. Still she doesn't make it. She almost gets there, but every time she doesn't make it. The flower hits the ground first.

seven

As cheesy as it sounds, I believe in miracles. I do. One happened to me once. Sometimes when a miracle happens, it's like lightning, fast and unexpected. That's what my miracle was like. Other times miracles are like a barrel filling with rainwater. The rain falls in; the water in the barrel gets deeper and deeper. Then one day it spills over the whole world in one big, wet gush. That's the tipping place.

Like today. I'm sitting next to Ann Mirette at the dreaded Ant Table. Sometimes this is the only place we can find a seat. *Ant* is short for *Antisocial.* On the other side of me is a kid whose name I don't even know. He has a misshapen Afro and glasses that make him look like a guy who secretly races hamsters in his basement. I scoot my chair a little closer to Ann Mirette's.

"Girl X will take your salad," she says. "But no dressing. Well, maybe a little vinaigrette."

"Sorry, nope. Like we even have vinaigrette."

"But ranch has thirty grams of fat per tablespoon. The idiots."

Girl X is the name of Ann Mirette's new blog. "It's short for *Girl Extended,*" she says. "Girl X is beyond appearance, beyond trends, fashion, anything. She's got range."

This is Ann Mirette's supersize dream, that someone—a guy, namely—is out there waiting for her. He will love her for her mind. Her three-point jump shot.

We start to eat, but there's some kind of ruckus across the way. Mr. Tim is leading Rickey Thigpen through the lunch line. Rickey's in special ed. Nobody seems to know what's wrong with him. He never speaks, never makes eye contact. His hair is cut tight against his broad skull, even shorter than Nix's. Rickey was built for earlier times, when strength meant everything. He's eighteen inches taller than me, weighs over three hundred pounds, and not one ounce is fat. Standing there in the line, his calf muscles look like flesh-colored pool floats. He's the prototype football god in a state where football players *are* gods. Coach Hindman's always bemoaning the fact that Rickey "would've made one hell of a DT." A DT is a defensive tackle. With a dad like mine, you learn a little something about the game, even if it's against your will.

"How y'all doing, how y'all doing, ladies?" Mr. Tim booms.

I like him. Mr. Tim is a black guy who is built like a linebacker. Ann Mirette says he's a competitive power lifter, but even Mr. Tim is no match for Rickey. We've all seen their wrestling matches. I don't think Rickey's actually mean, it's just that he could kill somebody without even realizing it. Last semester he broke Ms. Crawford's arm just by pulling her roughly through a doorway.

There's a vibe in the room when Rickey's here, a collected expectancy that is overpowering, like wind pushing ahead of a coastal storm. You can feel the raw concern of the lunch ladies; maybe today will be the day Rickey lifts the entire serving counter and dumps it in their laps. But everything's cool at the moment. He's grinning, smelling the food, mouth quivering. Mr. Tim heaps big mounds onto Rickey's plate, two, three, four times the regular servings. Then he steers him to a special table where Rickey can eat without terrifying anybody.

As always, Rickey sits up straight and rigid in his groaning plastic chair, ready to go. This is the one thing you can count on with him: lunch. He knows he's supposed to be here, won't leave without Mr. Tim. Hunger is driving his obedience. But today his pattern is broken. Our assistant principal, Ms. Wamer, who spikes her hair and gets away with it because she's a Yankee, hustles over and whispers in Mr. Tim's ear. Mr. Tim grimaces, then says something to Rickey, patting his arm, and hurries away with her. Rickey stays put, staring straight ahead. Eager. Smiling. Showing a little bit of wet pink tongue.

The vibe in the room intensifies, getting giggly and crazed. I already know what's going to happen—everybody does. Sure enough, Rickey raises his arms, elbows crooked, and brings his fists down on either side of his tray like twin sledgehammers. *Boom.* His plate actually hops from the force of the blow. *Boom.* Again. *Boom.* Again. Rickey picks up speed until the *booms* take on a familiar rhythm.

Boom boom *BOOM.*

Boom boom *BOOM.*

Boom boom *BOOM.*

This is what everybody has been waiting for. It's the rhythm of a famous rock song, one you hear on TV in football and basketball stadiums. The song is "We Will Rock You."

Boom boom *BOOM.*

Boom boom *BOOM.*

Boom boom *BOOM.*

The rest of the kids are picking up the beat now, led by a sprinkling of jocks, all banging their fists next to their trays.

Boom boom *BOOM.*

Boom boom *BOOM.*

Boom boom *BOOM.*

The noise becomes huge, challenging, aggressive. The teachers are up and out of their seats, arms extended, moving their hands down as if they could push the enormous sound to the floor. It isn't working. They're all afraid to go to Rickey's table. There's been a whispering campaign against him for months because of what happened to Ms. Crawford.

"Come on, Mr. Tim. *Come on,*" Ann Mirette says. "Get your ass back in here."

Rickey Thigpen grins in the center of the thunderstorm, desperate, alive.

Boom boom *BOOM.*

Boom boom *BOOM.*

Boom boom *BOOM.*

And then. And then. And then.

"Oh my God."

It's John Mullinix. He's clear across the lunchroom but moving quickly. He swims through the ocean of noise and marches right up to Rickey's table. He stands in front of him and stares straight into Rickey's face. Rickey is staring at a space over the top of Nix's head. The hundred-and-fifty-pound difference in their respective weights hangs in the air like an unopened can of whup-ass. I can't believe this.

Boom boom *BOOM*.

Boom boom *BOOM*.

Boom boom *BOOM*.

Nix slides into Mr. Tim's chair. He reaches over, actually reaches *toward* Rickey, and picks up a spoon from the jolting tray. Plunges it into the Kilimanjaro of mashed potatoes. Offers a bite. Rickey lunges at the spoon with his head, engulfs it practically all the way to Nix's hand. Withdraws. The spoon is clean.

Rickey's arms flop to his sides, and the booming stops. Just like that. Oh, the rest of the lunchroom is still pounding away for a few seconds longer, until a collective gulp of disbelief jumps the spark gap—this is actually, really, undeniably happening. Nix scoops up another bite. Offers it. Another. He's feeding this giant. *Feeding him.* Bite, bite, bite.

Nix works his way around the plate, offering a variety of tastes. Rickey grins ecstatically, still not looking at Nix, bobbing his massive head to the spoon each time. Nix lifts a swallow of lemonade up to Rickey's lips, gives him a good long drink, touches his mouth with a napkin. More bites. They keep going like this, on and on, until every last morsel of food is gone.

eight

I'm in the locker room, changing for gym. The room is a war of chatter and scents: who's going out with whom, lavender lip gloss, lime Tic Tacs, new clothes, tangerine body spray, sweat, Neutrogena. But most of all—

"He's a Cajun. That's what I heard. His family was so poor, they got flooded out and had to move north."

"Wrong. He's a total head job."

"He was handing out business cards in Freaky Leakey's class."

"No way."

"They just said one thing—*John Mullinix, Friend.*"

"Oh my freaking God."

"That is so not true."

"What is up with that hair? Is he a Rot-cee boy or something?"

"Yeah, I think so. But actually kind of cute, really."

"Kind of?"

All of this is washing over me, the lies, the half-truths, the whole ones, but mostly the growing awareness that my little discovery, okay, my *major* discovery, is slipping away, minute by minute. I'm worrying over this when Ann Mirette bounces in wearing a sweatshirt that reads THIS WAS MADE IN A SWEATSHOP, SO I GOT A REAL DEAL.

"Am I crazy?" I say, pulling on my shorts.

"Of course you are," she says. "I wouldn't hang with you otherwise."

"No, really. He's—what he did with Rickey Thigpen—he's *amazing*. I've never seen anybody like him—"

"I agree. Freaking *heroic*."

Ann Mirette makes a big *X* with her arms and skims the sweatshirt over her black sports bra. I wonder what it's like to have shoulders so broad, arms so long. Her head reappears.

"Damn, girl. You've got it bad. This is so monstrously cool. So what's your next move?"

"Quiet." I look around. "I don't know. Who said I've made any move?"

"You don't know. You've got the inside track, and you don't *know*? Let me tell you something—there are three hundred girls in this school trying to figure him out this very second. When they do—"

"I know, I *know*."

"Then do something about it. Tomorrow might be your last window of opp."

"It's crazy."

Ann Mirette starts stretching, one foot on the bench, expertly holding each position for a fifteen count. "I swear, Frances, if you say that word one more time, I'll—"

"But—"

"Don't question it. It's a freaking gift."

I feel my eyes cloud. "I'm not saying it's crazy to fall for him, Ann Mirette. Am I crazy to *hope?*"

I duck my way through the crowd of girls heading toward the gym.

fighting with daddy

We are going to the creek. I'm holding Ninny's hand and
Tan is coming along behind us. Suddle is in her crib.

"I want to stay," Tan says. She looks back at the little
white house.

"No," I say.

"No," Ninny says.

"But I want to hear what they are saying," Tan says. She
is yelling.

"I don't," I say.

"I don't," Ninny says.

Ninny copies everything I say. She is holding my hand
tightly, won't leave me for a minute. Momma is not feeling
good. Today is a good day to be outside when she is inside.
Momma says this is my *mother practice*. That's what she calls
it when she gives me Ninny or lets me hold Suddle.

"You're practicing to be a mother," Momma says. "It's the
most important work on earth." She is not smiling when she
says this.

Right now I don't feel like practicing. I don't like it when
Momma and Daddy fight. Because Momma never does any
of the fighting. She is quiet and goes somewhere inside herself, deep, deep inside, and she won't come out and fight,

and then she won't come out at all. Not until she can hear us again. Not until her eyes change.

Tan keeps her shoes on but goes in the creek anyway. She starts taking mud out of the creek and throwing it at me and Ninny. I don't feel like throwing mud. I would rather be drawing. I got a new box of crayons for my birthday, and I have hidden them. I want to pull them out and use them before they get all broken and lost. Tan throws more mud.

We're watching from the creek bank when Daddy comes out. He is in a big hurry. He gets in the red truck and leaves, going very fast, and the truck wheels throw up big dirt like feathers. I hope it's okay. To go back. To see where Momma is now. To see if we can get to where she is.

nine

"Saw you feeding your fat-ass boy in the lunchroom yesterday," Jamal says in chemistry the next morning. "How's that friend thing going?"

Nix shakes his head. "Not so good. So far you and Rickey are the only applicants."

Amanda shrieks with laughter. I shrink in my seat and rapidly flip the pages of my lab book. Lots of nervous snickers break out. Freaky Leakey is busy explaining electron shells to some right-brained kid at the front of the room, oblivious. All eyes are focused on Jamal. A tendon in his neck tightens and untightens. Finally he snort-laughs and grins. "Damn, Opie. That's cold-blooded."

A relieved laugh gushes over the room. Mr. Leakey looks up, perplexed. I wait for the class to settle down to its usual gabble. Then wait some more. *Say it*, I think. *Say it now.*

"That—that was amazing," I say, breathing a little faster. I make sure to keep my voice low. "What you did with Rickey, I mean. Really amazing. One of the most incredible things I've ever seen. How did you do that?"

Nix smiles lopsidedly. He has a length of rubber hose clenched between his teeth like a heroin junkie. I hope it's not the one we used to titrate sulfuric acid. "Easy," he says through the corner of his mouth. "He was hungry."

I shake my head. "No. Everybody knew that. God. How did you go over there and feed him like that? Weren't you afraid?"

Nix shrugs. "He's a big guy, all right. But I didn't think he would do anything."

"It was amazing. I've never seen anybody do something like that. How did you do it with everybody *watching*?"

Nix plays with a test tube, letting it roll through his fingers. "That wasn't the important thing, was it? The important thing was he was hungry."

"Come on."

He grins. "Okay, here's the thing—I used to be embarrassed by my brother."

"Why?"

"His name's Brandon. He's special needs, like Rickey. Only Brandon's a lot more high-functioning." Something in Nix's face changes; the goofy grin begins to freeze in place. He sets an evaporating dish on a piece of wire gauze over the Bunsen burner and sets the flame going with a little blue pop.

"Okay?" I say.

He doesn't look at me, just looks at the blue flame. When he speaks again, it's in a quiet, flat voice, all the Louisiana honey drained out. "For a long time it killed me. I thought it was so damn unfair—other kids got to have big brothers who showed them stuff, played with them. I had to look after mine. I got into fights in school because of Brandon. I hated—I hated being seen with him. What now?"

"Huh?"

He taps my lab notebook.

"Oh. Heat the evaporating dish for three minutes. Then we take it off and let it cool, then measure and record the mass of the dish."

Nix stares at the Bunsen burner, expressionless. He extends his fingers toward the flame, closer and closer, stopping just short of touching it.

"Believe it or not, there was a time I wanted to be the most invisible person on the planet," he says. "Once, at this really nice restaurant, I had to go to the restroom, and my mom sent Brandon in after me. I was . . . completely occupied . . . so Brandon shucked off his pants and did it—went to the bathroom in the damn urinal. I thought I was going to die. I was finally able to get out there and clean him up, but three guys in suits came in and saw us. My big brother bare-assed next to the sink, me with a stack of those brown paper towels. They didn't say anything, but they had these pissed-off faces, like I had purposefully ruined their dining experience. I wanted to stomp their guts out."

He takes the evaporating dish off the flame and sets it on the balance. Squints his eyes closed a moment. I want to hug him. Right there in Freaky Leakey's chemistry lab.

"I'm sorry. I'm sorry, Nix."

"But then . . ." he says, opening his eyes. His jaw loosens.

"What?"

"Brandon nearly died."

"God," I say. "God."

He looks away and measures two grams of copper sulfate hydrate into the evaporating dish. "It was some kind of viral infection—the thing about kids like Brandon is, they never tell you when they feel bad. If they're not bleeding or throwing up, you just have to guess."

"Oh no. What did you do?"

"I didn't do anything. One morning we just couldn't wake him up. It was the scariest day of my life. We rushed him to the hospital, and they barely caught it in time. For a few minutes we thought—we thought he was *gone*."

He puts the evaporating dish back on the wire gauze over the burner. I don't know what to say, so I read from the notes.

"It says to gently heat the dish gradually by moving the burner back and forth. Then we heat strongly for five minutes, or until the blue color disappears. We're supposed to avoid any popping or spattering."

Nix brightens. "Aw, what's the fun in that? I like popping and spattering. Especially spattering." It's good to see his real smile back.

I put my notes down. "So that's how you did it? What you did with Rickey?"

Nix slowly moves the burner around, watching the blue in the dish. "My mom used to have a Creole nanny named Mammy Ida. When I was a kid, it seemed to me like Ida was a hundred years old. Maybe she was. Skin like leather, skinny as a broom handle. I remember she always smelled like coffee and ironing. Anyhow, Mammy Ida always said you have to do something *right*. That's what we're here for. See, it could have been me instead of Brandon. I'm the lucky one. The shit he has gone through, and still he is happy every day. Every day. So doing something for somebody like Rickey, I'm not going to be afraid to do it. Even if I *am* afraid. If that makes sense. Hey, the blue is gone."

I raise my goggles and smudge at my eyes, trying to keep my voice from shaking. I check my notes. "We're supposed to let the evaporating dish cool for about a minute, then find the mass of the dish plus anhydrous salt."

Nix takes it off the burner and lets it cool, watching it. "Don't look at me that way," he says.

"What?" I didn't realize I was staring.

"Like I'm some kind of big altruistic deal or something."

"But . . . you took care of him. You didn't do anything wrong."

"I'm inclined to agree with you." His drawl stretches out the word *inclined* until it pulls at my heart. "Nope, I didn't do anything wrong. Lots of people don't do anything wrong."

"But—"

My heart feels as if it is expanding, filling with tenderness. I could listen to him say the words *altruistic deal* over and over again.

"It's selfish, really," Nix says. "Using the bad, scary things that happen to you as an excuse to be your real self."

I feel myself coloring. "Why? If something horrible happens to you, it's got to have an effect, doesn't it? You can't just go around acting like it never happened, like you didn't— you know—learn something from it."

"But it's easier," Nix says. "People feel sorry for you. You can even act a little crazy, and they cut you some slack."

I wonder what he would say if he knew about my mother. He grins wickedly, but I'm the only one who sees it. Maybe this will be the grin he saves for me. I'm overcome with the need to touch him. I pick up the crucible tongs instead.

ten

We're done, just cleaning up. Freaky will be collecting our lab books soon. I can't believe the block is already over. I want to keep talking.

"What about your father?" I say. "You never mention him."

Nix runs his tongue over his bottom lip, morphing the smile into something else. A sad, distant look.

"He—he's gone."

"Divorced?"

"Gone."

"Don't you ever see him?"

"No."

"Wow. I'm sorry. I didn't mean to—"

"I once read an article that said over eighty percent of families with special-needs kids end up with the parents splitting up," Nix says. "It's too much. Too hard. The tension and the shit and the guilt. But we always figured it was different with Brandon. Like he kind of held us together."

"Oh."

"But I guess in the end—well."

"I'm sorry."

He leans back until his stool squeaks, putting his hands behind his head. His eyes are shining. "Guess what?"

"Um—what?"

"Did I tell you that Mammy Ida was kind of psychic? No, really. She used the bones of a golden eagle to foretell the future. Got them from a Crow Indian chief. But I don't need bones. I can predict the future with nothing but pure mind power."

I smile, feeling myself starting to blush. "Okay."

"Yeah. Like right now, I'm going to ask you out, and I predict that you will say *yes*."

I feel as if I'm going to faint. My head is not just swimming, it's crossing the English Channel.

"Um—"

"See, it's the perfect time to ask," Nix says. "I don't know how much longer I can make you feel this sorry for me."

"I—um, I mean. Do you really—?"

"Do I? Yes, I do. I want to go out with you, Frances. A movie, pizza, something like that. How about it?"

"Okay." My voice has turned into the voice of a woman whispering through a crack in a stone wall.

"Huh?"

"Yes. Yes, I'll go."

"Thanks," Nix says, sitting up straight again. He touches my fingers, making me almost flinch with pleasure. "One point oh eight grams."

"What?"

"The mass, how much it weighs."

the bullard

"That's where he goes," Momma says, pointing with her long finger. "He comes from over there. Let's look."

"Who?" I say.

We follow along behind her, Ninny and Tan and me. Where she's pointing is where the sun goes down. It always sits right there, on the other side of the sassafras tree, white and squashy and blazing. And I can only watch the outside edges of it, or it burns up all your eyeballs, Tan says. Is Momma talking about the sun?

"Come here," she says.

The sun moves, gets a little flatter, smushing down into the hills, and the light beams shoot off in different ways, and now I can see it. There is a stump there. The biggest stump ever, sitting by itself at the edge of the woods.

Momma takes us over to see it. The stump is almost taller than me, and it spreads its roots over the whole ground around it. It's hollow up on top. I have to climb up to it, stepping on the big, hard roots and pulling myself up its side.

"This is where the *Bullard* lives," Momma says. "This is its home. The Bullard climbs out of its home every night. It climbs out and comes looking around. It wants to get into Fireless."

I stick my head over, and everything inside the stump is black. I'm hanging onto the top of it, and the insides are all black. The stump stinks of moss and old woody water. Tan climbs up with me and drops a stick in, and the blackness moves, and I can see Tan's head all rippled and moving in the water. It scares me. I don't like looking down into this place. If I fall into it, my legs will be sticking up over my head, and my face will be in the black water. I pull my head back.

"What is it?" Tan says, very excited. "What is the Bullard?" She's straining, trying to lift herself up to the top of the stump so she can keep looking down into the water. Ninny is still hanging onto the roots. That is as far as she can climb. "I can't see anything, Momma," Tan says. "I can see my face, but I can't see the Bullard. Where is it?"

"The Bullard is down there," Momma says. "Don't look too long, Tan. I don't want the Bullard to see you. If the Bullard sees you, it will remember you, and when it comes out at night, it will know you are somewhere up here and come looking to find you."

This is the scariest thing ever. I'm looking around. Everything is still and green, and the sun has mostly gone away. But the leaves are shaking in the trees. I don't like thinking about something—something called a Bullard coming up here after dark. Actually walking around up here. Looking for me and Tan and Ninny.

"What is it?" I say, trying not to sound so afraid.

"The Bullard," Momma says.

"But what does it look like?"

I straighten up from the stump, and Momma holds up

her arms without saying anything. She holds her arms up more and more, making herself bigger and bigger.

"Is that how big it is?" Tan says, excited. "Is it a *monster?*"

Momma doesn't say anything. She drops her arms now and opens her mouth, pulling her lips up away from her teeth, until a sound comes out of her that is not like any sound I've ever heard—a growling, snarling sound, like an animal in the forest, but worse than that. Worse than anything. And Momma's eyes are flat and square, and the sound comes out of her and out of her until I know she is not going to change back, ever.

"No," I say. "Stop. No more, Momma."

"Yes, yes, yes," Tan says, jumping up and down next to the stump. She starts hitting Momma with her fists, hitting her legs. "Get her," Tan screams. "Get the Bullard."

I'm backing away, saying, "Stop it, please stop it, Momma. I don't like you like this."

But Momma keeps coming toward us. Ninny is trying to make her body hook itself together with mine, pushing up into me, her fingers in her mouth, and her other hand grabbing my hand, trying to touch every part of me. Tan is hitting Momma, but it's not a fighting kind of hitting, it's just hitting, excited; she's happy and excited about anything new.

"The Bullard. The Bullard is coming. The Bullard, the Bullard," Tan yells, hitting each time she says "Bullard." She thinks it's a game. Is it a game? I don't think it is.

Momma stops. Her arms go down until they are hanging. Her mouth closes. Her eyes are almost closed. They go smaller, and her face doesn't have all the lines anymore from where she was twisting it so much. We stand looking at her, our backs against the stump. What are we supposed to do, Momma? What is happening? How do we fix it? What do we do to help?

"Momma?" I say.

She stands there not moving. The sun has gone away; it's getting hard to tell one tree from another—it's all becoming just one big piece of dark.

eleven

"Mullinix," Mom says, tapping her front teeth with a violet fingernail. "It seems to me I used to know some Mullinixes."

I notice with a sinking feeling she's wearing her tightest, shortest green skirt, showing off her genetically perfect legs, the ones I couldn't inherit. We're sitting in the vaulted living room, and I'm doing my best to survive my parents giving Nix the third degree. The last time a date of mine went through this was when Bobby McAllister took me to see his sister graduate. Bobby nearly passed out. I was home before dark.

My brothers have been banished upstairs for the duration. Nix has lived through Dad's atom-smashing handshake and the tour of our house's wonders. At last, we're in the homestretch.

"Yes, ma'am, we're all over," Nix says in that delicious accent, arms spread wide across the back of the sofa. He's actually *enjoying* himself, I realize. I'm starting to worry if we'll make the movie on time. "There's a big bunch of Mullinixes over in Mobile. But Mom says our family name used to be Mullineaux. *Mullineaux* is actually from Manchester, England. The Creole comes from her side. She's an Abellard."

Abellard. The way the name rolls off Nix's tongue, Mom

is officially in full swoon mode, but for Dad the interrogation is not quite over.

"Button tells us you and your mother moved up here from New Orleans." The way Dad says it, *New Orleans* could be a synonym for *Land of the Deviants*. "I've been down that way a time or two. Played a little football in the Sugar Bowl. You might've heard of it." He laughs a little too loudly.

"Yes, sir," Nix says. "That's what Frances tells me."

"You follow the SEC? Guess you pull for LSU, I would imagine. The Bayou Bengals."

"Um—" Nix glances my way. "Actually, I don't pay that much attention to sports, Mr. Robinson. Seems like I always have my hands full with so many other things."

"That right?" Dad eases back into the cushions. "You work a job somewhere?"

"No, sir."

"School got you booked solid?"

"No, sir. Not really." Nix runs his hand over his hair. "My brother, Brandon, keeps us on the jump. He's special needs. They don't have many programs for older guys. That's why we came up here, to be close to the Sparks Center in Birmingham. Brandon's been cooped up ever since he got out of school. He needed to get out of the house. Mom works with the post office, so it was pretty easy to transfer. Bethel is as close as we could get to Sparks. The people there are great. Brandon loves it."

"Ever plan on going back to New Orleans?" Dad says.

"Maybe someday, I don't know. I'd like to travel some. Just see what all is out there."

"That right? Just what are your plans for the fu—"

"That must have been so horrible for you, Nix," Mom says, crossing her legs and cutting Dad off with a look. "I watched the hurricane on CNN for days and days. All those poor people. Everything so filthy. Babies in the Superdome. I can't imagine."

"Guess there were a lot of crazies running loose with guns," Dad says.

"Not so much that we saw," Nix says. "Just confused, scared folks trying to get from one day to the next. Help one another. We got through it."

"Help themselves to a big-screen TV," Dad says, barking out a laugh. None of the rest of us makes a sound. He recovers lamely. "Well, ah, all the looting. You know."

Nix beams. "To tell you the truth, Mr. Robinson, the media people kind of blew that part of it out of proportion. All I managed to snag was an Xbox and a couple of Dual Shock controllers."

"He's kidding!" I practically shriek.

"Well, I guess your movie's probably about to start, honey," Mom says, looking at me sympathetically and standing. We all get up, Dad grudgingly.

"Eleven o'clock, Button," he says. "And no alcohol. I don't need to mention any of the other things, do I?"

"No, sir," Nix says, experiencing one last kung-fu grip on the way out. "You have my guarantee."

"Eleven o'clock," I agree with a sigh, hustling him toward the front door.

"And don't worry," Nix says. "My ride's got the highest-rated frontal-side-impact rating in its class—"

I shove him outside.

twelve

Nix holds the passenger door open to the spotted van. "Here we go."

"Oh," I say.

He doesn't hear me. The interior smells faintly of french fries, but at least it looks clean. He shuts me in and drives slowly, almost too slowly; I want those spots to look like blurs. I'm afraid to ask him why they are there.

Still, it's Friday night, and a few minutes later we've left the van behind. We're sitting in the All American Café at the mall eating fajitas and Southwest egg rolls. I like watching him chew. I'm afraid I'm laughing too hard and talking too fast. *Slow down, Frances,* I tell myself. I want this to last.

We walk across the parking lot to Cinema 8. The lobby is full of squawking, twisting, posturing, hair-shaking bodies. It's a warm night. Nix is wearing a button-down short-sleeved shirt with a paisley pattern, untucked; I can see the curling tag where it rides against the back of his Levi's. Black Converse high-tops, no socks. I feel decidedly uncool in a tangelo-colored shirt with no sleeves, but no cleavage, either. Some of the girls here are sixty-five-percent skin and up, soft little stomachs showing above their low-riders.

"Blow job virgins!" a guy yells.

"Don't you wish!" a girl yells back. I pretend not to notice.

I'm already stuffed, but Nix buys pretty much everything. We get to our seats, the guys come in to check the exits, the speakers rumble, and everything blurs into a kaleidoscope of sensations. Somewhere in the middle of the movie Nix passes a napkin across to me and leaves his hand behind. I don't let it go for the rest of the night.

He has me home by 11:09. I don't think Dad will mind. But this is the part I've worried about most. The part I've dreamed about. The part I've thought and wondered and cried about, long before Nix ever arrived on the scene.

He parks in the cul-de-sac instead of the driveway and cuts the engine. "The farther from the front door, the better," he says. I can't see his smile, but I can hear it.

The lights are on above the porch. Are they watching at the windows? Would they do that to me? Something in my head starts to buzz.

We get out and walk up the sidewalk. I can almost see Mom's special place in the triangular shadow beyond the garage. It's a spot Dad cleared out in the sloping woods with a bench and a carved wooden sign that says PIXIE GARDEN.

There might be pixies tonight. I want to pull Nix there, take him under the redbud trees and watch the darkness. Everything is extra tonight. I want to be extra too.

But instead of moving into the shadows, Nix turns up the steep brick steps to the front door. Will he take me all the way there, up on the porch in the light, and stare into my face? Will everybody be watching, the whole street, all of them seeing what happens and what doesn't happen? Will he know this is my first? My ridiculous, insane first kiss, nearly eighteen years old, what is wrong with me—?

"I like this house," Nix says. "I really do. It looks like a house without anything bad inside it."

I can feel the bricks pressing up through my shoes and my legs and my back. If I get dizzy here, dizzy at all, I'm going to topple down Dad's impressive colonial distressed entryway. End my beautiful night in the emergency room.

Nix is looking at me. Into my eyes. Maybe he senses I'm lifting off, moving away; he needs to pull me down—

"There's a guy in my neighborhood," he says. "His garage is full of motorcycle crap. He goes out there just about every night and works on them. It's not so bad, except the light from his garage shoots right into my window. And some nights he revs the damn things up over and over again. It rumbles through your bones and makes you crazy."

"Why don't you—do you ever call the cops?"

"Mom went over there and talked to him. He really isn't that bad of a guy. It worked for a few nights, but he just started up again after that." Nix pulls his eyes away again. "This is a nice place. No motorcycles." He puts his hands on my hips.

"I've never," I say.

It's not that I stop. There is no other part of that sentence. That really is all I am able to say. "I've never."

"It's okay," Nix says.

"I've—well, sure, guys have—you know—but nothing like—not the real thing. Just—you know what I mean."

He takes me in his arms and puts his face next to mine, squeezing tightly. "It's okay, Frances. It's okay. It's all right. We're here. Don't worry. I'm not going anywhere."

He holds me, and I can see the streetlamp shining through his hair. I feel his warm breath on my ear. I'm standing one step above him, and it makes us almost even. I realize he thought to do it this way. We hold and hold. I don't want to let go.

thirteen

"That's it? He didn't even kiss you?" Ann Mirette says.

"Well, kind of. A little one. It was quick. Our mouths were closed. But it was incredibly sweet."

"Sweet, hell."

She has her hunting bow at full draw, graphite arrow nocked, leathered fingers just barely touching her cheek to steady her line of sight. Her arms are rock steady as she holds it, holds it, holds it, peering straight down what looks like a three-hundred-foot stretch of bare white hallway. From here the target looks as big as a fingernail. She lets the arrow go. *Thok.* Almost before I can see it fly, it's sticking in the target, dead center. She pulls another arrow from her quiver.

"What's wrong with the guy? I was expecting some fireworks. Something I could put on the Web."

"There *were* fireworks."

Thok. Another arrow drives home. "Bullshit. He can do better than that. Anybody that crazy, that nuts—"

"He's not nuts, Ann Mirette. He's not crazy at all. You just don't know him. He doesn't act that way all the time. And I told you about Brandon. We talked for two hours last night," I say.

"Great, two whole hours." *Thok.*

"Well, you know Dad, no phone after ten."

"Christ Almighty. He's got to lighten up a little. What did you talk about?"

"You know, everything and nothing. His family. His relatives. Stuff about New Orleans. He's amazing. Funny. Crazy."

"Did you tell him?"

"Tell him what?"

"You know—about your . . . your first family. What happened." *Thok.*

I feel all the air leave my body in one huge exhale. "Are you insane? No, of course not. No. Why would I do that? What would he think?"

"You'll have to sooner or later. Hey, he's been honest with *you*."

"This has nothing to do with being honest."

"You told *me*."

"And it took me months to build up to it. This is a lot worse than anything he has told me. A *lot*."

"I know. But you have to do it eventually. He needs to know." *Thok.*

"Why?"

"Well. I don't know. It's just a big deal. A huge deal. He'll wonder why you didn't tell him if you wait too long. It could screw everything up. You can't keep it a secret forever."

"I can try."

We walk downrange to retrieve the arrows. On the wall is a huge poster of Orlando Bloom in his elf getup from *Lord of the Rings*. His hair is white, ears gorgeously pointed. He has his bow at full draw, aimed right at you, as if to say, "Wanna say something funny?"

Ann Mirette pulls out the shafts, gently wiggling the points to free them.

"Nice spacing," I say. The holes in the bull's-eye look like the five points of a pentagon.

"So what's next?" Ann Mirette says.

"He says he's got a surprise for me."

"Surprise, hell. Tell him you have a friend who says he better get his ass in gear, or I'll do his earrings for free—from fifty paces."

She isn't smiling, but I am.

crown of thorns

Today in Fireless we walk out into the sunshine, and Momma spreads a blanket for Suddle in front of the crown-of-thorns tree.

Suddle lies on her stomach, pushing herself up with her fat little arms, head bobbing. She's trying so hard to hold it up and keep looking around, but her head is too heavy; it sinks back down to the blanket. She starts right up again, trying to raise her head and look around. She wants to see the world so badly, you can see it in the almost-smile on her wet little mouth. How much everything interests her, the way her dark blue baby eyes move.

I lie on my stomach next to her to see what she is seeing. The world is so wonderful and different from here. There's grass and old leaves and flying things that come over and around us. Suddle likes it with my head next to hers. She works hard to keep her head up and keeps turning to look at me. Her hair is so wispy and light, it's almost not there. In the morning, when we take her out of her crib, Momma rubs Vaseline on top of Suddle's head, making her all sticky.

"For cradle cap," Momma says. "It's to keep her scalp from drying out, getting all scabby on top."

"What's inside a baby's head when it's drying out?" Tan

says. And that's all she can think about all day. "Does it dry out and make itself hollower and hollower? Then maybe her head won't be so heavy, if it's all hollow inside."

I like it here on the blanket. The sun is warm, and there's a breeze. Tan and Ninny come over and lie down with us, then all four of us are doing it, lifting our heads the same way Suddle does. We look around at the grass and leaves and butterflies, then let our heads feel heavy until our chins come down, down on the blanket. The blanket is raised off the ground in places because of the thick grass. It makes little white hills on the blanket. This is our kingdom.

"Fireless is a new country, an undiscovered country," Momma says. "It's the Country of Dreams where everyone goes when it's time to sleep. But you don't have to go anywhere different to be in Fireless. It's right here with us, all the time. All you have to do is learn how to sleep while you're awake."

So we put our heads down and slowly, with lots of giggling, fall asleep.

When I wake up, Momma's sitting with her back against the crown-of-thorns tree. The crown-of-thorns tree has long stickers growing out of its side and all its branches. The thorns are shaped like a cross from church, and they even have little smaller thorns at the tips for Jesus's hands. Tan tried to climb it once and came down laughing and bloody.

Now I'm watching Momma. She has broken off one of the thorns. She's holding it against her skin, sticking it against the skin of her arm. She's sitting there not moving, not doing anything about it. Not smiling, but her fingers are wrapped around the thorn, and she's holding the thorn and not moving.

"Momma," I say, getting up slowly.

I'm afraid of scaring Tan and Ninny and Suddle. I slide on my belly across the blanket very slowly so they won't notice. Momma is still holding the thorn. The big part of the thorn is fat as a pencil. She is looking somewhere over my head, and that's when I see her push. She pushes the thorn hard, and the sharp point goes into her arm. The thorn makes a dent in her arm first; then I can't see the sharp point any-more—it's sliding into her arm, sinking in deep.

"Momma."

I'm almost to her now. She pulls the thorn out. I can see dark blood on the end of the thorn, dark blood going up to the fat part of the thorn. The blood is shiny in the sun and running down the middle of Momma's arm to her wrist. She pushes the thorn in again harder and faster. She takes it out and does it again, faster, faster. Momma makes a sound every time she sticks the thorn in. I can't stand it. I'm going to throw up. I can't stand watching what she is doing to herself. Her eyes are black. They can't see me, I can tell they can't see me, they can't even see the world anymore. She's stabbing and stabbing her arm and grunting.

"Momma."

I can't help it, I'm loud now. My sisters hear me scream. Tan and Ninny jump up, and Suddle starts to cry.

fourteen

Nix and I are sitting in the van in front of a mammoth place called Barclay's.

"A *furniture* store?" I say. "This is the surprise?"

A woman with a Matterhorn of frosted hair watches us through the front window. Probably hoping if she stares long enough, we will disappear.

"So what's your secret name?" Nix says.

My heart freezes—for a moment I figure Ann Mirette must have said something to him. No. She couldn't—she wouldn't do that. She's too good a friend.

"I—um—I—"

"Everybody's got a secret name, right?"

"Well—"

"It's okay," Nix says. "Tell me when you're ready. But it better be good. Or what else is a secret name for?"

"Okay," I say, relieved. "So what's yours, then?"

"Connery," Nix says.

"Connery?" I turn to look at him—I adore his profile: the slightly curving nose, strong cheekbones, tight hairline that makes a perfect little semicircle around his ears.

"My mom loves Sean Connery," Nix says.

"The old bald guy? The guy who used to be James Bond,

like, a hundred years ago? But you don't look anything like—
I mean—" I feel myself flush.

"I know. But I can do this." Nix wrenches his face into a
scowl. "Not a fan of the ladies, are you, Trebek?" He sounds
as if his throat is coated with Scottish river gravel.

"That's amazing. You do—you sound just like him. But
who's Trebek?"

"You've never seen *The Best of Saturday Night Live*? No
way. Mom's got some tapes. I'll educate you. Anyhow, that's
where the name comes from." He touches the bones in the
backs of my hands, rolling the skin over them. "This is going
to be really fun. Don't worry."

"But—what's the big mystery? What are we going to do?"

"Something special."

I look at the woman at the window again. "You're not
going to do something crazy, are you?"

"No fear. Trust me. It'll be worth it."

"I'm not so good with trust."

He reaches over and kisses my arm. His mouth is warm.
"That's cool." The word sounds three miles long: *coooooool*.
"So don't trust me. Just do what I say."

"Sounds like you have control issues."

Nix grins. "I have issues I can't control."

I laugh a little but stop the minute we get out of the van.
He puts the tips of his fingers against my back, making me
go first.

The front door is at least six inches thick and very heavy.
Nix has to heave against it for us to squeeze through. I can
already smell the leather. Loads of dark wood, chandeliers

like upside-down wedding cakes, dining tables you could use to play hopscotch on. The recliners are ranked like Roman legions, levers upraised like swords. The golden-haired woman comes over. My eyes are level with her name tag, which says GAYLE.

"Well, hello there," she says. "I'm Gayle, here to help you any old way I can. Was there something in particular y'all are looking for?"

"Hello, Gayle." Nix takes her hand and shakes it vigorously. I'm not sure she was offering it. "I'm John Mullinix. Call me Nix. This is my friend, Frances Robinson. The truth is, Gayle, we have no money. Not one cent to our names. But I notice that you finance?" I feel myself shrinking.

Gayle bites her bottom lip. "We sure do. One year interest-free for any purchase over two thousand dollars, or ninety days same as cash."

"We won't be able to qualify for financing either, I bet," Nix says. "We don't have jobs. In fact, we're both still in high school."

"Really," Gayle says, voice gone flat, only a little sugar left around the edges.

"Actually, it would probably be a gigantic waste of your time to show us around."

"Oh."

"Except that"—Nix points a thumb at me—"this is her *dream*. Frances wants a home of her own someday, and wants to fill it with . . . Barclay! Barclay furniture. It would mean a lot to her if we could just look around and fantazise some. Would that be okay?"

I feel myself flush and pinch Nix hard on the arm. But Gayle brightens. She gives her hair a little flip.

"Sure. I'd be happy to show you around."

And so we look. She shows us headboards with scroll-work, accent pieces with marble tops, wire patio furniture heavy as welded rebar.

"This isn't so bad, is it?" Nix whispers.

"No," I say. "I just wish we could be by ourselves."

After a good twenty minutes, Gayle is ready to grab a Diet Coke. She tells us to "holler" if we need anything and walks away with an exaggerated sway to her hips.

"Well, she's pretty damn nice," Nix says.

"Let's go while she isn't looking."

"No. We have to keep going. Take your time. There's so much more."

"There is?" I say. "So what are we really doing here?"

"You'll see. It takes a little while. When I was really young, my mom used to take me to places like this." He runs his fingers over the smooth finish of a cherry table. "I hated it. It drove me nuts. What's a guy supposed to do in a furniture store, anyhow? I never understood why she made me go. Until."

"Until what?"

"You'll see in a minute. You don't feel it so much here. Let's keep going."

"You sound like you've been here before."

"Nope. But these big stores are all pretty much the same."

The next room is extremely long and feels cut off from

the rest of the store. There are no windows here. The deeper we go, moving between the beds and dressers and mirrors, the more it starts to feel like a kind of expedition. As if this place has never been visited.

"I don't know what you want me to feel, Nix. It's—"

"Don't worry about me. Keep going. The best places are the ones that are the farthest to reach."

Just when I think we can't go any farther, a final room opens up with just kid bedrooms. Bunk beds and brightly colored tables. Chests of drawers with sailing ships carved into the drawers. It feels lonely here. Otherworldly. There is nowhere to go but back the way we came.

"Okay, tell me," Nix says. "First thing off the top of your head."

"It's the end of the world," I say. "There's nowhere else to go. It feels—it feels *sad*. Is that it?"

Nix shakes his head. "All this stuff, all these rooms and furniture—it hasn't been imprinted yet," he says.

"Imprinted?"

"Whatever people put on it after they buy it. Feelings. Energy. Spirit. Whatever you want to call it. Someday—this is what my mom showed me—every piece of this furniture is going to be sitting in somebody's house somewhere. Scattered, lost, disconnected. But right now it's pristine. It's pure. It's alpha. It belongs to all of us. We're connected. Mom calls it the House of the World."

I turn away, eyes burning.

"What?" Nix says. "What's wrong? I thought you'd think it was cool."

"It's—I don't know," I say. "I'm sorry. I don't know what it is. I don't know how to say it."

He puts his hands on my shoulders from behind. "Try."

"God, it's so big, I can't get around it. I don't know what to do. I don't have words for it. What I'm feeling. It's so good that—I'm *afraid* of it. Do you know what I mean? I'm afraid, Nix. I'm afraid of feeling as good as I can feel. I'm afraid of it—afraid of it coming out. Nobody has ever understood— not my parents, not Ann Mirette. But you—"

He turns me around and kisses me. A deep, deep kiss, his lips opening, tongue touching the tip of my tongue hesitantly, bringing it out, coaxing, coaxing. I'm here, my heart is beating. Everything is going to be okay. It will. He kisses me again, then holds me, my face in his chest.

"Shine," I whisper. "My secret name is Shine."

fifteen

The furniture in my bedroom is Mom's idea of *Southern Living*: an old cherry vanity; a tall faux-antebellum mirror; a high-backed chair, armless and covered in white fabric, sitting in the dormer as if to catch a certain angle of light. Twin valances the color of old wine hang across the opening.

I'm standing by the window. A cat, a yellow-and-black one I've never seen before, is walking across the pixie garden. He stops at the bench and looks up as if someone is sitting there, someone I can't see.

"I couldn't tell him, Ann Mirette. I came so close, but I couldn't."

She gets up from the bed and hugs my shoulders. "Hey, don't worry about it. There's time. You'll get there. It's not too late."

"I wanted to. I really did. God, I'm so afraid of losing him. What do you think he'll say?"

She lets me go and lies back on the white chair, swinging her jump boots. "How about maybe that he *loves you*? That it's okay? Do you realize how goddamn lucky you are?"

"I know. I know I'm lucky. It's maybe even a miracle." I

make a noise and run my fingers violently through my hair until all I can see are wispy strands of brown hanging in front of my eyes. "Shit. I'm *afraid* of it. The more I hang around with Nix, the more I'm afraid of it."

"Afraid of what?"

I don't want to say. She already knows.

sixteen

We're sitting in the grass downtown, watching the Bethel Spring Fling. It's an arts and music festival, mostly face-painting and crappy ballet. But the town square is sparkling, and the clover feels good between my toes. Best of all, a powerful emotional gravity is continually pulling my body toward Nix. He strokes my bare knee with a stem of goldenrod. The sensation makes me twitch; it's almost too pleasurable.

"So how did you get the name Shine? Who calls you that? What's it supposed to mean?"

I tug at a frayed piece of leather coming off the edge of my sandal. "Shhhh, don't let anybody hear you. It's . . . a long story. I was going to tell you about it someday—"

"Someday? Damn, I feel arthritis creeping into my joints."

"It's just—hard, Nix, it's really hard." Maybe I can start by skirting around the edges of it. "Have you ever read *The Time Machine* by H. G. Wells?"

"Nope. What about it? I think maybe I've seen the movie."

"In *The Time Machine* the main guy travels eight hundred thousand years into the future, where he finds a race of people called the Eloi."

"Just a minute. Ee-low-eye?" Nix passes me a paper cup of sweet tea and a hamburger on a Chinette plate. The pleasant aroma of grilled hot dogs wafts by. I take a big bite, savoring the charred taste.

"God, I didn't know I was so hungry. Yeah, I think that's how you pronounce it. Okay, so the Eloi—they're docile and childlike and really kind of innocently stupid. They run around like kids, playing all day, eating fruit straight off the trees, dressing in loincloths—"

"Diddling each other," Ann Mirette says. She's wearing a shirt that says MY PARENTS WENT TO DISNEY WORLD AND ALL I GOT WAS THIS LOUSY ADHD. She squats Indian style next to us with a sagging plate. "You always leave out the best parts, Frances."

I glare at her. "Anyhow, *Nix*, the Eloi live on the surface in this kind of a paradise. Everything technological has been allowed to collapse into dust. But—"

"Ah," Ann Mirette says. "There's always a big-ass *but*, isn't there? Hey, I like that. Big-ass butt." She jabs me with her elbow. I'm starting to regret inviting her, but Nix is laughing.

"So what about them?" he says.

"*But*—every so often, there's this giant horn blast, and the Eloi line up next to a temple and march underground, where they get *eaten*. By the Morlocks. See, the evil people have survived too. But they've moved underground. And they feed off the Eloi."

Nix has a smudge of ketchup at the corner of his mouth. I brush it away with my thumb. "So, Morlocks bad, Eloi good," he says, taking another bite. "I think it's bullshit, actually. I don't think society could evolve that way. It can't be that black and white, can it? There are too many shades of gray in the real world. Everybody has some of both, good and bad."

"But what if somebody is all bad?" I say.

"We throw their asses underground," Ann Mirette says.

Nix chews, thinking. "But it sounds to me like the Morlocks *decided* to live underground."

"Maybe they had to," I say.

"Maybe they wanted to," Nix says. "To live in darkness. Feed off other folks. Maybe they reveled in it, thought it was kind of cool deep down inside. It was in their nature. But nobody is all Morlock, right?"

"I don't know," I say. "Maybe. Maybe there are some."

"Maybe, hell," Ann Mirette says.

when it came

Tonight in Fireless, I sit up in bed with a scream echoing inside my mind. My sister Tan is awake too. I can see her eyes; I see them move as she looks to the window. Something red is splashing on the walls.

The red thing splashes again and chases itself around the room. It's some kind of light coming through the window, blinking and flashing. I get up on my knees and see there is some kind of car in the yard. But after I rub the sleep from my eyes I see it's not a car, it's a big white truck. It has spinning red lights on top going around and around like on a fire truck in a parade.

"It's a amboo-lance," Tan says.

"Amboo-lance?" I say.

"A amboo-lance. A amboo-lance comes to get the sick people and carry them to the hospital. I saw one in Jamestown. Me and Daddy were getting ice cream. You were in the Dollar General with Momma. The amboo-lance came, and the white men jumped out, and they got this old man in the drugstore and took him away."

Took him away. This amboo-lance thing takes people away. They are here to take someone away.

I fly to Momma's room, the one she shares with Daddy when he's here, but she's not there. It's empty; her covers are bunched on the floor. Light is coming up the stairs from the kitchen. Tan hangs on to my T-shirt as we go down.

We stop at the bottom. Some men in white coats are there, just like Tan said. They have Momma on a little rolling bed with wheels. Two men are there with her, and she's tied to the bed, moving her head back and forth. Momma's feet don't have any shoes. Her hair looks wet. Her eyes are closed, but you can see them moving like little balls underneath the skin.

"She's sick," Tan says. "Momma is sick. The white men— they're taking her away."

I can't say anything; I can only run to where they are rolling the skinny little bed out of the door. I slip and almost fall—there is something all over the floor, little wet places and lots of little white things smaller than marbles, everywhere on the wooden floor. This is all crazy, it's crazy; then Daddy is there, and he's got my arms and is pulling me back and pulling Tan back too.

"Tanya. Francine," he says. Then he pulls us to him and hugs both of us hard, squeezing so much I almost can't breathe. He won't let us go, even though they have Momma out the door now on the little bed.

"Now listen, girls. Momma's sick. But she's going to be okay," Daddy says. He smells of work and dirt and dust-smoke. "You understand that? She's going to be okay. She ate something she wasn't supposed to eat. They're taking her to the hospital, where the doctors will take it out of her stomach and make her well again."

"Doctors!" Tan says.

Both of us are crying. I am not as loud as Tan, I never have been, but the talk about doctors and the hospital makes my stomach hurt.

"Can we go with her?" I say. "I want to go with her."

"No, Francine. You're going to stay with a friend of mine. She's coming here right now to keep you. Everything's going to be okay. You'll like her."

"No," Tan says.

She pulls loose and chases the rolling bed outdoors. Through the doorway I can see them raising Momma into the amboo-lance, the legs on the bed folding just like the legs of a spider that is dying. Daddy chases Tan down and gets her by the arm just as the amboo-lance rolls away.

The lady who is here to keep us while Momma is in the hospital is named Aunt Dot.

"This is your aunt Dot," Daddy says. Aunt Dot smokes and has lots of bracelets on both arms, and her hair is up in a huge thing that looks like a golden hornet's nest. She looks sleepy sitting there on the couch, fussing because we don't have a television anymore.

"Daddy got rid of it," Tan says.

Aunt Dot has brought us all barbecue with white sauce. But Tan won't eat, and I can't eat. We're thinking too hard about Momma in the hospital. What happened? What are they doing to her? Is she okay?

Now Ninny is crying all the time while Daddy is gone. She's so small, just a face with big black hair on top. Daddy calls Ninny Baby Elvis. Dot says Ninny must have the croup, which Tan says is a disease that makes you cry all the time.

It's hard to go to sleep. The next morning when we get up, the little white things are still all over the floor. Nobody has swept them up.

seventeen

After school on Monday I invite Ann Mirette home for Mom's famous spaghetti Bolognese. The weather is beautiful, so she convinces me to walk. For once, my backpack is light. Coming up Springwater Street maple seedpods are spinning around our heads like tiny helicopters. Everyone is outdoors, checking on flowers, kicking balls around, washing cars. My impossible contentment has spread through the whole town.

"So, what'd you think?" I say.

"About Nix? I've told you a hundred times already. He's a doll. Strange, cute. And that *voice*."

"The first time I heard it—oh, shit."

"My reaction *exactly*—"

I jerk her arm, making her stop. A black Volkswagen Beetle is parked in my driveway—the same black VW I saw at school.

"Shit. It has to be him," I say.

"Him who?" Ann Mirette says.

"The weird old guy I told you about with the white hair. First he shows up at school, then Mom says she saw a black Beetle here the other day. Shit."

"Mr. Freeze. I gotcha. So? What's the problem?"

"So what's he doing here?"

"How do I know? Collecting door-to-door for embalming fluid."

"God. We can't just stand out here in the yard. I guess we have to go inside."

"Don't worry, girl. I got your back."

We cross the lawn to the front door. My brother Terry bangs into us coming out. He smells of peanut butter and barbecue chips. "Somebody named *you* is in *trouble*," he says and shuffles around to the garage. I go cold all over.

Mom's standing in the foyer. She has her hand close to her mouth, the way she does when she's scared. Her eyes are red. She touches my arm; her skin is icy.

"What is it?" I say, voice trembling.

"Don't worry, Frances. We're right here with you."

My heart drops into my stomach. "But who—what is it? He's been following me, Mom. Showing up at school. What did I do?"

"He's a lawyer, darling. Your father is with him in the dining room. It's nothing you've done. We're here for you, whatever you need." She squeezes my hand and looks over my shoulder. "Hello, Ann Mirette. You need to run on upstairs for a little while, honey. We'll get you when supper is ready."

"All right, Ms. Robinson." Ann Mirette trudges upstairs. At the landing she flashes me a thumbs-up and a sympathetic smile.

Mom leads me into the dining room. I see the man from the black car standing next to one of the captain's chairs. He's maybe ten years older than my dad, tall, with thick white hair, dressed in a dark blue suit. I can instantly tell he has that kind of obsessive hygiene you see in some older guys, as if keeping fussy about their cleanliness will hide all the systems that are failing. No five o'clock shadow, not a lock out of place, hair trimmed just so, an exact distance from his collar. He probably flossed after lunch.

The only thing that breaks up the picture is his fingernails. The whites of his nails are almost as long as the nails themselves. The rest of the nails are deeply lined and slightly yellow. I can't help staring at them as he talks to my father. As I come closer, I inhale a powerful jumble of musk, expensive apple shampoo, and shaving cream.

"Button, this is Mr. Carruthers," my dad says.

"R. C. Carruthers," the clean man says. His eyes are flat and gray. His hand swallows mine up. His skin is much warmer than I expected. The pads of his fingers are puffy and soft. I feel a ripple of disgust as the long nails slide over my fingers.

"Hi," I say, heart beating faster. "You were at my school, weren't you?"

"Yes," Carruthers says. "I stopped by the office to confirm some information I had acquired. I'm here about your mother."

"Mom?" A bolt of fear pierces my abdomen. I turn to my mother, not comprehending.

I can tell she's about to cry, but she's holding back. She reaches over to press my hand. "No, honey. Not me. Your— your birth mother."

I've never heard her use those words before. They sound menacing, something to be afraid of.

"I'm an attorney representing your biological mother," Carruthers says. "Afton Genovese Jelks."

He says it so matter-of-factly, as if this name is spoken every day in this house. As if Afton Genovese Jelks could be a first cousin, a kindly aunt, a favorite teacher. A tremor goes through my legs.

"I don't understand."

We sit down. Carruthers puts a briefcase on the cherry table and opens it with a formal snap. It's mostly empty, just a loose stack of papers and a few envelopes, with the tops of three gold pens peeping out from leather pouches.

"I don't—" I start again, trying to make the squeak of my voice a little louder, but my dad cuts me off.

"My daughter—you have to understand, Mr. Carruthers. Button hasn't seen this . . . woman . . . in over ten years. We don't talk about her—Ms. Jelks—in this house. We've always done our best to protect my daughter from that kind of thing."

"I understand completely," Carruthers says. He looks up, smiling now. I can clearly see his eye sockets beneath the skin. "Then we'll try to make this as brief as possible. There is nothing to be concerned about, Frannie."

"Frances," I say, but nobody hears. Carruthers takes some papers out along with one of the envelopes.

"Now, Frannie, this communication . . ." He taps the white envelope. It's sealed, but there is no address, not even a name. "This is personal, for you. Addressed directly to you. Ms. Jelks has been granted—well, perhaps it would be better if we go over the other one first."

He pushes a single sheet of paper across to me and waits to let me read it. Mom and Dad read over my shoulder.

Judge Henry H. Langford
Ninth Circuit Court of Appeals
Suite 5003
102 Peachtree Street NE
Atlanta, Georgia 30309

Dear Francine R. Jelks:

This letter is your official notification that your parent/ former legal guardian, Afton Genovese Jelks, is being released from the Clover Mountain Correctional Facility on May 22, 2006. Ms. Jelks is being placed in a halfway home in an undisclosed location.

You are reminded that the order, Ninth Circuit Court of Appeals, prohibiting Ms. Jelks from contacting you remains in effect with the renewal of subsection 8(b), paragraph 12 of the original court order pursuant to this matter issued August 22, 1999.

For the near term, Ms. Jelks remains in a treatment program and is being kept upon her release on supervised house arrest mandated by the terms of her parole.
You will be updated regarding this matter should the status or condition of Ms. Jelks's probation change with regards to the terms and conditions of her parole. If you require

further clarification of this order, please contact the above address and reference case #17738921.

Sincerely,

Judge Henry H. Langford
Ninth Circuit Court of Appeals

I have no reply. My throat creaks, and my eyes flood with tears. I feel the muscles of my face tensing as I fight to keep everything in, to smother it.

"I know how hard this must be for you, Frannie," Carruthers says.

"I'm sorry," I say. I swipe at my eyes with the back of my hand. Then a little louder, "I'm sorry. I'm okay. I just didn't know—I never thought about it, really. About her getting . . . out. Not after . . ." My voice trails away.

"I understand. Please forgive me," Carruthers says. "I didn't intend on coming here today to make you feel . . . uncomfortable."

"It's okay."

"Ms. Jelks—your mother—has been a model prisoner in the treatment program over the last eleven years. It was felt that with the remission of her . . . ah, psychosis, that it would be proper and permissible to . . . take the action they have taken. There is no danger. Let me be very clear about that—there is no danger whatsoever. She is being housed several hundred miles from here and will be monitored on a daily basis."

"Several hundred miles? Do you know where she is?" Dad says, fingers subconsciously tightening into fists.

"I'm not at liberty to say." Carruthers taps the briefcase, as if this somehow explains it. His silver watchband flashes.

"But how can they let her out?" my dad says. "After what she did?"

"I don't know if you remember the terms of Ms. Jelks's sentence," Mr. Carruthers says. "This is not a criminal sentence. She was found not guilty by reason of insanity."

"We know that," Mom says. "But I thought they said it would be better to keep her . . . supervised. That there was never any question of her obtaining her release."

"But there was," Carruthers says. He cradles the briefcase, almost seems to be using it defensively. "The key determining factor was whether her psychosis was considered to be in remission."

"But who decides that?" my father says, fists tightening again. "Why weren't we notified?"

"As you aren't connected with the original case, then—"

"But what about my daughter? Aren't there victim's rights laws, notifications—couldn't we have challenged something like this?"

"There are, but they aren't relevant in a case like this. Not guilty by reason of insanity. The decision was made to provide supervised medical treatment until the defendant was judged to no longer be a danger to society. Ms. Jelks passed a competency evaluation administered by the state of Tennessee three times in the past year. I have been told the focus is on transitioning her back into society."

"But how—?"

Carruthers holds up his soft hands. I find myself focusing helplessly on the tiny gray hairs on his wrist, how they roll over his watchband in gentle waves.

"Please don't worry," he says. "It's not at all assured that Ms. Jelks will ever be allowed to be released on her own recognizance. As I said, arrangements were made to transfer her to a treatment facility—a kind of halfway house—where she is continually monitored. Her condition—well, that's not really why I'm here."

He brightens, leaning back in his chair, and touches the blank envelope again, looking around.

"You have quite a beautiful home here." He looks at me again and slides the envelope across the table. "They felt— your mother wanted to send you something, Frannie. A letter. We petitioned the court and received a special waiver allowing her to do this. It's something she wanted . . . to do. Felt she needed to do."

"I don't know about this," my father says, leaning forward protectively. "I don't like this. It's sealed. Have you read it? Do you know what's in it?"

"The letter—whatever Ms. Jelks has communicated—has been held in the strictest confidence," Carruthers says.

"That's not what I'm worried about," my father says. "Does Frances have to read it? Legally?"

"Oh no, not at all. It's Frannie's to do with as she pleases."

"Throw it away," my mother says, starting to take it from me, actually getting her lacquered fingernails on it.

"No."

They're all surprised at the volume of my voice this time. I pull the letter to me, almost crush it to my chest. "Please. I want it. It's for me. I want to read it."

"Are you sure, Button?" my father says.

"Yes."

"Well then," Carruthers says. He slides another sheet over, a legal form, and unclips one of the golden pens. "If you would just sign and date here, please." He marks an *X* on two lines at the bottom of the sheet.

"Why?" my mother says.

"For our records. For proof of receipt of the documents."

"Why is that important?"

"It's just part of what Ms. Jelks has retained us to do."

I uncap the pen, start to sign. I stop, confused. "Which—which name should I use?"

"Your name," Carruthers says.

"No, I mean, my name before or my name—after."

"The name printed below the signature line."

I look. *Francine R. Jelks.* I sign it this way, but I have to write the name slowly—I've never written it before. It's almost too legible, doesn't look like a real signature. But Carruthers accepts it without a glance when I slide the paper back to him.

"Thank you." He stands with the air of a man with places to go.

"You don't have to see what's inside it?" my father says.

"No. It's client-privileged. Personal. We want to respect Ms. Jelks's privacy. Well, thank you again for your time, Mr. and Ms. Robinson. Frannie."

He says good-bye, obviously wanting to shake hands again, but I keep my hands on the letter. Then he's gone. I listen to the heavy front door shut and watch him walking to the black car through the dining room window.

eighteen

Now that Carruthers has gone, the air floods with the aroma of garlic and tomatoes. The grandfather clock on the landing is ticking so loudly, I can hear it one floor away.

"Okay, let's see it," my dad says.

"Don, it's her letter," my mom says. "Let me see it, honey."

"I want to read it," I say.

"You *can* read it," my mom says. "Just let us read it first, make sure it's okay."

"But I want to read it. I'm okay. I want to see what it says."

"Then we'll all read it together," Mom says.

"The hell we will," Dad says. He tries to pull the letter from under my fingers, but I drag it back against my chest.

"No."

"Come on, Button. We need to see it. For your own safety. Who knows what that—what she wrote?"

"I want to read it. It's mine. Mr. Carruthers said it's for me. It's *personal*."

"Well, yes, it is, honey. I'm sure it is," Mom says. "But what have we always said? Our house, our rules."

"I know, Mom. But this is important. It's important."

"Hey—" Dad says.

"Let her read it, Don," Mom says. "We can read it later, can't we, honey? What's the harm?"

I get up from the table and run up the stairs to my room and shut the door. The envelope feels warm in my hand. I wait a few seconds, but I don't hear them coming after me.

"Okay, so what's the deal?" Ann Mirette says from the bed.

"It's—it's—" My eyes are stinging with tears.

"Come on, spit it out. It can't be *that* bad, right? What'd the old freakster want?"

"It's really—oh God."

I settle to my knees on the bed, then fall over on my stomach, crushing the envelope against my eyes. I press my face tighter and tighter, feeling little crunches in my throat.

"Aw, sweetie." Ann Mirette slides over and I can feel her big hands rubbing my back. "Talk to me. What's wrong? What is it?"

For a long time I can't sit up. Finally I do, but I can't look at her. I look out the window. "It's—it's from *her*," I say.

"Her?"

"You know. My mother. My real mother."

"Oh. God. Oh, shit. What is it? Is it a letter? What does she say?"

"I—I don't know. I haven't opened it yet."

I wipe my face, take a long breath, then tear the envelope open, pulling out several sheets of paper. They are folded into thirds, invitation style. This is something she has held, I tell myself, hesitating. There's an energy in here. Bad energy. The pages are folded a little crookedly. I'm not sure I want to unfold them.

"I'm scared, Ann Mirette. I want to see it so much, but— what could she possibly say to me? That she's sorry? That she doesn't know what came over her? That she wants me to forgive her?"

"Then let me read it first."

"No. Wait. No. I have to. It's mine. Shit."

The thought of reading every word, this many pages, is like sinking back into a nightmare that I thought I had awoken from long ago. I slowly unfold the paper and look at the first page.

It's blank. Completely blank.

"Holy crap," Ann Mirette says.

I put the first page down, feeling tears starting again. Pick up the second page and shake it open. It's blank too. Third page, blank. Fourth, blank; fifth—

No. It's not blank.

"Toward the bottom," Ann Mirette says. "There's something on the bottom."

Something written in large, shaky letters.

I need to see you. Please come right away.

We have to finish.

the birds

My sister Tan is sitting up in bed. Her bed in Fireless is across from mine in the same dark room. She does that sometimes, sits up and talks in her sleep. She is saying something, mumbling at first, but getting louder and louder.

"Please make them go away."

"What, Tan?"

"The birds. Please make them go away, Shine. I don't like them. Please."

I look around. "There aren't any birds in here," I say. "What are you talking about?"

"The birds. The birds."

And then she is screaming and screaming and there's nothing I can do. I try to wake her up, but she pulls away from me, jerking her arms. I'm afraid she's going to rip the curtains down. Where's Momma? I don't know what to do.

And then it's me, I'm the one who's waking up screaming. Tan's not there. I'm alone in this dark room. I look out the window.

There are people outside in the yard. Many, many people. Standing out there with lights. Everything is bright, so bright I almost can't see when they point the lights. Some of the people have candles, and the people with candles go back and back, all the way to the creek, which is so dark I can't see it. But I can see the candles even if I can't see the people. At night they light candles and hold them up and sing. Sing so much, sometimes I can't sleep.

Now I can see Daddy running out of the house, shouting, waving his cap at the people by the big trucks. Why is everybody so angry?

There are things piled on the lawn. Toys and animals and flowers, and pictures, lots and lots of pictures of kids I don't know. Food. Lots of food. Daddy won't let me eat any of it.

The pin oaks next to the crawdad stream are tied with ribbons, so many, it's like a rainbow has settled around their trunks.

The next day a big black car comes and Daddy and some men, some very big men, push through the people and they get me, carry me outside. Women grab at my arms, crying and screaming. It hurts: they are pulling too hard, holding too tightly, and one of the big men has to put his hand in their faces. And the other man too. He uses his hands to get us through the people, and then we are inside the black car and I can smell them sweating and hear their breath coming hard from all the fighting.

The car has to go very slowly down our driveway; the people won't let us leave. Nobody can hear me—my voice is too small, even though I'm making it as big as I can. Why is this happening? How could all of this have happened to us? I don't understand it.

Then the black car is on the highway and we are flying away from all the people and the little white house by the creek. I wonder if I will ever see Fireless again. I don't think I will. I don't think I can go back there. Can you see us, Momma? Flying away like birds?

nineteen

I feel light-headed. I let the letter go; it flutters to the floor. Ann Mirette picks the pages up.

"Oh, shit," she says. "'We have to finish'—oh, shit. You don't think she's talking about—God, surely she's not talking about—you know."

"I need to—I think I need to throw up." I clutch at my stomach, waiting for the feeling to pass. There's a thump on the stairs floating up to the hall.

"They're coming," I hiss at Ann Mirette. "Put it away. Put it away."

She shuffles the pages together and shoves them back into the envelope. All except the last page. She slips it under my pillow. I hear footsteps outside the door.

"Not there! I don't want it under there," I say.

Ann Mirette pulls the last page out and throws it under the bed just as they knock.

"Hey," Mom says, coming in, smiling softly. "Anybody hungry in here?"

"How're we doing, Button?" Dad says, coming over and putting his heavy arm around my shoulders, squeezing hard. I don't say anything. I can't. I sit up straighter and hand Mom the envelope. Dad lets me go and stands, looking over her shoulder as she takes out the blank pages.

"Nothing," Mom says. "Look, Don, it's nothing. All blank."

"Let me see that." He pulls the pages away from her and looks. "Lord." He flips them over, examining the backs, then holds them up to the light. "Carruthers must've fouled up."

"Maybe—could it mean something?" Mom says.

"What could it possibly mean?"

"That . . . she has nothing to say. There is nothing she *can* say. It's all over. Probably that's what it means."

"But why wouldn't she just say that? Why go to all this trouble just to send blank pages?"

"I don't know, Don. I don't know."

"Crazy. Insane."

We all look at one another for a while, then they both come over and put their arms around me. I'm embarrassed, knowing Ann Mirette is in the room. We stay like that until Dad pulls away.

"I'll never let anything happen to my little girl," he says, staring hard at me with his big, hard eyes, voice breaking a little. "There's nothing in this world you ever need to worry about—you understand me?"

"I know, Dad. I know that."

"It's over, Button. I don't want any of us to have to think about her ever again. I should never have let that joker in the house." He tears the blank pages into long strips and stuffs them in his shirt pocket. "You know we would never, ever—"

"Well, who's ready for supper?" Mom says.

Ann Mirette jumps up. "Me, Ms. Robinson. I'm starved."

She grabs my hand, and we slide past Mom and Dad before they can ask anything else.

twenty

The greenish light of my cell phone makes the room feel like a trench on the bottom of the ocean. I open the curtains to let in light from the street. I was supposed to be asleep two hours ago.

"Why did you hide the letter?" I say.

"You know what your parents are like," Ann Mirette says. "They would've locked you in for the rest of your life."

"Oh, come on. They're not that bad."

"They're worse. Hello. They're overprotective as hell. I'd never see you again."

"Maybe they're right? I'm scared. What does she mean, 'We have to finish'?"

A long sigh rattles the phone. "Probably nothing. She's nuts, right? Except now they say she's kind of okay?"

"Supposedly she's in remission. That's what Carruthers said. But how can she be okay? How can she ever be okay? I don't get it. There's no way you can do something like that and ever be okay again."

"Take some deep breaths. You're completely safe. It was a long time ago. That bitch can't hurt you anymore."

I hit the mattress as hard as I can; it doesn't make a sound. "I'm not afraid that she's going to come get me. I'm *not*. I just thought I'd never have to deal with this stuff ever again. I hate her. I hate her so much. I wish—I almost wish I could do it."

"What?"

"Kill her."

"Frances. Come on. You're not the type."

"Like you know the type."

"Hey, I know some things. Take your mind off it. It was a long time ago. Read a book. Fantasize about Nix. Get some rest."

"How? I can't stop thinking about it."

"Take a good strong hit of NyQuil. Works for me."

I stare up into the strip of light the streetlamp is throwing across my ceiling. "God, what about Nix?"

"You should have told him already."

"But I thought maybe I could—"

"Get by with never saying a word?" I can see her rolling her eyes through the connection. "Get real. Imagine if he hid something like that from you."

"He wouldn't. But why does he have to know?"

"He'll find out sooner or later anyway. And then how do you think he'll feel?"

"What did you think the first time I told you?"

There's a pause. "I don't remember—yes I do. We were making that papier-mâché head for Myth and Legend class."

"The Cyclops."

"Yeah. You didn't like me," Ann Mirette says. "You thought I was strange."

"You were."

"Okay, but then you found out how deliciously cool I am, admit it."

"I admit it. But I wanted to—I wanted to give you something back. You told me all that wild stuff about your dad. I wanted you to feel better. So what did you think?"

"I thought it was very messed up. What else could I think? But that had nothing to do with you. That's what friends do, they tell each other the deep-down dark unholy shit. That's what you have to do with Nix. He's been there. He'll understand."

I roll onto my back and stare out the window. I want to put my face into my pillow and push. Sometimes I think if I push hard enough, all the bad thoughts will leak out the back of my head. This is the kind of thing crazy people think about. Their heads leaking.

"You still there?" Ann Mirette says.

"Do you think she remembers anything from the time before she did what she did? My God, Ann Mirette. I'm a *piece* of her."

"You can't help it. She's your mom."

"Don't call her that. Don't ever call her that. It's just that—it makes me *sick*—it makes me sick her cells exist inside me."

Ann Mirette yawns. "But is that really true? Somewhere I heard every cell in your body is replaced every seven years."

"But this isn't something that can just flake off like dead skin. She's in my *genes*."

I start to cry, but I make sure I cry so silently, she doesn't know.

"Frances?"

"I've—I've got to go."

"Tell him."

"I'll try."

"Is no try, is only do."

"Thanks, Yoda."

After we hang up, I realize there is no foundation to anything—the world, the sky, the universe. Nothing is under-
pinned by anything. We believe there's something safe under
our feet, when nothing is truly ever safe. I sit inside this
house with alarm panels, security codes, direct links to the
sheriff's office—what does any of that mean?

twenty-one

The next day at lunch the whole world seems to be roaring. Ann Mirette forks in a mouthful of defenseless green beans.

"I had this dream about Colin Farrell last night," she says. "God, those eyebrows—save me, Jesus. Anyhow, we're in love, okay? And it's the best thing in the whole world. And he's not anything like you hear about. He has this ranch where we rope cattle, fix fences. I'm teaching him how to shoot."

"And?"

"I haven't even gotten to the good part yet. Where Colin takes his big hand, runs it up my side—"

"His hands aren't that big, are they?"

"Meat hooks."

"But what does this have to do with me telling Nix?"

"Nothing. Hey, it's not all about *you*, girl."

I make a face.

"You missed a good chance this morning," she says.

"I can't tell him in chemistry. I can't. I've got to get him alone."

"Then do it. What are you scared of? Really?"

I put a finger to my lips. "I guess—I'm afraid he'll think the whole thing is too weird. He'll think *I'm* weird. Like I might be permanently messed up, going through something like that."

"Stop worrying. Just be honest with him. He won't freak."

"I know he won't freak. That's the problem. You know Nix. He won't hurt my feelings, even if he thinks—"

"What? What could he think?"

"I don't know. I don't know."

"Trust me. Trust *him.*"

After last block I hurry down to the multimedia room where Nix has a class in video production. The door is open, but the big room is semi-dark. There's a single light burning in the control room next to the stage. I take a few steps into the gloom and call out.

"Nix?"

No answer. I walk down the side aisle, going over everything in my head one last time to get it exactly right. I can't just blurt the secret out. Better to start with something easy, something safe—

Just before I get to the stage I hear a noise in the aisle behind me. I turn and see a tall shape silhouetted against the rectangle of light coming through the hallway door.

"Nix?"

He doesn't say anything. He's standing in one spot, just waiting. I start to go to him, then a wave of raw cold pulses through my chest. The shape is too broad, too muscular. It isn't Nix. It's Rickey Thigpen.

"Rickey?"

Mr. Tim is nowhere in sight. It's just the two of us in this big dark room, my back against the stage. I feel the blood drain through the separate pieces of my heart. It makes a gurgling noise, like when you puff your cheeks with air and punch them—a bubbly machine-gun buzz. Rickey takes a couple of slow steps toward me, arms swinging like logs on a chain. I can hear his powerful, openmouthed breathing—

Dizziness washes over me, making my legs unsteady. It feels as if my face is getting numb. The room seems to be moving, changing into something different. Rickey takes another step as dark spots jiggle in front of my eyes—

Now it's not Rickey who is coming toward me; it's someone else. Someone with long bangs hanging in front of her face like dead black snakes. The irises in her eyes are so fat and crazy, they look almost square. She's standing between me and the door. She has a pillow in her hands, is bringing it toward me, saying my name. I scream and back up until I feel the edge of the stage against my legs—no, it's not the stage, it's the edge of a mattress. Momma takes the pillow as I fall onto the bed and puts it over my face—

"Shine."

"Frances?" someone says, taking hold of my hand.

I break away and run out into the hall and bang through the first door I see. It's the boys' restroom. Everything is cold, every inch of my skin. I'm shaking all over, so I crouch on the frigid tile floor and wrap my arms around myself, desperately trying to get warm. My heart is rattling a million beats a minute, my face dripping cold sweat. I'm going to die. I'm going to *die*. Right here. Right now.

I wait a long time in a cloud of pure fear; then the cloud

finally starts to clear a little. I can feel it lifting. I stagger to
the sink and splash cold water on my face. I spend a long
time holding the edges of the sink, dripping, not daring to
look in the mirror. I don't want to see what is looking back
at me.

At last my heart slows down. I dry off with paper towels
and wait a few beats holding on to nothing, gauging how
shaky my legs are. It's almost okay. Almost.

"You all right?" a voice says when I step into the hall.

Nix is standing there in a lemon-yellow shirt. I feel hid-
eously exposed. My consciousness throbs in the air between
us. Rickey Thigpen is nowhere around.

I reach for Nix's arm to steady myself. "I'm all right," I
say. "I'm okay." A pang of nausea twists the corner of my
mouth into a painful smile. "I'm—"

He catches me.

twenty-two

"Man, what a day," Nix says, stretching his arms.

We're sitting on my mother's bench in the Pixie Garden. The clouds look like cauliflowers. A white-tailed hawk is riding the air currents above the pine trees. Another bird, tiny by comparison, keeps flying at the hawk in a fury, squawking piteously. A mother protecting her babies.

"It could stay like this the whole year round, far as I'm concerned," Nix says. "So, you contagious?"

I shiver and lean into him, my arm crooked around his arm.

"I'm not sick," I say. "The doctor said it was a mild panic attack. I haven't been sleeping too good—"

"Mild?"

"Okay, so it was pretty bad. But he doesn't think it will happen again. If—well, it's more in the mind than anything medical. What I think about."

"It's my fault," Nix says.

"Why?"

"Leaving Rickey alone like that. I figured nobody else was around, so it wouldn't hurt if I ran up to grab a Coke for him. Mr. Tim was on his way back. He said Rickey wouldn't give me any trouble, would stay in his seat. Stupid. Stupid."

I wait, avoiding his eyes. The hawk circles again. "Look, Nix. It wasn't anything you did. That just brought it to the surface. There's something—something I've been needing to tell you."

"I figured, from what Ann Mirette said."

I feel a sharp intake of breath. "What's she been saying?"

"Hey, calm down. Nothing, really. Just hints. She's worried about you. So what is it? What's going on?"

Start with something simple, I think. The smallest piece of truth you can find.

"My name isn't Frances," I say.

twenty-three

A truck rumbles by on the other side of the woods. We wait, listening to it downshifting to climb the hill.

"It's not?" Nix says, smiling. "So what is it? Paris Hilton? Hermione Granger?"

I frown. "I'm not going to tell you if you don't take this seriously."

"Sorry." He puts three fingers over his heart like a Boy Scout. "Keep going."

"My real name is Francine. Francine Jelks."

"Wow. So why did you change it? That's a pretty cool name, Jelks. And Francine is not that different from Frances—"

"They thought I would get used to it faster if they kept my first name close to the original."

"They?"

"My parents. They changed it when I was seven. No, actually eight."

"I don't get it. Why would they change your last name too?"

My mouth is dry. I lick my lips. "They did it to protect me. Nix—God, I don't know how you're going to react to this. It's—it's pretty bad. No, it's more than pretty bad. It's horrible. I've been trying to find a way to tell you ever since the letter came."

"Letter?"

"Oh. That's right. You don't know about that either, do you? So you don't know about Carruthers."

"Carruthers?"

"The weird old guy who keeps showing up in that little black VW."

"The one Ann Mirette calls Mr. Freeze? You told me about him. I've never seen him, but you told me."

"Okay. Okay." I slump against him and let out a deep breath into his shirt. "I'm really messing this up. Shit. This is something nobody knows about. Well, my parents know, of course. And Ann Mirette. But that's about it."

"Know about what? A letter?"

"No—well, that's part of it. But it's—my parents. They—well, they aren't my *real* parents. I mean, they are, but—Jesus, Nix."

"What? What is it?"

"I'm adopted."

His arms drop, and I feel him relax around me. He puts on a face. "Oh, man, that's it. I can't hang with you anymore."

I slap him on the leg. "You told me you'd be serious."

"But come on—who cares if you're adopted? I wouldn't care if you were raised by wolves—"

"It's not being adopted. It's the *reason* I was adopted. Please—stay with me. I'm doing the best I can here."

"Okay. Okay. No pressure."

"Okay. See, the letter I got, Carruthers brought it to me

a few days ago. Carruthers is a lawyer. The letter is about my birth mother—they're letting her out."

"Letting her out?"

"She's been living in—well, it's a prison up in Tennessee, but she wasn't really in the prison part. They have a special kind of annex place for . . . mentally ill people. People who committed crimes."

"Oh," Nix says.

"Yeah." I tighten my hold on his arm. "It gets a lot worse."

"So your mom—your birth mother—did something, and they said she was not guilty because she was . . . insane? Is that it?"

"Pretty much. But they say she's better now. They moved her to some kind of halfway house."

"So what did she do? You don't have to tell me if you don't want to."

"Well."

"It's okay."

"I want to tell you. Um—I was the oldest kid in my family."

"I know."

"No, I mean—in my—my original family, up in Tennessee. I had three sisters, all younger than me."

"Wow. Three sisters and two adopted brothers. That's a lot of siblings. You still keep in touch with them?"

"Well."

"Oh, shit. Something happened."

I try to feel my breathing. It's still there. "We lived way

out in the country, and my father wasn't there much—he worked a lot of overtime doing construction on a nuclear plant. We only saw him on weekends. My mother—my first mother—God, this is so hard." I wait a few seconds, looking into his eyes. His expression doesn't change. "She—she had some problems. After my baby sister was born, she got worse and worse. I didn't know what to do, Nix. We were all alone. Nobody was around to help us. I guess I just figured that was the way things were—you just kind of had to get through it. Things would be okay. Daddy would come. But then one morning—God."

He squeezes my hand. "It's okay. Everything's okay."

"Okay. Jesus. There's something about saying it out loud. Guess there's no way to make it any easier. One morning she got up just like every other day and fixed us all some Frosted Flakes. And right after that. Well."

"Are you all right?"

I'm trembling all over. I try to stop it, but I can't. "I'm all right, Nix. Just don't let go."

"You don't have to talk about it."

"It's okay. I'm okay. So. Right after we had our cereal— Jesus." I feel the tears starting to come, and I chew my teeth to stop them. "Momma—she called my sisters up to her room, one after another. And. And—she smothered them with a pillow."

"Oh no. Oh, shit. Frances."

I put the heels of my hands into my eyes and press them there until I can go on.

"She did the same thing to me. She called me up there

last. Some guy happened to be coming to the house that day and heard what was going on and saved me. If he had gotten there even thirty seconds later—"

A breeze rattles the redbuds. Somewhere a dog is barking. Nix puts his hand on the back of my head and holds it there, holds my head against his chest. I listen to the bird's cries as it battles the hawk.

twenty-four

We're quiet a long while. Finally Nix pulls away. "I'm thirsty. Are you thirsty?"

We go inside for some lemonade. It feels so much better standing next to him not speaking, just doing simple things. Normal things. Stirring lemonade, taking glasses out of the cupboard, holding them up to the refrigerator door for ice. Mom isn't home yet, and my brothers are in the backyard. We go up to my room and sit on the white settee next to the dormer. Drinking lemonade and listening to the clock tick.

"Just like a place in a magazine," Nix says. "How do you do something like this? I wouldn't know how to do this. Figure out which colors go together, what looks good. How to hang that stuff—" He points at the dormer ceiling, which is draped with a purplish fabric. "How do you even know to do something like that? What do you call it?"

"A valance."

"Damn. Smooth." It sounds like this: *smooo-ooth.*

"My mom—she did all of it," I say, touching my streaky cheekbones. "I don't know how you do stuff like that either."

"Mom," Nix says. "She likes to dream. She has all her favorite shows on HGTV. *Design to Sell. Curb Appeal. Divine*

Design. She would watch that stuff all day long if she could. Someday we will do this or that, get a nice place."

"Do you think you will?" I say.

"No. Not really. Or I guess I will be gone by then, probably."

"Where?"

"No idea," Nix says.

"You mean you haven't even thought about it? College? What you're going to do? What about the counselors at school, what have they told you?"

He smiles, touches my hand, leaving it feeling electric.

"I haven't, um, actually checked in with them yet."

"But time's running out. This stuff takes time to do, scholarships, getting accepted, registration. Aren't you worried you won't be able to get in this fall?"

"I'm not going this fall," he says.

"Oh. I'm sorry—I mean, why?"

"Why are you sorry? I'm just interested in too many things. I'm not ready to narrow down anything yet."

"But don't you have to—"

"No. You don't, you really don't. Lots of people take a year off before they even think about school."

"I know," I say. "But I couldn't—I can't imagine asking my parents to let me do something like that."

"Why?"

I take a sip of lemonade. "I just want to—get on with things, you know? Just regular things. All the junk normal people take for granted—it's—"

He waits for me to finish, but I don't. I stand and look

out the window. My brothers are bouncing on the trampoline in their soccer cleats. "Mom is going to kill—" I stop and put my face against the glass and close my eyes. "Jesus, Nix. What—what do you think about what I just told you?"

Nix stands up behind me and puts his hands on my shoulders. They're heavy. I lean back, bumping his chest.

"You don't cry much, do you?" he says.

"Not if I can help it. Not if anybody can see me."

"Ever?"

"Ever."

"Why?"

"Embarrassing. It's too embarrassing."

"Because why? You don't deserve to if something really shitty happens? What are you afraid of?"

"People. People—who maybe want to help me. Not like you—I don't mean that—but people who don't understand—they want to help, but they don't understand. I just wanted to forget all that stuff. Just be like everybody else. And now, since I got that letter, I feel like it's starting up all over again."

"Can I see it?"

I walk over to my dresser and dig the letter out of the bottom of my pajama drawer. "It was mostly blank. I hid the last page from my parents."

Nix looks at it a long time. "Damn. That's pretty messed up." He lays the page down and starts to rub my shoulders very gently. My relief is so huge, I let every muscle go limp. All I want to do is fall back against him.

"So what do you think she means?" Nix says.

"Who knows?" I close my eyes. "Maybe I should."

"Should what?"

"Oh my God," I say.

"What?"

"Oh my God. Oh my God."

"Tell me."

"No. Wait. Just wait." I pat his arm. "Please. Just wait."

I hug him as hard as I can. My teeth touch his collarbone through his shirt. I put the letter away, and we go downstairs.

twenty-five

"I want you to run away with me," I say.

We're sitting on a little concrete wall behind the school. The buses rumble by, one after another, leaving an industrial stink behind. Across the way a boy runs around the track, shoes making a *chuff chuff* sound.

"I've got something to show you," I say.

I hand the brochure to Nix. On the front is a spiky-haired kid wearing an orange life preserver and paddling a yellow inflatable raft, white water exploding in the background.

"The spring rafting trip to Nantahala Falls," I say. "Only we don't really go to North Carolina. We go looking for *her* instead."

I watch the running boy, his skinny legs uncoiling in the afternoon sun.

"Damn," Nix says. "You're serious?"

"Ann Mirette's going with them. She can cover for us, tell us things about the trip."

"Okay. Damn. It's perfect."

"My parents would never let me go. It's the only way, Nix."

"What about stuff like the paperwork? Won't we have to—?"

"You know we can figure that out. That's nothing. The big thing is—meeting her. That's going to be the hard part. I won't pretend I'm not scared to pieces. But I want to do it. I have to do it. Don't try to talk me out of it. Just say yes before I can think about what I'm saying."

I watch his face. The horizontal sunlight spreading over his shoulders, around his hair, makes him look like an angel.

"Yes," he says.

He turns the brochure over. "So we'd leave early on a Friday. We'd have a three-day weekend, basically. You could call them every night."

"I don't like lying. I completely suck at it." I sigh.

"What's wrong?"

"I guess part of me was hoping you'd say it's a stupid idea."

"It's not stupid. It's good. It's *bold*."

Another bus rumbles by. The tattoo on the driver's shoulder looks like an oil stain. I think about all the times I haven't been bold. All the things I could tell him. Like when somebody is trying to murder you, how everything inside your body comes gushing out—one final, devastating humiliation. As if the horror isn't enough.

"It's insane," I say. "But I still want to go. What if it's something—what if it's something she's passed on to *me*? I want to know."

"You'll never be her," Nix says softly. "I know that. But you need to know it."

My eyes are misting over. "Imagine if this is all my life will ever be. Being connected to something filthy and disgusting and evil—this can't be the only thing my life is about. It can't."

"Hey, hey, hey." He puts his arms around me and kisses my hair. "It's okay. That's why—I think that's maybe the reason we met. Maybe I'm here to help you do this."

I pull away. "Don't say that. You're not responsible for me. I'm tired of people being responsible for me, protecting me. I want more than that. Especially from you."

"Okay."

Another bus goes growling by. We watch the boy run.

twenty-six

I'm sitting cross-legged next to my bookshelf, compulsively arranging the titles by height. I do this sometimes when I'm stressing. Somebody turns on the water somewhere in the house—I can hear it roaring through the walls. I call Ann Mirette on my cell.

"So he's up for it," she says. "The rafting trip."

"Yes."

"Fantastic! How'd your parents take it?"

"About like you'd expect. After all the hyperventilating, they finally started to come around. It's just that I've never asked to do anything like this before. I convinced them it's a good thing. Fresh air. Social skills. Teamwork."

"Right, all that bullshit. Now you just have to find her, and you're home free."

I jerk out another novel. I have a lot of books about time travel, I realize. Maybe because I'd practically kill to be able to go back and change everything. How I screaming hunger for the chance.

"I wouldn't exactly say home free," I say. "We're talking about going to see the person who pretended to love me, then one day tried to murder me."

"But maybe she really did love you," Ann Mirette says.

"That just makes it worse. How can that much good and evil exist in one person?"

"Hang on." I hear a door slam. "That's what happens when it's locked," Ann Mirette yells. "Hey, I'm back. Guess what? Girl X got her first e-mail from the blog today. A total freak. Probably my dad's age, bald, scratching himself while he types one-handed. Half the stuff he talks about, I don't even know if it's medically possible. So it's out there, Frances. Evil. Craziness. Shit. You're going to run into it sooner or later. But you can't sit back and hide. Life equals risk."

"Yeah, yeah, yeah. So how come I'm having all these second thoughts?"

"Okay, so what's your biggest fear?"

"That it—that it will all be so twisted, I'll come back *changed*. Weird. Somebody nobody will want to know. Maybe I'll never set foot outside my house again."

"That's going to happen if you *don't* go. You think it's bad now, that little panic thing at school was just the beginning. Your room is gonna turn into your personal little cocoon. Your womb. Your bedwomb."

I laugh in spite of myself.

"I'm serious," Ann Mirette says. "You've got to put yourself out there. Human beings—it's a mixed bag."

I shove *The Island of Dr. Moreau* into place. "Yeah, I know. Everybody has a little bad in them. But not *monster* bad. Not *evil* bad."

"Maybe people can get better. Even the evil ones."

I stand, feeling unsteady; my left foot has gone to sleep. "They should have given her the death penalty. But that's disgusting too. And—God—she can't be there with *them*."

I've never thought about that before. Momma and my sisters—all of them in the same place for eternity.

"Then she'd just have to go somewhere else," Ann Mirette says. "There *are* other accommodations." I can hear the wicked smile in her voice. She's a fallen-away Baptist.

"I don't know if I believe in hell," I say. "It's too horrible."

"Maybe there's another place. Not heaven or hell, but a place where somebody like her can flush it out of their system before they move on. Maybe way back in the dawn of time 'go to hell' used to mean 'go to *heal*.'"

I sit on the bed and pull my knees up. "I don't think she deserves another chance. You can never recover after you do something like that. It's over. Her soul is cooked. Toast."

"You're making me hungry."

"God, you're so messed up."

"And you love me for it."

"I do. I really do. Thanks."

"No prob. Get some sleep."

But after a long time thrashing around on my bed—freaked, excited, afraid—I realize I've reached that point Kafka wrote about in Mom's Little Zen Calendar. There is no longer any turning back.

twenty-seven

We're standing in front of storage unit number thirty-six of the Bethel Ready-Lock. I take a deep breath and pop the combination lock open and set it on the ground. Nix pulls the yellow rope to raise the door.

"Damn."

The unit is small, only eight feet by eight feet, but it's almost completely empty. The trunk is sitting against the back wall. It's about the size of a bale of hay, padlocked and spray-painted a light blue.

"So this is it," Nix says.

"Yeah. This box is basically all I have left from—from back then. Aunt Dot saved it for me, thinking I would want to have it someday. Of course, my dad locked it up. He doesn't want me to see any of this before I turn twenty-one."

"It must be weird, not being able to talk to your folks," Nix says.

"We talk," I say, fumbling with the key ring.

"About what? Football?"

"It's . . . complicated."

"So how long have we got?"

I try the keys one after another on the padlock. "As long

as I get the keys back in her jewelry box without her missing them, everything will be fine."

"I thought you didn't have any aunts or uncles?"

"She's not my aunt. Aunt Dot is just a family friend. I went to live with her before I got . . . adopted. She would know where my mother is, if anybody does."

"Do you know how to get in touch with her?"

"I can't even remember her last name. That's what I'm hoping to find in here."

It's stuffy in the storage unit, but not that hot. Still, my hands are sweating as I take each key out and put it in the lock.

"You want me to drag it out into the light?" Nix says.

"No. Let's just open it first."

I don't know if I want much light. Not right away. *There.* The lock falls open. I take it off and set it on the concrete. Nix helps me undo the latch and lift the lid. I let out a long, fluttery exhale. The first thing we see is a stack of drawings, the kind a kid would do with colors and those fat first-grade pencils. I hesitate. The box smells of dust and disuse.

I slowly start to dig through it. Broken toys, picture books torn to pieces from reading, scraps of paper with my writing on them, greeting cards, dried flowers. Proof of my existence.

"Can I help?" Nix says.

We sift through it together. I'm afraid to let him know how fragile I feel touching these things. Like a piece of fine glass that has just been thumped, I'm vibrating, waiting for just the right frequency that will shatter me to pieces. We keep going.

"I feel like a geologist," Nix says. "Digging through your strata."

Pressed flowers, buttons, a piggy bank, hair ribbons, a

couple of jump rope handles—the most powerful emotion connected with seeing this stuff is the dead certainty that everything in here has *stopped*. Is no longer part of the living.

"Oh. Oh, Nix."

I feel a stabbing pain in the center of my chest. He's holding a photo of Tan and Ninny. Tan is standing next to the kerosene heater in pigtails and shorts and nothing else. Her legs are scratched and muddy, her cheekbones peppered with freckles. Ninny is wearing green OshKosh B'Gosh overalls. She's smiling at something—not the camera—her hair black and lustrous, teeth small and bright and square. She has tiny red shoes. I remember tying those shoes a dozen times a day, how hard it was to get the laces through the holes.

Nix touches the picture. "This is Tan, right?"

I nod, pressing my hand to my sternum. "She was always so . . . good."

"Yeah?"

"That's not what I mean—she was so good at *doing* things. Tan could fix things. It was amazing how quickly she could figure out mechanical things."

"She was six, right?"

I don't know what to say to this. Tan was six. That's all she was. That's as far as she ever got. The number sticks in my throat.

"Help me." I start pawing frantically through the rest of the stuff in the trunk, piling it beside me on the cement floor. "It's not here," I say.

"What?"

"I can't find any picture of Suddle."

"Oh. Maybe she was just too—maybe they didn't get a chance to . . . to take any."

"She's gone, then," I say, feeling my face tighten. "Completely."

"I'm sorry," he says.

I rub my eyes on my sleeve. "Let's keep going."

My fingers close over what feels like a length of blue satin. I pull it out slowly; it's some kind of banner with big, ornate letters. We spread it across our laps.

DEDICATED TO THE LOVING MEMORY OF TANYA LEE JELKS, RHONDA MARIE JELKS, AND SUSAN DAWN JELKS. MAY THE BLESSED ETERNAL FATHER ENFOLD HIS CHILDREN IN HIS LOVING ARMS FOREVER.

"Jesus," Nix says.

A shiver rolls across my back. Seeing my sisters' real names brings up images of their unclosed eyes. I fight to control myself, shuddering. "I guess—I guess it must be from the funeral."

"You okay?" Nix says.

I nod, putting the banner down. Then I see it. Near the bottom of the box—it doesn't look like much—a crumpled yellow square of paper with my bus number written on it. Bus number 84-57. From the first time I ever went to a real school, even though I was nearly eight. The paper still has a white safety pin from where it was fastened to my sundress. And on the back, something even more important. Aunt Dot's address and phone number.

twenty-eight

I hold the slip up. "Oh my God, Nix. Cooper. That's her. Dot Cooper. Why couldn't I remember that?"

"Excellent," Nix says. "White House, Tennessee. Wonder if she's still at the same number?"

"I bet she hasn't moved. She didn't have a lot of money."

"So, you going to call her?"

"Now?"

"It's better than calling from home."

I gulp and take out my phone. "Okay." I dial the number. The phone starts ringing. I put it on speaker and shove my cell at Nix. "You."

"Nope."

"But you'll do it better than me."

He holds his hands up, refusing.

Someone picks up. "Hello?"

I hurry to put my head against Nix's and cradle the phone between us.

"Um. Yes. Hi. May I please speak to—" I actually have to stop and think. "—to Ms. Dorothy Cooper? Please?"

"You got her, honey." The voice is deeper, raspier than I remembered. "If you're selling satellite TV, you can just hang up right now," the woman says. "I'm on the national do-not-call list. We don't take phone solicitations here."

"No, no, ma'am. Not at all. I'm—" I wonder what name I should give her, then realize she only knows me by one name. "Aunt Dot. This is me, Francine Jelks. I'm—Afton Jelks's daughter."

A long pause, then we can hear what sounds like a dishwasher being unloaded. "What's that again?" Aunt Dot says. "I moved you to my good ear and didn't catch everything." I hear silverware being dumped in a drawer.

I look appealingly at Nix. He shrugs his shoulders. "This is Francine, Aunt Dot. Francine Jelks. Do you remember—?"

"Okay." There's an exasperated sigh, and all the fumbling with the dishes instantly stops. "This is the last time I want to hear anything about this. Do you understand me now?"

"But this is me, Aunt Dot. It's Francine. It really is me. Please—"

"Girl, do you know how many times I've answered the phone over the years with somebody claiming to be Francine Jelks? Or asking questions about her mother? That all happened years ago. It's over. I didn't have anything to do with it, except taking care of a little girl who needed a mother when she didn't have one. I've told y'all, I'm not going to talk about it anymore, not to the TV or newspapers or anybody else." The dishwasher noises start up again.

"But it's true. It's me, Aunt Dot. I need to speak to you. Please believe me."

"No, you listen to me, honey. You've wasted just about enough of my time today."

"Please."

"Okay, you want to prove it to me? Then you come up here. I don't even need to tell you the address. The real Francine Jelks would know it. You show yourself to me, I'll believe you. Otherwise—"

She hangs up without saying good-bye.

twenty-nine

We're sitting in front of the computer in Nix's bedroom. The room is small, the ceiling low, with only a single window. Brandon thumps by in the hall without looking in, rapidly flicking the fingers of his right hand in front of his face as if trying to shake something off.

"Stimming," Nix says. "It's something kids like Brandon do. Doctors think they're stimulating something in their heads, watching their fingers move like that."

From up the hall comes a string of jarring speech: "I'll *lam* into you something fierce," the deep voice says. "And you know I can do it too." The voice trails away into a series of low grunts.

"He loves to mimic his favorite characters from movies," Nix says. "Especially the pissed-off ones."

"He's good. Scary good."

"You should hear him do James Earl Jones." Nix maneuvers the mouse, selecting from a group of Google links. "This looks like a good one."

He clicks on it, and we see a marble-white Web site shot through with veins of purple. A line of tiny cartoon butterflies is chasing the cursor wherever it goes. Fat little cherubs with stubby wings are winking in and out at the top of the page, tooting on celestial horns. The whole thing is framed by big splashes of cartoon roses, red, yellow, and white.

"Don't turn up the—"

Nix turns up the sound. Oh my God. There is some kind of MIDI music tinkling electronically in the background. It sounds like a rendition of "Amazing Grace" being played on a dozen Game Boys. Inside a sewer drain.

"Whoa," Nix says. "Brains and eggs for breakfast. Sorry." He turns the sound down.

"God, what kind of person would make something like this?" I say.

"You never know," Nix says. "You sure you're ready for this?"

"No. But I want you to see it. You need to know what she looks like."

He pauses, hand on the mouse. "You can close your eyes."

"No. Go ahead. It's okay."

But I do close my eyes, waiting for the click. Even through my shut eyelids I can see that the dark background is still there. Then something light pops up. I open my eyes, squinting at first where I see the whole world through my lashes.

There she is. The camera flash is huge. Momma's hands are behind her back. Her hair is long and stringy. It doesn't look like she's taken a bath in days. She's turning toward the camera. It's a picture taken the day she walked into the sheriff's office—the day it happened. I want to look away. I force myself to look, eyes burning, raw.

Her lips are in a line. Her skin is mottled and dotted here and there with tiny moles and blackheads. Her nose looks dirty and slightly squashed. A tangle of crazy black bangs hangs across her moist forehead. Her eyes are the worst—crazed and staring. The irises somehow look square and black. Something square and dark and evil has come to squat inside her head. That's the only thing I can believe. Momma looks as if she is living in a place beyond shock.

"She's pretty," Nix says.

"*Pretty?*"

"Well. I can tell that she *was* pretty. At one time."

My stomach moves.

"Hey, here's another link." He looks at me questioningly.

"Go ahead," I say.

Nix clicks the link, and a blank Windows Media Player comes up. "Oh, shit—it must be a video," he says.

"I don't know—I don't know if I can see it," I say. I close my eyes and wait. "Is the sound turned up? What's going on?"

"It's getting there. My computer is kind of slow."

"Oh, Nix. God."

"It's okay. I'm right here."

"I know. I know. But God. I never expected to find anything like this."

He touches my fingers again, and I let him take them, clenching hard. "Jeez, come on. There. There it is. Oh, man. You can open your eyes, Frances."

I do, but looking down at the bottom edge of the monitor. I'm aware of dark movement on the screen, a kind of scissoring motion. It's her. And she's *moving*.

My heart flutters as I slowly raise my eyes. The video is in color, but somehow it almost looks black and white. Momma is wearing a dark jumpsuit and sitting at a long, bare table. There is something odd about the angle of the shot, as if it was taken by a security camera that had been knocked slightly off level. Everything is slanting to the right. A blocky man is sitting across from her, but a little to the left. I can still see most of her body, including her long legs under the table. She's shockingly thin.

The man is wearing a dark suit that is stretched across his barrel-shaped back. He could be a psychologist. Lawyer. Cop. Corrections official. Anything. He has a pen and a pad of yellow paper.

I see all this in a blurry instant, but Momma's hair—that's the first thing I really look at hard. She still has bangs. But these bangs are so very unnaturally long—they hang straight down over her eyes all the way to the tip of her nose. When she moves her head, the bangs move too. A shimmery black fence. I'm watching an animal. Some creature, a monster, caged, cornered, dangerous, crazy.

Her lips—there is something different about her mouth too. Her lips are thinner. She has lines at the corners of her mouth, and the lines run down to her jaw.

There is a moment of complete, horrifying silence; then the man taps the pad with the pen and says, "So, Ms. Jelks, that was when you first got this idea? This idea of doing something to your—your children?"

A sound starts up, a kind of rat-a-tat-tat beat, fast, almost mechanical. Then, under the table, I can see it—the toe of

Momma's right shoe is tapping against the leg of the table, tapping faster and faster. It's the only part of her body that is moving.

"Ms. Jelks? Do you understand the question?" the man in the suit says.

Tap tap tap. "Uh-huh," Momma says.

I had expected something terrible, monstrous, snarling, her voice ripping through me, knocking me down with evil. But this voice is flat, like that of someone who has spent all day Christmas Eve shopping at Wal-Mart.

The man in the suit starts up again. "When was the first time you ever thought about doing something—"

"Number twenty-five," a deep male voice barks. "Number twenty-five."

Neither of them flinches. The voice seems electronically amplified, maybe coming from a loudspeaker the camera doesn't see. "Number twenty-five. Number twenty-five," the voice shrieks. Then everything is quiet again, except for the tapping of the table leg.

"Ms. Jelks. Do I need to repeat the question?" the man says. Momma doesn't say anything.

"Ms. Jelks?"

"Uh-huh."

"When did you first have these thoughts?"

"About. About my children?"

"Yes."

"I—I'm not really sure. The first time was maybe—it was about right after I had. After I had Ninny."

"Ninny?"

"Uh-huh. Ninny."

"Who is Ninny, Ms. Jelks?"

Tap tap tap, getting faster and faster. As if the very last part of her mind, the very last wisps of her true soul, are trying to make their way out into the room through her foot. "Ninny is—Ninny is Ninny," Momma says.

The man looks at his pad, staring closely. "Rhonda. Is that who you are talking about, Ms. Jelks? Rhonda, your third child?"

Tap tap tap. "Yes. Ninny," Momma says.

"All right, Ninny," the man says. He speaks to the pad. "Notation. Let the record show, the patient is referring to her third child, Rhonda Marie Jelks." He looks at Momma again. "And what happened immediately after Rhonda— after Ninny was born, Ms. Jelks?"

Tap tap tap. "I tried. I tried to do it."

"What did you try to do, Ms. Jelks?"

"The voice. The voice told me I had to do it to Ninny."

"What voice?"

"The voice I heard."

"Was this the voice of another person, Ms. Jelks?"

"Uh-huh."

"A person who was there with you at the time?"

"A voice," Momma says. *Tap tap tap.*

"And what did the voice say?"

"I had to take her—I had to take her away."

"Take her away from what, Ms. Jelks?"

"From the—I had to protect her, take her away."

"Why did you have to protect her?"

Tap tap tap. "I had to protect her."

"What did you do?"

"I—" *Tap tap tap.* "I put Ninny on the bed. I told her I was going to take her away. I got the pillow." Long silence.

"What did you do with the pillow?"

Tap tap tap. "I got the pillow."

"What did you do with it?"

Tap tap tap. "I put the pillow. I put it over her face."

"What happened when you put the pillow over Ninny's face?"

Momma opens her mouth and slowly licks her narrow lips. "He came in."

"Who came in, Ms. Jelks? Your husband? Your husband came in?"

"Uh-huh. He came in. He came in, and I took the pillow away."

"Did you want to kill your children, Ms. Jelks?"

No answer. *Tap tap tap.* "Did you want to kill them?" the man says, leaning across the table.

"My children?"

"Yes."

"No. I—I had to take them away." *Tap tap tap.*

She's tapping so hard now, the table is shaking. The video runs out and stops.

A fury comes up in me. A fury so huge, I want to kill her. Right now I want to kill her. I want to feel my hands around her throat; I want to make her not exist anymore. It makes me sick with the need to shriek to think of her still here, sharing this planet with me, this life, this existence.

We're breathing the same air. Living under the same sky. She should be dead, dead, dead. Gone. Worse than gone. If she were dead, she would still have a grave. People could come to see it. Photograph it. Maybe even leave flowers. She should never have been.

"Are you okay?" Nix says.

Before I can answer, Brandon is in the room. He comes straight at me, leans over, and gets right in my face. His face is large, and his breath smells of bananas. "Are you going to go home?" he says. "Good-bye."

I almost hit him. But I jerk my head away from his dark eyes and look at the floor.

"Hey, Bubby," Nix says, jumping up and taking Brandon by the arm. "Come on, let's leave Frances alone. You need to go out. I'll take you bike riding later."

"So I don't need to worry about her?" Brandon says. "She will be okay?"

"Yeah, Bubby, yeah." Nix is pulling him to the door. "She'll be fine. Frances brought you the bubble-blowing stuff, remember?"

"Good-bye," Brandon says and disappears down the hall.

"I'm sorry," Nix says, turning and kneeling in front of me. "Are you all right?"

"I'm—please."

He takes me in his arms. I'm clenching my teeth so hard trying not to cry, my neck is starting to cramp.

thirty

It helps this morning that my parents are in a bit of a rush. They're taking Terry to a chess tournament in Birmingham. Nix shakes hands with Dad, hugs my mom. She has a delightedly embarrassed look when he lets her go.

"Where's your mom?" I say to Nix.

"Asleep," he says. "She's working swings lately. We said good-bye yesterday."

Ann Mirette bounces over to play her part. "Oh my God, Ms. Robinson. We're going to have so much fun." What a liar. I'd believe her myself.

"Will you girls be rooming together?"

Ann Mirette stares at me, green eyes flashing. Message received: it's my turn to tell a whopper. "Well, um, sure," I say. "They set it up that way."

"It's the same with the boats, Ms. Robinson," Ann Mirette says. "They pair everybody up—two by two, biblical as shi—as Noah, according to, um, your room. So we'll be paddling across from each other the whole time. It's a buddy system. Frances is my buddy. I've got the stronger stroke, so no doubt we'll be going in circles."

I touch my elbow to her ribs, whispering, "Don't overdo it."

"Honey, let me call you," Mom says, taking out her cell. "To make sure your ringer's on."

"I checked it, Mom."

"Just in case."

She calls my number and we don't hear anything.

"It's on vibrate. In my pocket."

"Well, take it out, Frances."

I check, and sure enough, one missed call. "It's working."

"Put it on ringer, Button," Dad says. "What if there's an emergency and we can't get a hold of you?"

"I'll just check it every once in a while. I hate it when it goes off in public places."

"There's nothing to be embarrassed about, sugar," Mom says.

"We're running late, Marjorie," Dad says, glancing at his watch. I'm afraid to look him in the face. He trusts me so much—what if he finds out? What will he do?

Mom hugs me. Her hair tickles my nose. She smells of lilacs and bath powder. Dad kisses me on top of my head and squeezes my shoulders. I focus on walking slowly with Ann Mirette to the bus, walking down the center aisle past the jostling kids. We sit and wave through the little rectangular windows until they have sped out of sight, streaking toward Birmingham. I stand to go.

"Be careful," Ann Mirette says. "Keep close to Nix. Watch out for the rest stops. Steel toilets—bleh."

"So you know what to do?" I say.

"Yep. My cell is locked and loaded. I'll beam you plenty of digital pics. Raul the rafting guide hauling the boat off the bus. Plunging over the Nantahala Falls. Indulging in an epic throw-down at the Bryson City Wendy's."

"Perfect. But you don't have to flood me with them. Just enough to be convincing." I let out a sigh. "I wish I really could go. I'm going to miss you, A. M."

"It's only three days. It'll be okay."

"Yeah, only the three weirdest, scariest days of my life."

"Call me. I can't believe you are really doing it, you and Nix—oh, shit, did I just say that? But it's so incredibly juicy. Beds. Sweat. Showers."

I put my hands to her throat, pretending to strangle her. "Very funny. You breathe one word—"

"Sigh. I know. How come the goddamn scaredy-cats get all the *real* adventures?"

"Don't drown."

"I'm naturally buoyant. Here's something for your trip." She sticks something crackly in my pocket. "Be safe."

"What is it? A snack?" I start to pull it out, but she grabs my hand.

"Not here! Somebody might see." She hugs me again hard enough to collapse both lungs. Her jacket smells of WD-40. "God, what a trip," she says. "Wish I could go with you. I'd blog every mile."

The mass of her red hair blurs my vision. Or maybe it's the hint of tears. I let her go and race to Nix's van and hop in, watching her large silhouette making its way to a seat. Nix circles the North Carolina bus and points us toward the interstate. I reach my hand into my pocket and pull out the crackly package. A condom.

thirty-one

I've never felt worse. I've never felt better. I didn't know it was possible to have both these feelings at the same time. We're doing it. Oh my God, we're doing it.

We're sitting at the last stoplight before merging onto the interstate. A golden dog drifts across the road in front of us, snuffling something on the shoulder. I can see morning mist rising from a cow pond in the distance. Everything is so indistinct and quiet and green. It reminds me of a Yeats poem, "Lake Isle of Innisfree." Where "peace comes dropping slow."

I pull out the Trip Tik we printed from the AAA Web site and unfold it. "It's not too hard, Nix. Just stay on Sixty-five all the way through Nashville, then exit kind of northeast onto Highway—let's see—Seventy-six—just a few miles to White House."

The light turns green, but Nix doesn't go. A car behind us blares its horn, then angrily pulls around. Nix reaches over and starts to pull me across the stick shift.

"Hey."

"Unsnap your seat belt," he says.

"Why?"

"Just do it."

I do it, and he reaches under his seat for the lever and scoots the seat back. Then he pulls me over until I'm sitting in front of him in his lap. Now he's putting my hands on the wheel. He pulls the belt across both of us and snaps it in. His stomach is warm against my back. The light turns green again.

"Now go," he says.

"Are you kidding? I can't reach the pedals."

"Try."

I slide forward on his long thighs, reaching with my foot, but I can't feel anything. I slide forward some more until I can just touch the rubber of the gas pedal.

"Are you sure?" I say. "I don't know how to drive a stick."

"Your left foot goes on the clutch," Nix says. "You push it down all the way, then give it some gas with your right. The trick is, you only let about halfway back on the clutch while you're giving it gas. Go."

I put in the clutch, stomping hard to make sure it's all the way down. And start to push the gas pedal. The van lurches into the intersection a few feet and stalls with a massive, jerking shudder. I scream, then start to laugh.

"No big thing," Nix says. "Nobody's around. Try again."

We lurch and buck across the intersection, stalling several more times, until finally we're rolling along in first gear. I have a little trouble getting it into second—the gears squeal—until I remember to tromp on the clutch. My hands have gone white on the steering wheel.

"Okay. You're doing great," Nix says. "Listen to the engine—when it sounds like it's revving too fast, hit the clutch again."

We're picking up speed now. Getting into third and fourth goes a little more smoothly. Nix takes his hands off the stick. We pass the McDonald's, its morning lights glowing a lonely yellow.

Now it's a journey. We're going, we're moving. We don't pass any other cars for a while. In twenty minutes Nix lets me back in the passenger seat, and we're tearing down the interstate between the ribbons of hills and asphalt and the road markers with no traffic lights. It's all different, and we might as well be in South Dakota.

The houses close to the interstate are small and old and removed from one another, some of them buried deep in Johnson grass or honeysuckle or kudzu. The kudzu is the strangest—the way it rolls over everything and holds it down and hides it and finally swallows it. It's strange, but I can understand a plant like that. I can understand being beneath it, motionless, feeling the rot come. But not today.

thirty-two

The landscape unrolls before us. Pretty soon we've crossed the border into Tennessee. I never knew this state had so many hills. I mean, I knew it intellectually, sure. But now I know it with my body. It's nice coming up a long slope with no idea what's on the other side. Nix's van struggles to pull the grades; I find myself unconsciously moving back and forth in my seat, straining to help it.

"This baby is a four-cylinder," he says. Which means the engine knocks like crazy, and the people behind us stack up and tailgate.

But then we top out, and the mystery is revealed: green, foresty bumps cut through with massive shelves of tan stone where they blasted a way for the interstate. Sometimes the geologic layers are tilted at crazy angles, as if monster earthquakes have rocked them up from the depths.

I like reading the exit signs for the towns we pass: Dellrose, Frankewing, Cornersville, Culleoka. I wonder what the people are like here. The places that fascinate me most are the tiny little gray houses perched high on the sides of steep hills.

After the big green strangeness of the countryside, I don't like coming into the city—it's too bland and anonymous and impersonal. Everything to either side of the highway seems covered in grime or made of rusted iron, and the radio station billboards with their leering heads make me worry about the state of Western civilization.

But I can't spend a lot of time on the scenery. As navigator, it's tough keeping straight which lane we're supposed to be in to avoid losing the interstate. And the roads are crowded with greasy trucks and scowling drivers hell-bent on getting somewhere.

"Crazy," I say when a guy in a Honda Element nearly takes our door handles off.

"Life in the big city," Nix says. "You should see New Orleans." It sounds like *Nawlins* when he says it. "And if you have a wreck, everybody is suddenly *cooyon*."

"Huh?"

"Dumb, stupid. And nobody can speak English anymore when the cops get there."

We exit the interstate and eat at the first Cracker Barrel we find. Back on the road we don't speak much as I have to concentrate to keep us from winding up in Kentucky while Nix makes sure we don't become a hood ornament for a semitruck. He visibly relaxes once the traffic finally thins out.

Checking the Trip Tik, I realize with a jolt that we're less than ten miles from the highway that takes us to White House. It comes to me forcefully again that we are really doing this. This is the new place. The road that doesn't take you back into town.

"Did you say something?" Nix says.

"No. I don't think so. Maybe I made a noise."

"I think that classifies as a yelp. Are you okay?"

"I'm just . . . a little freaked, I guess."

"On a scale of one to ten."

"Um." Grilled trout shifts coldly in my stomach. "Call it an eight point seven. A notch or two below sheer hysteria. Talk to me. Tell me something about Mammy Ida."

"She was about a hundred when I knew her. Skinny as a rail."

"I thought all mammies were supposed to look like Hattie McDaniel in *Gone with the Wind*."

He laughs. "You talk like somebody from Alabama. A mammy can be anything she wants to be. Especially ones who know how to work the gris-gris."

"Gree-gree?"

"Black magic. Evil spells."

"Was she a witch?"

"Shoot, no. Went to church every Wednesday night and twice on Sunday. Mammy Ida died sitting straight up in the backseat of a Crown Vic on the way to Mount Nebo Bible Baptist Church. I was one of the ushers at her funeral."

"So why did she mess with black magic?"

"Didn't say she did." He smiles. "Didn't say she didn't either. Mammy Ida knew a lot of stuff. You never could tell what she was thinking if she wanted to hide her thoughts from you."

"You don't believe in evil spells, do you?"

"What if I did? Would it make a difference?"

"But you don't?"

Nix scratches his ear, thinking. "There are some strange things out there, I'll admit that. But I'm kind of a wait-and-see type. Like ghosts. New Orleans is supposed to be full of 'em. Mammy Ida once saw Prince Suleyman in a house on Dauphine Street. You should've heard her tell about it. Pirates, a harem, rooms washed with buckets of blood. But I never saw a damn thing."

"It must be nice," I say, watching the road.

"What?"

"To—um—to know people like that. To be connected to them. People who aren't anything like you."

"It's downright unavoidable in New Orleans."

"Maybe you can take me there someday."

"Someday, sure. We'll ride the trolley up to Tulane; then I'll teach you to eat beignets at the Cafe du Monde in the French Quarter."

The green world whizzes by outside my window. I curl a lock of hair around my finger. "I want to start building some memories. New ones. Somewhere other than places like Epcot or Splash Mountain or the Smithsonian."

"Then here you go," Nix says. "Your wish is my command."

"What?"

"Look."

He points at a sign. The exit marker for Highway 76.

thirty-three

The house hasn't changed. It's an older one-story brick place with a wide front porch, mini columns, a gabled front entry, and a long garden in the back. So Aunt Dot is still growing Silver Queen. The corn plants are small, their leaves shiny, dark green, and tender. The big red oak in the front yard is still there. I see the window where I was standing when Daddy left the last time.

Nix turns into the wide circle drive, tires crunching on the gravel, and cuts off the engine. The only sound we hear as we get out of the van is that of a yellow sprinkler flopping back and forth. We cross the grassy yard and step up onto the porch. Nix searches the edges of the door frame for the bell.

"I guess you have to knock," I say.

I rap the knocker hard a couple of times and let the screen settle back in its frame. My breathing speeds up, but nothing happens. I'm just about to knock again when Aunt Dot jerks open the door. The scent of faux oranges sweeps over us from inside the house.

I have to suppress a gasp. Aunt Dot's a photo negative of herself—she was so dark when I was seven; now her skin is wrinkled and brittle, her hair so ghostly light, it's almost floating. Her nose is broad and red, lips lined and slack. She's wearing a lime-green housecoat. Her eyes are younger than her face, sharp and watchful.

"Can I help you?"

I back away a couple of feet; the scratchy voice really projects.

"Yes, hello, I—"

"Do I know you, honey?"

"Yes. Yes, ma'am, you do. I called you on the phone a couple of days ago, and you asked us to come up and see you." It feels strangely formal to say my real name to her after all these years. "I'm Francine Jelks, Aunt Dot."

"Who? No. No. My baby. That was *you*?"

She throws the door back and takes me in her arms—her skin is stubbled with goose bumps.

"Oh my God, my darling, my baby darling, how are you? I'm so sorry I was short with you on the phone—all those nuts—you wouldn't believe what I've had to put up with over the years, sugar. You haven't changed one bit. Where have you been? What have you been doing? Come on in here, sweetheart, and tell me everything."

She's hauling me inside by my wrist, Nix completely forgotten. The minute I'm through, Aunt Dot lets the screen door slap in his face.

"You used to call me Aunt, you remembered that."

The room is dark and square, smaller than I remember. I sink into an overstuffed chair; even with a cushion behind me, my feet are dangling above the floor. I see Nix slip through the doorway to stand in the foyer.

"Tell me everything," she says again. "How long has it been? My goodness, girl."

"Well. I've been living in Alabama. With my family. My—my family."

"Let me look at you." Aunt Dot stands again and comes over and pulls me up. "Well. You certainly got your height from your grandmother." She takes my cheeks in her fingers and pulls. "You know, I could just eat you up. Oh, you come on in," she says to Nix, waving him to the couch. "Are y'all related?"

"He's—he's my friend from school. Nix, this is my aunt Dot."

"Hello, ma'am," Nix says, modulating the setting on his drawl to Weak-in-the-Knees. "Nice to meet you. We're—"

"Now, what does your father do, honey?" Aunt Dot says, looking back to me. "Who was that he was working for— DuPont? Reynolds Aluminum?"

"No, ma'am. He works for a dog food company." I'm careful not to say the name, but now I don't know what to add to it. "He makes dog food," I say lamely.

This sends Aunt Dot into peals of craggy laughter. "Dog food." She rearranges some magazines on the coffee table, kicks off her shoes, and props her legs up. Her shanks are translucent and veiny.

"And what's your daddy's name? Your adopted daddy."

I'm ready for this. "Thigpen," I say, in case she decides to check up on things. "Thomas Thigpen."

"And where does he live?"

"Birmingham."

"Birmingham. The Magic City. How about that. Well. So you landed on your feet, darling. That's so good. I can't believe how long it's been. I just can't believe it. Have you heard from your father, Francine?"

For a split second I'm confused. "Oh. Daddy? No, ma'am, I—"

"There was a time, years and years ago, he used to talk about you a lot. He was going to go to court, was going to do all kinds of things—an appeal, you know. To get you back. But I never heard what happened. He was still working at Belfonte when the government shut it down. Shut everybody down. The whole town over there—Red Vine—it's really been hurting since they lost the nuclear plant."

I shake my head sympathetically.

"You know, it's so good of you to look me up like this," Aunt Dot says. "I can't wait for old Wayne to see you. How long can you stay? He'll be here any minute. He'd be so happy to see you, girl. This would just make his day. Can I get y'all anything to eat?"

"No, thank you," I say. "We had a big lunch in Nashville."

"Just look at you. Way off down there in the Yellowhammer state—that's what they call it, isn't it?"

"Yes, ma'am."

Silence. We wait, looking at each other. I glance at Nix. I guess it's time. I look down at my dangling feet, willing them to be still.

"Aunt Dot, the reason we're here—really, we want to know where my mother is. I heard they moved her somewhere. I just wanted to know if maybe you had heard anything?"

Dot's face immediately pinches in on itself, changing from joy to a gloomy concern.

"Oh. Oh, darling. Don't worry. Please don't worry. That poor woman isn't going to do one bad thing to you anymore. It's so different now. She's—they've given her so many treatments. She's still under medication, last I heard. You're safe. That was a onetime thing. A horrible tragedy, an accident."

"No, Aunt Dot—really, that's not what we're worried about," I say, then realize I shouldn't have said "worried." "We're not worried about anything, actually. It's just that, well—"

"Do you know where she is, ma'am?" Nix says.

She turns to look at him, eyes tightening. "Why do you need to know? What are you hoping to do?"

"We—we'd just like to know," I say. "Really, it's just that I need to see her. I haven't seen her since that day. Only a few pictures. I want to—to know how she is doing."

"Are you sure you should, Francine honey?" Aunt Dot says. "Wouldn't that just start things up again? Maybe—it might hurt her. Did you ever think of that? That maybe whatever progress she has made, maybe it will all go backwards if she sees you? Too many bad memories. Too much pain."

"On the flip side, maybe it will be good for her," Nix says, smiling helpfully. "Maybe it'll be just what she needs."

Aunt Dot stops smiling. She stares hard at Nix and slides

her feet off the coffee table, sitting up straight. "Just what is it to you—Nick, did you say your name is Nick?"

"*Nix*, ma'am. With an *x*—"

Dot's face collapses into a sour mass of wrinkles. "I'm just wondering what you children are up to, I have to admit."

I fidget, sweat starting at my temples, trying to think of what I should say. "Well, yes, ma'am. I mean, no, ma'am. Well. The thing about it is—Aunt Dot—we—"

"Francine and me are getting married," Nix says.

thirty-four

Every rib in my chest contracts as a gasp escapes my lips. Aunt Dot is staring at me, expecting me to speak. I can't.

"We wanted to wait until June," Nix says, showing all his teeth. He winks at me. "But I guess it's okay letting the secret out a little early."

"But—" Dot says. "For real? You really are? Aren't you a little young?"

"Well," I say.

"I'm eighteen, ma'am," Nix says. "And Francine is eighteen. We've been planning it for a while. Nobody really knows yet. It's a secret. We're having so much fun letting everybody in on it. So please don't tell anybody."

Aunt Dot waits, gauging us, then hops up. "Oh my Lord, well, congratulations." She comes over and grabs me for at least the third time today. It's like being hugged by a set of sofa cushions. I almost fall back into the chair when she lets me go.

"Wait a minute now," Aunt Dot says. "This isn't one of those things—you don't *have* to get married, do you?"

"Hell, no," Nix says, Louisiana indignant. "Excuse my French, ma'am. But this is goddamn true love."

I have an idea. "Um. We wanted to tell Momma and

Daddy about it. But it's been so long—I was so little—we don't know where they are."

"Oh," Dot says. "You were hoping I could find them for you?"

"Well."

"I'm sorry, Francine. I haven't seen your daddy in three or four years. Maybe longer. The last I knew, he was still up in Red Vine. Your momma—I don't know, honey. We—we don't keep in touch."

"Do you have an address, ma'am?" Nix says. "Even if it's old, maybe we could still use it to track—to send an invitation."

"It—it would mean a lot to me," I manage to say. "Momma—I just want her to know about it. But I was hoping Daddy could come to the wedding and . . . give me away."

Aunt Dot settles back onto the love seat. "I don't remember the name of the place where they are keeping her. I'm sorry, honey." I watch her eyes, trying to tell whether she is lying. "You could try going through the Tennessee Department of Corrections. There used to be a number for Prison Health Services—"

"We tried them, ma'am," Nix says, sorrowfully. "No luck. They wouldn't release the information."

"Can't say I blame them, truly," Aunt Dot says. "So many crazy folks out there just won't let this thing . . . die."

"Aunt Dot." I get up and cross the room and sit beside her. "What did he do? Daddy? Why did he let me go?"

"Well." She lets out a long sigh. "That man—he was

always one of the best men I ever knew, darling. And one of the worst."

"What do you mean?"

"Let me see. I've known your father since he was knee-high. Larry Jelks was a good Methodist boy. Growing up we played Ping-Pong every Sunday night in the fellowship basement. Cocky—my Lord. He drove all the girls crazy. Then he went on a wild tear when he got out on his own. But what people never really knew was he just was a big old kid at heart, full of fun. That's why everybody liked him so much. But he had some big fears inside too—things that never cropped up till after he had a family. He was obsessed with keeping y'all safe. Simply obsessed. But he shouldn't have never—" She stops, touching her face as if she doesn't want to go on.

"Never what?" I say quietly.

"Taken all y'all girls out to the boondocks like that. Not another house in sight. Nobody around for that poor momma of yours to talk to but a bunch of babies. Afton, she was . . . special. She could do so many things. Class valedictorian of her high school up in Illinois." She pronounces Illinois as if it should rhyme with the word *voice*. "Do they even have them anymore?"

I nod.

"Anyhow, smart as a whip. She could have been anything she wanted. But all she wanted was Larry—your father. When it all happened—that poor, helpless man—he didn't know what to do. Sick. He was just sick over it. Even so, lots of folks blamed him for the whole thing. He couldn't stop them asking questions, making the most awful accusations. Finally it was just too much to bear. So Larry got weak and made some bad—some bad judgments. He let things get out of control, keeping you out of school, dragging you all over creation defending himself on TV. People were paying too much attention. There was so much pressure; he couldn't fight it."

"He was forced to give me up?"

"That's the size of it. They went through the courts, all right, but some said it was rubber-stamped before he ever got there. It broke Larry's heart. I thought he would die. I never—well, he just wasn't the same man after that. And you—everybody wanted you, honey. You were the cutest little thing. Cards and letters came from all over. You wouldn't believe it. Egypt—I remember one came from *Egypt*. Everybody wanted to take care of you. Me and Wayne—we weren't married yet, so us raising you, that was out."

The screen door slaps open, and a man is standing in the foyer. It's Wayne. Crap. I was hoping we could get an address and get away before he got here.

"Oh, goodness, Wayne," Aunt Dot says, standing. "Look who we've got here."

Wayne's a little heavier, a little redder around the neck. His skin is unnaturally rosy. The lines circling his throat make it look as if he has spent the last eleven years wrapped in twine. Dot makes introductions, and Wayne crushes me to him.

I'm smothered under the weight of his big arms. "Francine Jelks. Well, come here, sugar." His chest smells of dried sweat and Aqua Velva—the scent makes me shiver; there are too many memories connected to it. "How've you been? You sure turned out to be a sweet little thing."

He lets me go with a final suggestive squeeze. We sit back down and rewind the conversation we already had with Aunt Dot. Wayne takes off his CAT DIESEL hat and drops it on the coffee table. Underneath is a red line dividing white from purple skin.

"Francine and Nick here are getting married," Aunt Dot says.

"Well, come here," Wayne says. I have to endure the Hulk Hogan routine all over again. He shakes hands with Nix, slapping him on the back. "Congratulations. I know you're gonna name your first baby after me, Francine. Tell the truth."

First baby—the thought flattens my heart. "I—I don't know," is all I can manage to say.

"Wayne." Aunt Dot lights a cigarette, and little puffs squirt out between her dry lips. "Francine was just asking about Larry—her daddy. Maybe you can fill her in some. I remember one of the first things you said to me when it happened—'What is Larry going to do without her?' That's just the way you said it."

"That man was lost," Wayne says.

"Sounds like you knew him well," Nix says.

Wayne looks at him and settles back, ready to tell a story. "Son, I spent eight years working with that boy, give or take. Browns Ferry, Buck Island, Belfonte. He was younger than me, of course. I kind of showed him the ropes around the job site. Larry was something of a hell-raiser back in the day. Don't get me wrong—he'd be right there in church every Sunday, regular as taxes. But every night after work, Larry and some of them other boys—they'd go out clubbing." Wayne laughs a little, then smiles sadly. "Hell, what else were they going to do? Working jobs in the middle of some shit backwoods counties. Money burning a hole in their pockets, nothing else to spend it on. They hit every place they could find. Some of 'em more than once, if the pickings was good. I figured if he kept at it like he was, his damn pecker would fall off."

Aunt Dot slaps him playfully on the leg. "Wayne."

"Well, it would have," Wayne says. Then he quiets down, eyes slightly wet, looking into the distance. "But then he met her."

"My mother?" I say.

"Yes, darling." He coughs several times into his hand. "Larry found her up in Fentress County, in a smoky little bar called Napoleon's Nook, trying to sing. Mercy. All that black hair, pretty eyes—Larry Jelks figured she was the most beautiful thing on earth. An angel."

I'm trying to picture my mother—young, unattached, beautiful, a free spirit. It's hard.

"So he stopped? Just like that?" Aunt Dot says.

"Just like that." Aunt Dot gives him a look. Wayne puts his hand on his chest. "If I'm lying, I'm dying. Afton was living in a room so little you could've set the whole shebang right here in front of us. I saw it once. Paintings all over, a potter's wheel—you want to talk artistic—one wall was plumb covered over with feathers, I shit you not. Larry said it was like waking up inside a goddamn chicken."

Everybody laughs.

"Anyway, Afton was like no woman Larry had ever seen before. She come down from S'cargo—"

"Scargo?" Nix says.

"Up in Illinois. Where her folks was from. She was trying to get a job singing bluegrass, but Jamestown was the closest she ever got to Nashville. Larry married her as soon as he could—it took six months to wear her down, but he did it with them old-time Appalachian tunes."

"I never knew he liked music," I say.

"It's true. 'Shady Grove,' 'Sourwood Mountain,' 'Booth Shot Lincoln.' You ask your father about it sometime. Afton went just wild over that shit. So imagine that. Larry Jelks hooked up with a goddamn Yankee. But you talk about love. It was like he found religion. That's exactly what it was like. I knew he would be flat tore up if anything ever happened to that girl."

I don't know what I should say. I've never heard any of this. "Really?"

"He worshiped your momma," Wayne says. "That's why he took her off to Benton County to live. Benton's a dry county. Only fourteen thousand people. No hell-raisers for miles. Quiet as death."

A look passes around the four of us. Wayne grunts shame-facedly and goes on.

"Larry, he said he knew what the world was like. He had seen it, the things men were capable of. Not to mention he was jealous as hell. He wanted to take Afton away from every-thing. Protect her. Protect all of y'all. He was always scared something was going to happen. But that's the crazy part—Benton was so far from work, and the shifts at Belfonte were so long, he could only come home on the weekends. It killed him that he had to be away so much. Absolutely killed him. That wild, beautiful girl out there all by herself, surrounded by you kids. He especially worried every time right after she had a baby—hey. What's wrong? Dot?"

Aunt Dot is sniffing into a Kleenex. "Something hap-pened," she says.

thirty-five

Aunt Dot wipes at her face. The skin between the bones of her fingers is slack, almost webbed. "It's just that they don't know, Wayne," she says. "I don't think they know."

"What?" Wayne says.

"How bad it got. How sick Afton was. The things she did—before."

"Oh," Wayne says. "You mean like when she took the knife and—"

"Don't say it." Aunt Dot's smoky voice rises almost to a squeal.

"All right," Wayne says. "Let's just say your mother—she got—different. Something broke inside her. I think the first time was right along after the third baby was born. Isn't that right, Dot?"

Aunt Dot looks tired. "Yes. That's the way I remember it. She was never the same after that."

"Afton starting having times when she couldn't tell real things from make-believe," Wayne says. "It got to where it happened more and more often. The doctors—they told Larry she needed watching. But what was he going to do, working that kind of schedule? Besides, Larry Jelks didn't trust doctors. Never has. Well, it turns out it was way worse than anybody knew. There is no telling what she was up to when nobody but you kids was around. Nobody really knows. But if it was me, I'd say—"

Aunt Dot stands. Her eyes are red, pleading. "All right. That's enough about all that. This is supposed to be a happy time for Francine. So I'm going to do something special for her. Let me see, sugar." She comes over and touches my arm still holding the Kleenex, and I can feel the dampness of the tissue. "Stay here. Just a minute." And she goes off into a room in the back.

Wayne rises and goes into the kitchen. I look at Nix, and he shrugs his shoulders. It feels funny being in this strange room by ourselves. I desperately want to be out of this house, back on the road, but we still haven't gotten what we came for. We can hear Wayne rummaging around in the refrigerator.

"Any of those deviled eggs left?"

Nix and I glance at each other, half afraid to speak. Then Aunt Dot comes back holding a scrap of paper.

"Francine, honey, this is old, but it's likely he stayed in the same place. So you can send him the invitation."

Daddy's address.

thirty-six

The sun is low in the sky, perched on a reef of clouds rimming an orange sea. We've been driving a couple of hours, heading steadily east-southeast across something called the Cumberland Plateau. I really like all the green. It's not as hilly here, but every bit as hard-bitten. We just passed a church that has a giant hand carved out of plywood standing in the front yard. CHURCH OF THE HAND, the sign says.

"Well, of course, what else would it be?" Nix says. "That's the great thing about traveling by car: everything is a big unknown. You never know what you'll discover."

Right now we're discovering that the outskirts of Red Vine, Tennessee, are littered with disemboweled cars, shotgunned mobile homes, abandoned fruit stands, decaying outbuildings of every shape and description. As we get closer to town, the structures undergo a kind of evolutionary process, from slack-jawed wood to sheet metal, then finally blood-colored brick that was probably fired about the last time Stonewall Jackson came through.

"Red Vine might be too nice a name for this place," I say.

"How about Bonemeal Springs?" Nix says. "Sulfur Flats, Burning Landfill."

"Or maybe just Stinking," I say, rolling my window up. "Stinking, Tennessee."

Nix laughs. "Homa the Aroma."

"Whew. What *is* that smell?"

"Paper mill. They always smell that way. Something in the chemical process working with the pulp. We had them all over down in Louisiana. I'm just glad you didn't think it was me."

I'm thinking about my birth father, living in a place like this for years and years. "God, imagine living with a stink like that all the time."

"You get used to it," Nix says. "Like most things. Besides, I bet it's not as close to town as it seems. Usually they put them way out in the sticks, fifty miles from civilization. But when the wind is right—"

"Bleh. If this isn't the sticks, I don't know what is. I think I'll skip dinner. Oh well, small price to pay for living in a literate society."

"Ha," Nix says. "Ninety percent of their production is going to make toilet paper."

A state trooper's silvery prowl car comes alongside us in the fast lane, its radio antenna bent across the roof and fastened down. Through the passenger window we can see the trooper's round campaign hat and Chuck Norris chin. Nix throttles back to forty-five miles an hour.

"Nothing like spending our first night in the hoosegow," he says.

"The what?"

"Hoosegow. That's Louisiana speak for *jail*, honeylamb."

I shudder deliciously. "Oooh, Cap'n Butler, say it again."

"How you holding up?"

"Pretty good, actually." I'm starting to feel as if I can really do this. At least one piece of it at a time.

Nix has been jonesing for hillbilly ice cream, so we stop at the local Dairy Barn for malts. A group of slouchy men is sitting at the outdoor tables smoking. I can imagine what they must be thinking about Nix's spotted van. They're all wearing baseball caps and have tired, dirty eyes and sunburnt faces. The tattoos look self-inflicted. I'm afraid to get out.

"Damn, that's so good," Nix says, getting back in and taking a long pull on his malt. "A few more years, all these great little places will be gone. It's a shame. Nothing on earth can touch a Jethro milk shake."

"Um," I say, holding my malt but not drinking.

"Okay, spit it out," Nix says. "What's wrong?"

I look at the low hills in the distance. If you're going to insult someone, is it better if you look at them when you do it? "It's the spots," I say finally, looking straight into his eyes. "I—I've just always wondered why you put spots on your van."

"Good question," Nix says. "The spots weren't my idea."

"Then who did it?"

"I did."

"I don't understand."

"Well, let's just say I allowed it to happen." He leans back, stretching his arms, and takes another long pull at his malt. "Mmmm, baby. Okay. Here's the thing about Brandon. He hardly ever starts anything on his own. That's the big thing with a lot of autistic spectrum kids. You have to jump-start them, let them kind of borrow your motivation. Or a lot of the time they will just stay in one spot, doing nothing but stimming themselves, rocking, staring off into space, repeating stuff they heard on TV, et cetera."

"Okay."

"So whenever Brandon does come outside of himself, does something completely on his own, me and Mom, we have an agreement. Whatever he is doing, we have to honor it, no matter what it is. As long as it's nothing dangerous or gross. We want to give him that. It's the only power someone like him really has."

"That's—that's really sweet."

"So one day a couple of years ago, he came home from school with a whole backpack full of these colored stickers. And he took one over to my van and pasted it on. And another and another, and kept on going."

"Oh." I'm starting to get the picture. "So now the spots are kind of—"

"Sacred," Nix says. "I'll keep them on her till the bottom rusts out."

I feel my eyes misting. I try to distract myself by looking at a dirty girl in blond pigtails licking a waffle cone. "You're so good," I say.

"Ha, just wait till you really know me."

"I mean it. You're not like—you're not like anybody I've ever known before."

He reaches across to squeeze my fingers. "Look at you. Look at what you've been through—but you're still so . . .

I don't know, *untouched.* Like all the bad stuff out there has never gotten through to you. It doesn't reach you. It's like you give off this energy, you radiate something. I wish I could say what it is, but—"

"More like hermetically sealed, maybe. Until you opened me."

He runs his index finger along my temple and starts up the van. "I opened you. I like that."

I do too.

thirty-seven

Two minutes later, and we've reached the center of Red Vine. The town square is truly a square—a block of elderly greenery lined with prehistoric furniture stores, a bank once knocked over by Jesse James, and shops that are just now catching on to mood rings, Beanie Babies, and Cabbage Patch Kids.

"Damn," Nix says. "We've found the capital city of eBay."

I check the directions I scrawled after looking up the address Aunt Dot gave us. I almost can't believe we're this close. "We head on down Main Street, then take the first left past the square."

Nix makes the turn, and we're in a place of old subdivisions now, little frame houses slipping quietly back into the earth of their beat-down yards. The trees are large and monstrously disfigured into half moons and saddle shapes where the power lines cut through. Daddy's house is easy to find.

"Oh my God."

There it is: 408 Front Street. A small wood frame house painted blue—and not just any blue, but the kind that comes in really small cans in the sale bin at Home Depot. The driveway is two lines of wrinkled concrete with a thick Mohawk of grass between them.

Nix turns in. There's only room for the van and the red pickup in front of us. Daddy's pickup. So banged and scarred, it looks as if it's been resting on the bottom of the Gulf of Mexico for the last eleven years. The back window is spiderwebbed with cracks. There's a gun rack, but no gun. A bald tire in the truck bed is looped with a monster chain. Nix cuts the engine, and we sit there.

"Wow," Nix says. "Just—wow." I'm speechless. Nix looks at me. "You okay? Breathe, Frances. How bad can it really be?"

"Pretty bad," I say in a shaky voice. "Hurry and get out before I change my mind."

We get out and make our way through the crabgrass to the concrete stoop. My feet feel like blocks of cement. I reach for the bell, then realize the front door is open behind the screen. It's so dim inside, it's hard to see anything. Nix raps on the door frame.

"Yeah," a voice instantly yells, startling me. It's higher pitched than I remember, and scratchy with the need to cough. "Come on in, door's open."

I pull the screen door open and slip through, my heart trip-hammering. There is no foyer; we are immediately standing in the main room of the house.

The living room. What a terrible name for this little space. I can't imagine much living goes on in here. There's a couch, green and saggy, that looks as if it has been sitting in the same spot since the invention of microwave ovens. Something squat and cylindrical stands against the far wall—a woodstove, I realize, with a blackened pipe that bores through the ceiling. The door of the little stove hangs open like a mouth, a tongue of cedar firewood showing pinkly.

It's the chair in the corner I don't want to look at—someone is sitting in it. My daddy. The daddy who lost me or simply gave me up. He was such a big man in my memories—not tall, but big-boned, squat, powerful. I remember the line of his shoulders was a long, slanting upside-down V that became a football player's neck.

But the man I see before me now—the chair could swallow him whole. I can imagine him sitting there year after year until finally he disappears into its stomach. Eaten.

I wonder why he isn't saying anything. None of us is saying anything. The effect of the room is crushing—even Nix has to feel it. This is not a room to make jokes in. The single-paned windows are flyspecked and fogged, letting in blocks of feeble light.

There's something strange, unnaturally stiff, about the way Daddy's sitting. Like a man in a wheelchair with no wheels. I can't stop looking at his arms. The way they are resting on the arms of the chair reminds me of the Sphinx, as if he can only hold them a certain way.

"Yeah?" Daddy says, his voice a high-pitched croak. "What you kids need?" He coughs three times, lungs sounding as if his alveoli are being ground into sausage. I look around, but there's no smoke, no cigarettes.

"Hello, um, we're looking for Mr. Larry Jelks?"

"Nobody's called me 'mister' since Miss Nicholson, 'long about third grade," the shriveled man says. "But if you're looking for Larry Jelks, you sure as hell found him. What can I do for you?"

He's waiting for me to say something, but I want to run instead. Standing in this room is like holding a wire pulsing with an electrical charge—I want to drop it and get away, but it's stuck to my hand.

"We've come from Alabama—" I say, catching myself as if afraid of saying, *A banjo on my knee.* "To—see you."

"Come here, girl," Daddy says, his voice cracking a little on the word *girl.* "My eyes are shot, and I don't have my glasses handy."

I take a reluctant step forward. The only electric light is coming from a TV sitting in the corner. The left side of the screen says, *Four easy payments of $69.95.* The right shows a hugely muscled guy on an exercise machine, rocking his legs back and forth as if skiing in midair. His skin is purple. He doesn't look remotely human.

"Aunt Dot," I say finally. "We went to see Aunt Dot, and she told us where you live."

I keep glancing at the TV because it's safe. I don't want to look at the man with the locked arms. But then I have to because he's talking to me.

"Are you?" he says quietly.

"Yes. Yes, I am, Daddy," I say.

daddy crying

When Daddy comes home, the door opens and he comes in, and then he comes out, and there is another car there, all hot in the dust from the driveway and bouncing from driving so fast and stopping hard. The sheriff gets out and goes to Daddy, and then Daddy is bending over next to his truck, then he is falling into the grass next to the house, and the sheriff has his arm on Daddy. A woman is getting out of the car.

I've never heard Daddy make noises like that. It's like an animal sound, an animal that is badly broken or hurt or scared or maybe just about all dead. The sheriff, the man and the woman in their sheriff suits, get over next to Daddy and they are standing on their knees now, the sheriff on one knee and the sheriff woman on two knees. And they are holding Daddy's arms and saying something, but I can't hear what they are saying. I don't want to hear.

It's a long time before I will come out again, out from the crawdad creek to where the sheriff is, to where Daddy is lying on the ground. Where he is crying and making noises, and all the cars are parked. It's too many cars. I can't come out. I might just stay here and never come out. Maybe there is no Fireless, but this creek is here, and this is a place where nothing bad has ever happened. My feet are in the water.

They have been in the water a very long time, and the sun has moved across the sky. Through the bushes and the trees I can see people coming in and out of our house, and Daddy is sitting up now. He is drinking something from a cup that someone has given him. A man is talking to him now, someone with a uniform, touching Daddy on the shoulder. Daddy is standing now; he drops the cup; he's going all around the house, trying to get in; he's fighting to get in with other people, but they won't let him. Now he's by the cars and looking in the cars, and he's saying something, and he's getting louder and louder saying it.

"Francine!"

That's what he's saying. "Francine! Francine!"

They are trying to talk to him and hold him and now they are suddenly changing, wanting to do the same things Daddy is doing. "Francine! Francine!" he says. I can hear him perfectly right now. It's like his voice is inside me, pulling my insides to him. But I don't go. I can't go yet, I can just watch now, all of them looking. All of them looking for me.

thirty-eight

"Come closer," Daddy says.

But this is as close as I want to come. Nix touches my fingers, letting me know it's okay, he's here with me, won't let anything bad happen.

"Turn on that light," Daddy says.

He lifts one arm, and it's as if he's wearing a stone costume. He's trying to point at a lamp on the wall, but his arm only goes up so far. Nix fumbles with the lamp, and when it clicks on, the room is screamingly bright. Oh my God. A little chirp of surprise slips from my mouth. I wish Nix would turn off the light. I wish I wasn't seeing this.

Daddy's eyes are puffy and allergic, his nose broader, the pores large, skin tinged a reddish violet. His hair is sparser on top; the thick curls I remember are now mostly in a gray ruff above his ears and around the back of his neck. His lips are dry and thin. He seems to have lost a ton of weight. But none of that is part of the shock that hits me when I see his arms.

"Don't even want to touch me, do you, Francine?" Daddy says.

I start to say something, but it's impossible.

"Can't say I blame you," Daddy goes on. "Look a little bit like Frankenstein Junior, don't I?"

He's wearing a long-sleeve shirt, but the sleeves are unbuttoned and rolled back sloppily to the elbows. His wrists—

"Oh my God."

Daddy's wrists—there's something wrong with them. He's got—there's metal sticking out of his arms. It looks like—it is—

"Screws," Daddy says. "They put them in my wrists basically to hold the bones together. I fell thirty-seven feet at Belfonte. Doesn't sound like much, does it? But I fell right through the goddamn roof at the new control room at Tower Three onto a concrete pad. I tried to catch myself. Now isn't that the stupidest thing? But that's what you do, even when you fall that far. You get your hands down to try to catch yourself. Shattered both wrists. Broke my back. Stove in a bunch of ribs—I had a collapsed lung. And I never even lost consciousness."

"Oh, Daddy. I'm so sorry—"

"The doctors said they had never seen anybody live through a fall like that. I'll never work again. The bones won't fuse. They can't do anything about it. It's okay. You can come closer. You can look."

I glance at Nix. His mouth is hanging open. He takes my hand and we go forward together.

"Does it—does it hurt?" It's the only thing I can think of to say.

Daddy holds up his arm again. "Not so much on a day like today. But when a thunderstorm rolls in—Lord, you talk about aching. They've done everything they could, goddamn doctors. Five separate operations. Any more than that, and I've eaten through my cap on the insurance."

Nix whistles sympathetically under his breath.

"I still have that little house up in Benton County. The place where we used to live. It's been up for sale off and on for ten years, but nobody will buy it, even though I'm practically giving it away. Hey, could one of y'all bring me a sip of water? I keep it in the 'frigerator so it's ice cold. Grab you one if you want." I go and get it and Nix hands the bottle to him.

"Ah. Man. That's good." Daddy wipes his mouth. "Thanks. Doctors. I used to tell people, what are doctors good for? Just easy stuff like fixing bones, that's it. They can't treat anything complicated. Now I wonder if they can even do bones. But everything's too smashed up. I can't lift anything more than a bottle of beer. Doesn't that beat all? After all this time, I bet you never thought when we finally saw each other, it would be like this, did you? Who's your friend?"

I realize I haven't introduced Nix. "Nix," he says, coming over and extending his hand. "From New Orleans. We go to school together."

Daddy takes Nix's hand, and it's painful watching him trying to shake it. The screw on his wrist glints in the lamplight. Nix's face never changes. He amazes me.

"Well, hell. Storm blew in a damn coonass, huh?" Daddy smiles, but it's not a mean smile, and the words don't sound mean.

"Creole, actually," Nix says.

"Same difference. Which part?"

"On my momma's side."

"I mean, which part of NOLA. I've been down that way a time or two for the Sugar Bowl."

"Metairie. Smack in the middle of the Pontchartrain Basin."

Daddy grunts and shifts in the chair by lifting himself on his elbows. He turns his attention back to me. "Well, Francine, looks like you landed in high cotton. Look at you. I'd know you from a million other girls. You look just like . . . her. Only shorter. So you took after the mackerel-snapper side of the family."

"Mackerel?"

"Catholics. Always got to eat fish on Fridays. A hamburger, they go straight to hell."

"Oh."

"I'm just kidding you. I've imagined this so many times—how long's it been? Too long. Way too damn long. I would say I'm sorry, but I can't anymore. I don't feel it. Look at what you would've had to put up with. I couldn't give you what those people gave you. There was a day I would have torn out my eyes to hang on to you. But—it was right. What they did was right."

I'm not ready to talk about that. I'm still looking at his wasted arms, his awful wrists. The screws—they're jutting out of his puckery skin at least an inch, terrifyingly metallic against the pallor of his flesh and slathered with something that looks like Vaseline.

"Antibacterial ointment," Daddy says. "I have to apply it twice a day to keep infection from setting in. How would you like to live that way?"

"I'm sorry."

"Workman's comp only goes so far. But you look good,

Francine. That makes me happy. Couldn't you come a little closer?"

I force myself to walk toward him, slowly cutting the distance in half. I'm not quite sure why I'm freaking out. I just know I don't want him touching me. Ever.

"Does it—" I start to ask if it hurts much, then realize I've already asked this. Maybe with some situations you can only go back to the pain, over and over.

Daddy squints appraisingly. "So one day you just got a wild hair and decided to run off and come see your old man? You say you saw Dot? Dot Cooper? Damn, I haven't seen her in years. How's she and that old bullshitter Wayne doing?"

"Fine," I say.

"Do you visit them much?"

"That's the first time, actually. Really, the thing is— Daddy—I want to see Momma."

His face instantly changes. It's as if every muscle under the skin around his eyes and mouth goes slack and droops. "Your mother," he says. It's not a question, not a statement, not anything—it's words coming from a stone—no, a piece of fiberglass. Something that was never alive.

"She's dead," Daddy says.

thirty-nine

If feelings can ever be like fireworks, that's what mine are right now—but not the kind exploding with color and light and joy, but the aftermath—the hot, powder-burn ash bits falling back down on my head.

"No," I say. "No."

"Hold on," Daddy says, lifting both arms with a great wooden effort. "I'm sorry. It just came out that way. I didn't mean it the way you're thinking. I mean—the mother you had—she's gone. She's dead. She doesn't exist anymore. She killed herself that day as much as she killed—well, you know. She's just not here anymore."

Oh. God. Okay. I'm breathing a little more regularly now. I swipe at my eyes with the back of my hand. "But—how—do you still see her? Is she—does she talk to you?"

Daddy eases back in his chair and brings his arms down Sphinx-like again. "It's been quite a while. Well, maybe not all that long. I used to try to get over there whenever I could, but ever since the accident—I just haven't had the stamina for it. And don't forget, permanent kidney damage—have you seen her?"

The question catches me off guard. "No, Daddy. Not since—everything happened. I haven't seen her one time. I just want to see her. I want to talk to her."

"I don't know if that's such a good idea."

"But—what's she like? Can you talk to her? Does she— react? Does she say anything about what happened? About me?" There's suddenly nothing in his eyes—it's as if he's left his body; he's not dead, he's gone.

"Daddy?"

I wait a long moment looking at him, willing him back. At last he slowly licks his lips and starts to speak, as if trying to find the correct frequency on his personal radio.

"In the early days, I told myself I was going to see her every day, every week, every possible chance I got," he says wearily.

"So you still loved her? Even after she—"

He coughs violently, blotting out my question. When he stops coughing, his voice is a little less wheezy. "I did. I loved her. I still do. You have to understand—I loved the *memory* of her. I've imagined all kinds of things we could do—ways we could even start over again, the three of us. Build our family back together."

"You don't really believe that," I say. "You couldn't, Daddy."

His left hand rises shakily, then settles again. "I did," he says. "I still do. I'm sorry if that bothers you."

"But why?"

"Because I had to believe she would come back to me. To us. All the way back. The woman I knew was gone. Another person did those things. But I knew the real Afton would come back. I knew it. She had to. I was patient. Sometimes there would be flashes, I'd see her peep out again. For a minute or two. Sometimes just a few seconds. That kept me hoping. And she needed me so much. For a while right after it happened, your momma wouldn't eat. I don't think she even knew what she was doing, but she was starving herself to death. I was the only one who could get her to eat. You don't know how hard it was. I had to coax her, sometimes hours on end. Then finally she would let me feed her. Spoon it into her mouth, just like feeding a baby. I was up there feeding her every day. I'm the only thing that kept her alive, Francine."

I feel something sickening rising from deep inside. A poison oil is dripping down my throat into my stomach, making me sick, queasy. I take a small step backwards, then a bigger one.

"So that's what you were doing, Daddy," I say. "All those weeks I was living with Aunt Dot. You were with *her*. Talking to *her*. Feeding *her*. Taking care of *her*. Instead of me."

"I had no choice, Francine. Don't you see that? She would have died otherwise."

I turn to Nix, whispering, "I have to go. I can't stand to be here anymore."

"But we haven't—" Nix starts.

"I have to leave, Nix. Please."

I start to walk out, but Nix takes my arm, whispering soothingly, "I know, I know. Wait." He brushes a lock of hair out of my eyes and turns to face my father.

"Mr. Jelks?"

Daddy looks at Nix but doesn't speak.

"Do you know how long they'll be keeping her at the new place?" Nix says. "Your wife?"

Daddy grunts to clear his throat. "It's open-ended, far as I know. All depends on the remission of her psychosis."

"Great. Well, I'm sure she's in good hands," Nix says. "We've heard some wonderful things about Three Oaks."

"Three Oaks?"

"The new facility in Chattanooga."

Daddy frowns and seems to rise a little in his chair. "I don't know who's been pulling your chain, son, but my wife's in Fire Tree Recovery Center in Charleston. They wouldn't have moved her again without telling me."

"Oh, right," Nix says. "My bad. Fire Tree. Charleston. That's in South Carolina."

"Last time I checked."

And there, with those easy-sounding words, we have it at last—the place where they are keeping her. Now it's nothing but driving and some time. There is nothing else standing between us and my mother but some walls.

forty

As we turn to go, Daddy calls to us.

"Wait."

He looks at me a long time, eyes watery. "Please—please let me hold you just once, Francine," he says. "Before you go. You don't know how many times I've thought about you—wanted to help you. But things—everything has been so complicated. A man can't be expected to go through something like that and come out the other side with—I don't know." He trails off.

I look at Nix, not knowing what to do.

"Things change so much," Daddy says, his large head drooping. "You start out young, full of fire, gonna live forever and burn the place down a time or two along the way. But—things change, and your life isn't your own anymore. I promised myself so many things. You were a big part of those promises. But they took you away from me before I could get my life together again. You'll never know what that was like, losing you. Please, at least let me take your hand for a second."

I'm frightened and—I have to admit it—a little bit grossed out.

But it's more than physical revulsion. I'm sickened by this

man, this person who was supposed to be my father for all time. I was supposed to see him grow old, bury him, grieve over him, and nothing, there's nothing there.

I look pleadingly at Nix. His face doesn't change one millimeter, his eyes don't move, he doesn't even breathe differently. But I know what he thinks I should do. I know what *he* would do. So I walk over to this man, this broken person, and let him take me in his arms.

forty-one

On the way out Daddy asks us to turn off the lamp again for him. "It's weak on my eyes," he says, whatever that means.

He laughs a little, surprising me. But I remember how he used to do that. He would laugh right in the middle of something awful. Something Momma did, something else that was happening. And he'd laugh. It was his way, I guess, of trying to make the bad things smaller, more manageable.

"Hey, but we will keep in touch now, okay?" he says, his voice stopping me at the screen door. I see his dark eyes glittering in the shadows of his little corner, his arms laid out in front of him. I don't want to say yes or no, so I just nod a little and say, "Well."

"A book—you know, that's what we need to do," he says. "Hey, yeah. Write a book. We could do that. That's something a man can always do, no matter what. What do you say? We could put both our names on it. It would sell by the boatload, Francine. What do you think?"

"I don't know, Daddy," I say. "I don't know if I could write about it. I don't know if I should."

"But—maybe it could help. It could help both of us. Think on it. It would be inspiring to folks to know—to know you've done so good. Like that little girl in Texas who fell down the well. I saw her on Fox—she just got married. People love uplifting shit like that. You wouldn't have to write so much, just remember. I could fill in the gaps. I've got a tape recorder. A good tape recorder. It has cue and everything. A book. Can you imagine? We'd be on all the networks again, you know that? Everybody would want the story."

Nix is holding the screen door open for me. My escape hatch. "I've got to go," I say. "I hope your wrists get better."

"Well, you think on it. My number—it will be different—but I'm getting a phone again soon. But just remember my address. Four-oh-eight Front Street. Write me. Think about it, and write me. I'll send you a tape."

"'Bye, Daddy."

I let the door slap closed behind me. He makes a sound like he needs to say more, but I'm gone before he can.

"That was definitely pretty weird," Nix says in the van.

I snap my seat belt, feeling a shudder pass through my back. I know I'll never see this little blue house again. "Thank God it's over. Jesus. You're brilliant, by the way. Where'd you come up with that stuff about Three Oaks?"

Nix looks over his shoulder backing out of the drive. "Oh, you know, those places are always named something like that. Burning River. Six Feathers. Wounded Creek. He was acting so . . . proprietary about your mom, I figured he might not give us the address unless we tricked him into saying it."

"You're a genius."

"Yeah, and now we have a name for our journey."

"We do?"

"Sure," Nix says. "The Road to Fire Tree."

forty-two

We're hungry, but we can't get out of Red Vine fast enough. I feel better the farther away we get.

The sun is lower in the sky, and the clouds above the plateau look as if they are burning. It feels as if we've lived this entire day on the road. Nix starts to say something, but I don't feel like it, so we ride for half an hour not speaking. I don't want to think; I just want to absorb everything around me. Crowd the other thoughts out.

We see little houses that are barely more than trailers without the wheels. But you can tell they're someone's pride and joy, clean and neat, with flowers and new-looking cars in the drive. We see churches smaller than gas stations. We see churches that used to *be* gas stations.

Watching the world roll by in the fading sun, I realize it. This feels like a separate country. There are two Americas, and I have feet in both of them. But this is the one I came from.

As we start to descend the Cumberland Plateau into the Sequatchie Valley, my throat tightens. The road is so steep, I can imagine the wheel slipping in Nix's hand and the van tumbling hundreds of feet down a ravine. Nobody would notice us for weeks, months. Maybe years. I'm gripping the dashboard so hard, I'm leaving nail prints.

"I read about this place," Nix says, trying to puncture the tension. "The Sequatchie is one of only two rift valleys in the whole world. The other one is the Great Victoria Valley in Africa."

"God, just keep your eyes on the road," I say. "What's a rift valley?"

"It's where a plateau tears itself apart, leaving a skinny little valley in between. The Sequatchie never gets wider than five miles."

"Speaking of tearing itself apart—is that the brakes I smell?"

At last the road bottoms out with glossy fields and shimmering mountains on either side, and I can relax again. We pass farms and creeks and chicken houses—superlong buildings painted gray, with tin roofs, and gigantic fans on one end.

"It's weird."

"What?" Nix says.

"How bad I want to slow down and take it all in."

"Maybe you just don't want to get to where you're going," he says. I glare at him. "I'm kidding," he says. "I knew you'd like it."

"How'd you know? You've never been through here before."

"I just knew."

"This is the stuff I fly over," I say. "But it's almost too much."

"Sensory overload?"

"I guess. For some reason it makes me want to know every little story about everything we see. The history of each place—all the lives that have ever been there. Who they loved, how they lived. How they died. And then it's all gone in seconds, blurring past the window before I can barely think. New stuff instantly takes its place, and it starts all over again. Like, what's the deal with that house over there?"

"The one with the falling-down porch?"

"Yeah. The black porch. Why is that porch so black? And look how big the house is. It's the kind of house somebody was really proud of. Now it's falling to pieces. How does a house like that—why did they ever let it die?"

"No telling," Nix says. "Divorce. Death. Legal junk where the heirs can't agree on anything. Sometimes a house just gets so old, there's no fixing it up anymore."

"Nix, promise me something."

"Okay."

"Promise me you'll never get one of those vans with a TV or a DVD player."

"Couldn't afford it."

"But even when you're old and fat and bald and have a bunch of kids climbing on you, screaming all over the place. Promise me."

"Okay. I promise."

I unbuckle myself, lean across the stick, and give him a kiss. Something is buzzing. I look around at Nix wondering. The buzzing is coming from my purse.

"Oh God, Nix, I forgot to turn on the ringer." I grab my cell and answer it.

"Yes, we got here fine," I say to my mom, looking guiltily at Nix. "No, it's wonderful. No, it was okay. Really. I'm sorry. No. No. Just eating, having fun with the kids, getting stuff unloaded. It's really beautiful up here. I'll send some. I'm sorry. I know. Really, no, I know. I've turned it on now. Yes. I'm sorry. She's . . . up the hall with some of the other kids. No, she'll be staying with me. I just meant right at the moment she's off messing around. No. God, Mom, no. Okay. Watch a movie, probably. I know, I know. It's locked. Yeah. We promise not to get into it. Yep, first thing in the morning. Probably. No, not that cold. I did. I did. Don't worry. Please don't worry. Okay. I will. Yeah. Yeah. Okay. Tell him I love him too. 'Bye. Okay. 'Bye."

"Are you sorry?" Nix says, grinning.

"Quiet, you." I check for messages. Three calls from my mother, each one a little more freaked. "God, I feel so guilty. We're just lucky she didn't try to call the hotel. I'll keep it on ringer from now on."

"What's locked that you promised not to get into?"

"The bar in the room. Jeez, I hate being such a liar."

Now my view has been lost in the gloom of the evening. I close my eyes and let myself drift for a few miles, trying not to think about what a horrible person I am or my rumbling stomach.

"Do you ever think about having kids?" I say.

"Sometimes," he says.

"You don't sound too sure."

"I'm not."

"But you would be so great with them."

"Maybe. But sometimes you need to be strong in ways you never believed you could be. I've seen that with my mom and Brandon. I don't know if I'm that kind of strong. But I've always thought I would make a very cool grandfather."

I roll down my window. The twilight air feels good rushing past my face. Somewhere in the night a dog screams as if being attacked by dog vampires. I unfold a gas station map and flip on the overhead light.

"Why can't we cut across the corner of North Carolina? That seems like the logical way to go."

"The guy at the station said dipping down into Georgia is better. You save time because you don't have to take the curvy mountain roads."

"But we could stop in and say hi to Ann Mirette."

"Ha. No messages from her yet?"

"No."

"Maybe she dropped her cell in the Nantahala," he says.

"Don't even say that. I bet she's just busy letting Raul get her all wet. God, that didn't come out right."

Nix laughs. I like to hear him laugh more than just about anything else.

We stop to eat close to the Georgia border at a place called Uncle Jimmy's. Every table has a roll of paper towels on a spike, presumably to mop up the grease.

"They oughta add 'Sucks' to the name," Nix says. "Don't get me wrong, grease is an essential element to certain forms of comfort foods. But limp onion rings? Blasphemers."

The other customers look like guys who tried out for the Hells Angels and didn't quite make the final cut. I nibble at the edible bits, trying not to think about what we're doing, where we're going. But night has fallen, I'm hundreds of miles from home with a guy who is hot-wired to my insides. Everything is different, even cheeseburgers.

forty-three

Nix lifts his head from his food to look at me.

"Hey, can I ask you a question? Kind of a weird one."

"Okay."

"What was it like afterwards?" he says. "You don't have to talk about it if you don't want to."

I wait, fork halfway to my mouth. Then set it down.

"I can't really remember immediately afterwards," I say. "I guess I kind of blocked it out. I don't remember her being arrested or the police coming. I just remember when everything got really crazy."

"TV and everything?"

"It was insane. We couldn't stay in the house anymore. People in the yard night and day, getting inside, Daddy running them off. Then after I went to stay with Aunt Dot I didn't see him much for a while. I guess that's when—when he was taking care of—"

"I know."

"Well, somewhere in there he came back and we started traveling all over doing interviews. I think—maybe it was just kind of his way of getting through it, you know? Because you almost couldn't stop and think, everything was moving so fast. It's funny—I mean, strange funny—but the things I remember the most are the kinds of stuff you'd remember if you were seven and had never been anywhere before."

"Like what?"

"You know, how thick the wires were running all over the floor at CNN—how I had to be careful not to trip. How hot the lights were. I remember the lady who powdered my face—she kept calling me 'poor little dear' and smudging her eyes with a napkin. I got to meet Larry King."

"Really?"

"Really. I know what his breath smells like. Not bad, actually. I think he must tote around a pack of Altoids in his shirt pocket. I remember thinking it would be fun to pop his suspenders. I know what Dan Rather's shoes look like. I know the shape of Ted Koppel's head from the back. Weird stuff like that."

"Whoa."

"But the things that really got me—it was just regular stuff. Like some guy holding my hand when I stepped out on the curb in Atlanta—my neck hurt from looking up at the buildings. I remember a bald guy who brought me a warm Coke. Everybody said I was such a brave little girl. I didn't feel brave at all. I felt confused, mostly. I was so used to just being around Momma and my sisters. I missed a ton of school. Didn't you ever wonder why I'm eighteen, but I'm only a junior?"

"Oh. Right."

"I remember being hustled from airport to airport. I was so scared every time we took off—it was too much, too big, too heavy, no way could we lift that airplane into the sky. I remember the smell of luggage and how the material of the pant legs around me felt as we stood waiting to get off."

"Damn. I guess I never really thought about stuff like that," Nix says. "You see things on the news, you never think about how the people feel, what they are really going through. So nobody knows where you are now?"

"Not since I moved to Alabama. Unless my parents just didn't tell me about it. Carruthers was the first."

"I wonder how he found out."

"Who knows. Maybe there was something in the courts where they had to keep a record of my adopted family. Maybe Carruthers went through some kind of legal deal to find out."

"It's getting pretty late. You ready?"

We dump our trash and head out into the night, Nix holding my hand. Back on the road my head starts to slump against the seat, and I drift away dreaming of birds.

forty-four

When I wake up, Nix tells me we've crossed over into the eastern time zone. It's nearly ten o'clock. "I wish you'd let me drive some," I say.

"I'm all right," he says. "But we should probably start looking for a place to stay."

I swallow hard and try not to think about it. There are no other cars now. The highway is spooky. It's so black beyond the shoulders of the road, it feels as if we're riding on a narrow strip of land between two unseen oceans. Then a tangle of fairy lights appears in the distance. The patterns the lights make in the complete darkness are strangely thrilling.

"What is it?" I say.

"Could be anything," Nix says. "An alien spacecraft."

"Narnia. Middle Earth."

"An offshore oil rig. The world's biggest ocean liner."

"On land?"

I can sense him smiling. "Maybe we've driven off the edge of the world."

"No—I've got it. It's a city in an alternate universe. A city that only appears on certain nights at certain times. You have to be there at just the exact moment to see it. The rest of the time it's still there, but you can't see it, 'cause it moves in time and space."

"Oh yeah, I like that," Nix says. "A city that exists, but doesn't exist. Perfect."

"I wish we could get closer to it."

He turns his head to me. "Maybe we're better off not knowing? Because then it's still a mystery—"

"Nix."

"What?"

"What would you do if the end of the world was coming, and you knew it?" I say.

He moves against the seat, stretching his back. "Why'd you ask that?"

"I don't know. But what would you do?"

"Okay." He stares into the cone of the headlights. "I'd make oatmeal cookies."

"*Cookies?*"

"I would. That's just what I would do."

"Why?"

He lifts one hand from the steering wheel and pinches his chin. "Because the world is changing so fast all the time. There's nothing you can do but just say, 'Cool,' and roll with it. But some things can stay the same, *should* stay the same. Flour is still flour. Vanilla still smells like vanilla. Say a giant fireball is motoring toward us right now from Alpha Centauri. Okay, universe. You expect us to run and scream and kill one another? Sorry, we're making oatmeal freaking cookies."

"Why oatmeal?"

"Only kind I can make without screwing it up. Besides, they're Brandon's favorite." He points at the city of lights. "Look. It's going away."

"Maybe it's time," I say. "Maybe this is when it flickers and goes out, and nobody will ever know a city was there."

"Nobody but us."

"Oh, Nix."

"You okay?"

I feel light-headed. I crank my window down to get some air. I can hear birds, the wind, crickets. I had forgotten how loud the nighttime is in a place like this. A place like Fireless.

forty-five

We see the sign—its electric glow—from several miles away. There is nothing else close to it, so it looks like a strange fluorescent boat floating on a very black sea. I want to tell Nix that it's okay, that he can keep going, that we can make better time at night when there are no other cars. But I realize again that he's tired—it's not fair of me to want him to keep going only because I'm afraid.

The name of the place is the Shayland Motel. When we pull into the parking lot, I notice the name is actually Shadyland, but the "d" in the sign is messed up, burnt out. A wormy dread works its way up my spine.

"It'll be okay," Nix says, sensing my fear. "I've traveled enough to know a good place from a bad place."

"Which kind is this?"

He doesn't say anything but gets out smiling and arches his back. I roll down the window and call to him. "Wait."

"What?"

"What are you going to tell them?"

"That we would like their goddamn finest suite, please."

I laugh a little. It feels better, but then it feels worse again. "I don't think there's any difference."

"I agree," he says, tugging at my door. "So come on."

"Maybe I should stay in the van."

"Hey, it's not the nineteen fifties anymore. They aren't going to say anything."

"If they see me, they might scream statutory rape."

"No way. You look at least . . . fourteen. Come on."

I snarl a little under my breath. "Do I have to?"

"Like I said, you don't have to do anything. But I wish you would."

"Oh, all right. Move."

He steps to one side, swinging the door open before I can put my hand on the handle.

"This way, milady."

Nix bows ridiculously and takes my hand, guiding me over to the dirty sidewalk. It looks as if all the road grease in the world has settled there. There are only two other cars in the parking lot. One of them has duct tape and garbage bags for a back window.

"What do you expect for twenty-five bucks a night, the Luxor?" Nix says, winking and pushing his way into the office.

The door jingles when we come through. The man behind the counter is not really a man. He doesn't look any older than Nix. He has washed-out spiky blond hair, washed-out papery skin, and washed-out pale gray eyes. Everything about him screams out to be handled on the delicate cycle. He's leaning against the counter, his knobby elbows pinning the classified ads from a newspaper. Here and there are red circles on the paper as if he has been checking the job openings. I wonder if he will take out the shower curtain ring earrings when he goes for his interview.

It hits me: I've never been to a motel room before by myself. Do we get two rooms or—?

But Nix is already answering for me.

"A single," he says to the sleepy clerk.

"Single bed or two?" the clerk says, the corner of his mouth turning up. I wonder if he's deciding if I am Nix's baby sister.

"What's the difference?"

"Costs the same. Two fulls or one queen."

Nix looks at me and turns smoothly and says, "Two."

This could mean so many things. It could mean he respects me. It could mean I don't mean as much to him as I think. It could mean he's just giving me a chance, one way or the other.

"That'll be thirty-seven twenty," the boy-man says. "And we don't take checks. Cash or charge."

"I thought it said twenty-five for a single?" Nix says.

"Taxes and state fees. You want it or not?" The clerk smirks a little, and I wonder if he's trying to figure out whether we need the room for the whole night or just an hour. Maybe even less. I don't like the way he's looking at me. I study the office. A dusty fake plant is standing in the corner. A bunch of brochures for an antique car show that happened three weeks ago are fanned next to the cash register. Through a narrow door behind him, I can see the light of a TV dancing and moving.

I pay with the credit card my dad lets me use. "You know they can check online now, right?" Nix says. I have to smile about this.

"My parents are lucky if they can even get the thing to boot up," I say. "It will be a whole month before they see where I've been, if they bother to check the bill at all."

One room. I'm thinking about little else as Nix fills out the paperwork, writing in a fake address. The clerk gives us a key, a real metal key, not a key card. It's attached to a green, diamond-shaped piece of plastic embossed with the golden number 16. Nix hands it to me.

"Keeper of the Kingdom," he says, and we go out. The door bangs behind us, making me jump.

Everything is thrilling and terrifying at once. I've never done anything remotely like this before. I wonder if Nix has. Surely he hasn't. That's not the kind of person he is. Is it? The key feels as if it is vibrating in my hand. Am I really doing this?

There's a long bank of flickering yellow lights along the roof of the motel. Behind the building is a mass of dark trees jutting out from hills that can't be separated from the gloom. I don't like looking back there; it's too dark and deep and unknown.

"What is it about a place that makes you feel you are somewhere completely, utterly different?" I say. "Especially at night."

"The swastikas spray-painted in the parking lot," Nix says. "Here we are."

I fumble with the key. At first it doesn't seem to fit; then I can't turn it. "Here." Nix turns the key one way, then the other. The lock gives, but the door is surprisingly heavy. Or maybe I just want it to be heavy. Maybe I want it to take an effort to do this, to enter this room. My parents are not within two hundred miles of this door once it closes.

Unlike a hotel door, this one doesn't close by itself. Nix gives it a kick with his heel to shut it. I scrabble around for the light switch, and a small lamp pops on. The little beds with their tragic red velour spreads throw blocky shadows on the floor. The carpet is decorated with paisley teardrop shapes. There's a flat slab of tinny-looking metal on the far side of the beds with a rank of black plastic buttons across the top.

"I'll get the bags," Nix says, swallowing.

"I'll help."

"No, you can—you know." He lifts his shoulder at the dark space that must be the tiny bathroom.

"Okay."

But I don't go to the bathroom in there. I turn on the light and see the flecked mirror and the pink shower curtain, and it makes me never want to go into another bathroom ever again. I go back into the room and find a chair. The bottom has no springs, and it feels as if I might fall through. I sit and realize I will be doing nothing when he comes back. Should I turn down the covers? Both beds? Or just mine?

I step between the beds instead and turn on the bedside lamp. I don't know if this is better or worse, being able to see more. The room seems to be clean, at least. There is no television, just a big iron bracket on the wall where the TV used to be. I pull out a drawer; there's a receipt inside. It's for a water park in Wisconsin called Wisconsin Dells. Wisconsin? The nightstand holds a maroon-colored Bible. My hand flips the pages at random until my eye falls on a line from First Corinthians, chapter five:

"Yet not altogether with the fornicators of this world, or with the covetous, or extortioners, or with idolaters; for then must ye needs go out of the world."

Fornicators is outlined in red.

"Checking the Ten Commandments?" Nix says when he comes back in. "How many have we broken so far?"

I put the Bible back in the drawer and slide it shut and don't say anything. I can't look at his eyes. He lugs the suitcases onto one of the beds.

So here we are. Together for the first time behind a closed door that isn't in one of our houses. Hundreds of miles from our parents. Have I done the right thing? I haven't. I know I haven't. The night tells me I haven't—every bad thing that can exist is out there, right now, in the darkness.

Nix goes into the bathroom. I fall down on the bed, pulling the thin covers over my clothes, trying to keep from crying until my face burns.

forty-six

Nix is holding a can of something called Fresca. I blink, sitting up. I must have drifted off. He puts his free hand on my neck—it's wetly cold—and hands me the can of soda as if it were medicine. I take it because I don't know what else to do, and sip. It tastes of synthetic grapefruit.

"It's good," I say. "Thanks." And try to sip some more.

"It was all they had left. All the good stuff was lit up."

"That's okay. It's important."

"What's important?"

"I mean, it's important that you did it. I'm sorry I'm ruining everything."

"You haven't ruined anything. Everything is fine. This is a first for me too, you know."

"Really? You promise?"

"My mom would be scared shitless." He flops back on the other bed, propping himself up on his elbows, his neck bent. He uses his Connery voice. "No matter how old I get, I'll always be her baby."

"What would she say? I mean, if she knew."

"Don't let her fool you. She's easygoing, sure, but if you push her too far, she'll kill you. Shit. I'm sorry."

"Don't be. It's okay."

I take another sip and grimace getting it down.

"Billy Idol is damn stingy with towels," Nix says. "But I managed to snag us a couple."

"Towels," I say. My head floods with images: undressing, showering, drying off. All with Nix right there. "You want to go home?" I say, blurting it out before I can stop. "What do you think? We've come this far, you know? That's pretty good, isn't it? I never thought I would do it in the first place. I really didn't. You've been so great. I couldn't have done this without you. What do you think?"

He comes over and sits down on the bed next to me; it sinks alarmingly under our combined weight.

"You're just tired," he says. "We both are. It's a good thing we stopped."

"But it's so hard. I didn't know it was going to be so hard." I want to say that it's not just my mother, it's something about the night, the dark, this depressing little room, how it's all too much, how everything is closing in around me.

"Nothing wrong with being scared," Nix says. "If a tornado is bearing down on you, you'd be stupid not to be terrified. That's straight-up survival. But I bet a million bucks for every tornado, there're a thousand things that don't deserve that kind of fear. Stuff in our imaginations."

"You're right. It's pretty stupid. But what if the kind of survival I'm worried about is more than physical? What if—what if—"

"It's mental?"

"Yeah."

"You order pizza."

"What?"

"Sure. You order some goddamn pizza. You say, okay, going to have a crack-up? Might as well go to pieces while throwing down some kick-ass pepperoni."

"Nix, I'm serious."

"Okay, Deep Dish Supreme."

forty-seven

Big Ed's Pizzeria is several miles up the road, but our food's still warm by the time we get back. The pizza box is sitting on the bed between us. Both of us are looking at the space where the TV used to be.

"First restaurant I've ever seen where they can also rotate your tires," Nix says, laughing.

I pull a long, bubbling hot string of cheese up to my mouth. "God, this is so good. I guess I didn't eat enough at the hamburger place."

"Sometimes that's the way it is," Nix says. "You explore and find those good places you never would've tried otherwise."

I pull off another slice and bite the drooping triangular tip, inhaling the sausagey flavor, tasting it more with my nose than my tongue. I'm watching Nix's small eyes, how they widen and narrow, depending on what he is looking at, how hard he is thinking.

"Who was it?" he says, wiping his hands on a paper towel.

"Who?"

"The man who came in. The guy who saved you."

"Saved me? Oh—I don't know." I take a big bite, chewing

thoughtfully. "He was coming to read the electric meter or something and heard what was going on."

"So you were saved by a total stranger?"

"Yeah. That's why I believe in miracles."

"And you don't even know his name? Did you ever get to meet him after that?"

"Yeah. We were on TV together some. Doing interviews and things. He was a big hero, but he didn't think about it that way. All he ever said was how badly he wished he could have saved them—my sisters. I don't know anything else about him."

"Aren't you curious?"

"I guess. I haven't thought about him in a long time."

"Maybe we could look him up sometime."

I halfway clean my fingers with a napkin and fall over on my back. There's a tiny line of faded red-brown splatters dotted across the ceiling. "Ketchup—or blood?" I say.

"Blood," Nix says.

"How do you know?"

"That's way more than you could get out of one of those little ketchup packets."

"Maybe—maybe they had a bottle and squirted it up there."

"Why?"

"I don't know. Why does anybody do anything? Are you sleepy?"

Nix closes the pizza box. "Are you mad at me? You sound kind of mad at me."

"At you? No. Never. I—I don't know what I am."

A motorcycle engine suddenly burps to life outside. The growl gets louder and louder—I swear, some idiot is driving up and down the sidewalk.

"Is the door locked? Did you lock the van?" I say.

"Yeah. Sorry about this." Nix waves his arms around to indicate the room. Finally the motorcycle blessedly whines away into the distance. Now I'm thinking about this bed I'm lying on. How many people have slept in it? How often it has been used for—

"Look at me," Nix says.

I turn my head. He's in front of the window, wearing shorts and a T-shirt that says PROPERTY OF USPS. His mom gave it to him.

"I can't believe any of this," I say.

"It's pretty much real," Nix says.

"Why do you say pretty much?"

He plunks down in the saggy chair. "Because sometimes I wonder what is ever really real. Okay, you want to know something that terrifies me?"

"If you want to talk about it."

"Hypnotism."

"Hypnotism? No way." I start to laugh, then put my fingers to my lips, realizing Nix is serious. I roll over to look at him. "Why would anybody be afraid of hypnotism?"

"I used to be. Truly terrified. When I was a little kid, one of my friends down in Metairie got on this hypnotism kick. He carried around a little gold medallion—I think it was something stupid, like the symbol for the Power Rangers— but it was on a little golden chain. He would swing it trying to hypnotize the other kids. But I would never let him do it to me. So he would sneak up behind me and reach over my head and start swinging the medallion, and I would practically freak."

"Why?"

Nix dusts pizza flour from his hands. "Let's see if I can explain it. I was afraid of losing reality, you know what I mean?"

"No."

"I was afraid I would go under, and he wouldn't be able to wake me up for some stupid reason. And I would be living in this awful dreamworld that didn't really exist. And I could never get back out of it. But that's not the worst."

"What's the worst?"

Nix closes his eyes. "The worst was thinking, What if I wake up, but I never *really* wake up? What if it looks just like home—same house, same friends, same family. But I'm not really awake, I'm still hypnotized. And they can't get me to wake up, but I'm living in a world that looks just like my world? What if that has already happened? What if none of this really exists?" He touches the slick wooden arm of the chair. "I could still be sitting in Jackie Barlow's weird old basement all this time."

I sit up and come over and take his head in my arms, cradling it. "God. Whatever made you think of something like that?"

Nix talks into my shirt, voice muffled. "I don't know. Maybe—maybe subconsciously I needed to believe that bad things, like what happened to you and your sisters,

Columbine, 9/11, serial killers, what happened to Brandon—maybe I needed to know that shit like that is only a bad dream. It can't happen in real life. Only in some weird, bizarro world. And it would be so great if I could just wake up."

I bring my face closer and closer to his until I can feel his lips. Then my eyes close, and there is nothing, nothing at all, but Nix holding me so close I can barely breathe.

forty-eight

My cell starts playing the Indigo Girls' "Chickenman" in my purse. I jump a little, pulling away from Nix, and move too quickly to answer it.

"Hey, girl," a voice says the moment I open it. "Got your freak on?"

"Ann Mirette. Jeez."

"So tell me, I've got my Spy Shop digital recorder rolling: boxers or tighty-whities?"

"We—" I realize with Nix in the room, I have no idea what to say.

"You mean you haven't even gotten down to it yet?" Ann Mirette says. "I almost didn't call, afraid I was going to interrupt the hunka chunka."

"God, you're so terrible," I say. But I'm smiling when I say it. "Where've you been? What's going on?"

"It took a million years getting through the mountains. For a long time I couldn't get a signal. The switchbacks were impossible, and every five feet there's a church bus strapped with forty-two rubber rafts blocking the way. Somebody taught the Baptists how to procreate."

"Have you been in the river yet?"

"Only wading. The rocks are covered with this slimy

underwater moss, slippery as owl crap. Donnie Johnson busted himself. It was high-larious. We ate at Denny's, Frances. *Denny's.*"

"Oh my God."

"Oh my God is right. But the hotel is cool. Even has an indoor swimming pool. We shut it down. They finally had to run us off. I just got back."

"Pictures?"

"I'm uploading a bunch to your phone. Wait'll you see Jameson the Bear in swim trunks. Talk about a Roswell moment—I nearly lost my Lumberjack Slam breakfast."

"Great. Thanks."

"Damn, girl, I'm so hungry for details—but I guess the spotted wonder is standing right there?"

"Yes. Yeah, well, sitting, actually."

"Okay, then at least tell me the safe stuff. What about your aunt? Did you find her? Was she nice? Where are you?"

I fill Ann Mirette in on our day.

"Charleston," she says. "Talk about synchronicity. I went there last summer for an archery meet. Fort Sumter is right there on a little island in the harbor—you have got to go see it. There are still pieces of busted brick lying all over from the bombardment. You can pick them up! They still have the flag that was flying when the Civil War—"

"I don't know if we'll do much of that kind of thing. I'll be happy just to survive meeting my mother."

"Oh. Yeah. You're right, eyes on the prize. I wish I could be with you. Look, I've gotta go—I'm keeping Raul awake—

you take care, okay? But do something outrageous and horrifying. Preferably naked. Call me."

"I will."

We hang up. Nix looks at me, and I start to repeat the
conversation, but he cuts me off with a motion of his hand.
"I heard most of it. That girl has got some lungs." He laughs.
"Neither."

"Huh?"

"She wanted to know about my drawers. Boxers or tighty-
whities. Neither. I wear Jockeys."

He lifts his T-shirt to show me the logo stenciled on the
waistband. I feel myself blushing. Just a little while ago I was
kissing him so long and hard, I couldn't feel my lips. But
with the phone ringing, Ann Mirette's insane gabbling—the
mood is gone.

"I've got to . . . go," I say.

I brave the white little bathroom and slip into my
nightshirt. A little bolt of alien terror runs up my throat
when I see Nix's toothbrush perched on the edge of the
sink. What's the matter with me? He's the same wonderful guy. Everything's okay. I put my own brush on
the other side, carefully balanced in the Ziploc baggie I
brought it in.

When I come out, Nix has opened a window and stripped
off his T-shirt. His chest is smooth except for a small oval of
blondish hair that becomes a honey-colored arrow pointing
at his navel. I've never seen him undressed before.

"I can't figure out the air conditioner," he says. He
thumbs one of the black buttons, and immediately a huge

noise floods the room; it sounds like a garbage truck com-
pacting its load. Nix turns it off.

"That's okay," I say. "The night breeze feels good. What
time is it?"

Nix digs his watch out of his shoe. "Whoa. Nearly two.
I keep forgetting we crossed the international date line or
something. Ready for bed?"

I gulp almost audibly and manage to nod. He gets up and
pulls back the covers on the other bed. I can hear him shifting around, getting comfortable, and then all is still. "Night-
night," he says, and clicks off the light. "Wait." For a split
second everything inside me goes to DEFCON 5. But Nix
only slides over and kisses me on the forehead; then his bed
creaks again.

Now I'm twisted in the sheets on my bed in the dark,
my face to the wall, praying. Praying he'll believe I'm asleep.
And then I am.

forty-nine

"Francine."

I wake with a start. The only light I can see is an unfamiliar fuzzy rectangle hanging in space. I don't know where I am. Worse—a long arm is draped over my side. I can feel a big hand flat against my stomach. There are long legs nestled against the backs of my legs. A snuffling sound in my ear—

The noise I make is more grunt than scream. I try to sit up, arms flailing. "Nix." And then I realize what has happened. Sometime in the middle of the night, he has gotten in bed with me.

He makes a snuffling sound, and I feel his body tighten against mine. "Um. Hey."

My heart is pounding. "When did you—how did we—?"

Nix makes lip-smacking sleepy sounds. "Huh? Oh. Yeah. I think maybe . . . you were kind of whimpering. I think maybe you had a bad dream."

"How long have we been like this?"

"I . . . don't know."

"God. God, you scared me."

I can feel his arms reach over his head, stretching. "Me? Want to switch?"

"Switch what?" My pulse begins to slow down. I'm in

bed with Nix. *With Nix.* Along one edge of the curtains I can see a sliver of oily parking lot glowing under a mercury streetlamp like dribbly blood. "You're so warm," I say.

I feel his chest expand, as if he needs lots of air to talk. "Mom always called me. Human Bed Warmer. When I was a kid." He's barely awake. So tired he can only speak in chunks of thought the same size as his breaths. "I twitch."

"What?"

"Just warning you."

I laugh quietly, feeling a little better. I reach behind me to give his cheek a pat. He could stand a shave. "You're crazy, you know that?"

"Yeah. Can you. Sleep like this?"

"I can try," I say. "Why did you call me Francine?"

"Bluh?"

"Just as I was waking up, you called me Francine."

But he's gone. I lie there unable to sleep, actually letting myself be held, circuits completely fried. I'm safe. I'm lost. I'm sane. I'm freaking out of my mind. I've never been held this way before. I have dreamed of this for so many years. It can't be happening, but it is. Nix's unearthly heat, his gentle snore, the touch of his distinctly nonfeminine legs are my evidence.

Time passes. I drift in and out of sleep, waking frequently to reposition my body. This is a huge surprise—sleeping entwined like this. It's pure heaven for about ten minutes; then it's completely uncomfortable.

Nix's long, hot leg is across my ankle, making me feel slightly claustrophobic. I don't dare move it. Not because

I'm afraid of waking him, but because I'm afraid of losing contact with his body. It's as if breaking free would mean I never get a second chance. I don't know what to do, so I do nothing.

I adjust my pillow for the forty-seventh time. Nix stirs against my hip. He lifts his leg and lays it across my thigh. I'm instantly paralyzed, my mind a blizzard of conflicting emotions. Is he asleep? I push against him.

"Nix?"

He curls into me and kisses my neck. He's touching me through my nightshirt. He moves his hand to my stomach, setting off a delicious autonomic quiver; I feel my back muscles contract pleasurably, my shoulder blades moving together as if connected to his lips by a wire. It's almost more than I can stand.

"Nix?"

Oh my God. He's kissing my spine. Vertebrae by vertebrae. I love the size of his hands, the length of his fingers—I love his strength, but I'm terrified. He can do anything he wants. What does he want?

He brings one hand down. I can feel it hanging in space above my left breast. Then I feel his fingers touch me. I feel their warmth against my tingling skin. I feel my response, the way my back lifts to bring us closer together.

I turn in his arms and kiss him. We kiss long and deeply as his powerful thigh comes up between my legs, pressing into me. The pressure of his leg rearranges things inside my body. I can feel it all the way to the tips of my fingers and toes. Nerves I've never used before are springing alive and sending messages. Messages about blood and breathing and rustling sheets.

I'm stupid. I don't know what to do—I don't know what to do. Is this the place? The place where it finally happens? Is this the real reason we have come all this way? This room?

"Please," I say. "Please."

I wonder if he understands the word is going in two directions at once. Nix touches my knee, slowly brings his hand up the inside of my bare thigh. My legs are shaking. My breathing is coming in rags. Too fast. I'm not ready. I can't do this. I'll mess it up. He'll hate me forever, he'll run, he'll—

But it's happening. It's really happening—and then—

She is there. Squatting on her hairy Morlock spider legs in the corner, watching us. Her dark bangs like a nasty picket fence. Her eyes black and rectangular, mouth hanging open, tasting the air, licking her thin lips. She's smiling. She wants this to happen. She needs it to happen. She wants his hand there, between my legs. To begin everything.

How could I have done this? How could I have come here? How stupid can I be? This is exactly what she wanted, isn't it? She knew this would happen. She knew all she had to do was get me away from them, my parents, get me out here alone and lost and terrified, and—

"I can't," I say into his chest, fighting to control myself.

"What?" he says. "Did I do something—what is it?" Even in the dark I can tell he's trying to find my eyes, but I'm hiding them from him.

"It's not you. You have to understand. Please. I can't. I have to stop. Please. Please forgive me."

He starts to speak, but I cover his lips with my fingers. I've got to get it all out or never say it again. "I'm so afraid. Please. I don't know what's wrong with me. It's all wrong. It's shit. Everything, everything."

"Shhhh, shhhh," he says, brushing a tear from my cheek.

"I've destroyed everything. I'm terrible. I can't do this. Please. Please tell me it's going to be okay. Please. Please tell me it doesn't matter."

"It doesn't matter," he says, rolling over onto his back. "Actually, everything matters. It matters to me if it matters to you."

"Please hold me."

I lie across his chest, my ear suction-cupped to his sternum. I listen to his heart and feel his breathing moving my hair. "Please don't hate me," I say.

Nix sighs, stroking my cheek. "I don't hate you. I could never hate you."

"I'm so sorry to disappoint you. I know—I know you must have been thinking about it, or you wouldn't have gotten into bed with me."

He doesn't speak, but he slides out of bed. I hear him fumbling with the lamp, and it flares to life. And now I can see—this is *his* bed I'm lying in, not mine. It was me. I was the one who came over.

fifty

I have never felt so monstrously alone. Nix is snoring right over there, a million miles away. It's a gentle, funny, whistling little snore; if I was an ant and could stand on the very top branches of a tree and listen to the wind, it might sound like that.

I'm crying because I know the very best day of my whole life is over. I just killed it. And everybody knows there are no second very best days.

fifty-one

Nix is taking a shower. I drag myself out of bed, eyes aching from lack of sleep, and pull the curtains back. No monsters, just an overcast day loaded with dark, furry-looking clouds. The hills that were menacing and mysterious last night turn out to be strewn with rusting tractor parts. Some kind of farmer junkyard. Shayland has gone—Shadyland has taken its place. The road out front is not a pathway to a magical city, just asphalt with bad skin. We clean up and leave without speaking much.

Maybe I won't see her today, but we'll be in the same town for the first time in over a decade.

I yawn miserably listening to the whine of the van's tires as we nip off the corner of Georgia. The names of the towns don't thrill me so much today. Adairsville, Cartersville, Buford, Suwanee, Sugar Hill, Canton, Waleska—does anybody really live on a road called Parks Cemetery Street?

Crossing into South Carolina, everything is suddenly for sale. Everything. We drive past miles of scungy farms without seeing a single piece of property anybody wants to keep. Some of the real estate signs are rotted. I can't help feeling it's a bad omen.

Neither of us has spoken about what happened last night.

But the voice in my head is beating my soul into sushi—
I love you, Nix. I love you, Nix.

Over and over. Those four words have become the back-
beat to my consciousness. As if by saying them enough times,
I can somehow keep him with me. Nix is so quiet. I try to
concentrate, to remember this is the last leg of a difficult
journey, but I keep thinking about him instead. Wondering
if things between us have changed.

The countryside gets flatter, grassier. A little more poor.
We see peeling whitewashed churches. Dusty, barefoot kids
playing with the guts of a glassless TV. A massive concrete
football stadium in a place that probably can't afford libraries
or fire protection. Nix exits and turns into a Taco Bell surrounded by exotic-looking plants with sawtooth leaves.

"Is that a palm tree?" I say when we sit down with our
food.

"Sabal palmetto. State tree of South Carolina. How far
do we have to go, navigator?"

I unfold the map and use my knuckles to measure the
distance. "A little over a hundred miles."

"If the traffic's not too crazy, we'll be there in a couple of
hours," Nix says.

I can't believe we're this close. This close to Fire Tree. My
mother, the Morlock. I dump the rest of my lunch in the
trash.

Back on the road, I remember to open my phone and
check out the pictures Ann Mirette uploaded: a blue church
bus with white crosses painted on the exit door; laughing kids with half-wet T-shirts stumbling across shallow,

frothy water; sunburned girls mugging at Denny's; Coach Jameson's prehistoric belly. It all seems to be happening on another planet.

Heading out of town, the clouds finally burst, drenching the flat landscape and blurring my view. Lightning forks above the highway, hanging in the sky for long seconds, like an after-exposure. The road ahead looks as if it is vanishing into strands of dark hair. I close my eyes.

I realize I've been asleep when the van lurches. I unstick my bottom lip from the window and roll it down. Instantly the air feels heavier, muggy. I can smell steam coming off the street, but the rain is gone. Nix is turning into the parking lot of a Best Western. We're here. Charleston, South Carolina.

fifty-two

Nix pulls into a parking space near the office. I can see the shapes of people moving around in the lobby.

"Hi," I say, stretching.

"Well, hello," he says, tugging on my left earlobe.

"Why didn't you let me drive? You must be dead."

"Actually I feel pretty good. Think I got my second wind in Columbia, knowing we were so close."

"I can't believe we're here. I really can't believe it."

"We are. You figure they have beds inside?"

We get out stiffly and walk into the lobby. Nix sends me to the front desk to get a room while he checks the phone book for Fire Tree.

"We need a room," I say, feeling bold. If the counter were a foot higher, I wouldn't be able to see over it.

"Greetings and welcome to the Best Western Lowcountry Ocean International," a dark-haired, bright-eyed lady says in a crisp Hindu accent. "How may I be of service to you?"

"Ocean?" I say. I've completely forgotten Charleston is on the coast.

"Most assuredly." She raps away on her keyboard. "Folly Beach, Sullivan Island, Kiawah—all only a short drive away. Here is a brochure." She pushes it across to me and goes back to clacking away. "Be sure to check the tide maps. You may perhaps also be interested in a tour of the Charleston Slave Market, ghost tours of the French Quarter, the U.S.S. *North Carolina* in Charleston Harbor, or—"

"Oh. Really, we're not on vacation—we're here to visit a sick relative."

"Oh my goodness, I am most sorry to hear so. Is it serious?"

I'm sorry I brought it up. "Well, it's—it's my mother—we don't know, really."

"Well, may I wish her a swift recovery, and hope that you do necessarily otherwise enjoy your stay with us. Now. Do you require a single or a double?"

"Um. A double. I mean, single. It's just me. Me and my . . . brother." I point at Nix, who is getting a drink at the water fountain. "Whatever is regular, I mean—whatever you have."

"Hi, sweetheart," Nix says, coming over and kissing me on the mouth.

fifty-three

Our room is up on the third floor. I fumble with the electronic key. The light on the door is still blinking red. "God, Nix, you had to kiss me, didn't you?"

"How was I supposed to know?" he says, smiling. "Hey. Slow up. I think maybe you're putting it in upside down, Sis."

"What? Oh." I try it the other way, and the door blinks green. I swing it open with a click and hurry through.

"Oh no, Nix—there's only one bed."

He sets the bags down next to the dresser. "What can I say? You picked a single."

"But I thought they meant—I thought she was talking about rooms. God, this is embarrassing—I can only imagine what she must be thinking."

Nix laughs. "Probably something to do with incest. But the bed is plenty big." He walks over and flops on the mattress. "Ah. Nice and cushy too. Especially compared to Shayland. But damn, it's cold in here."

He's right: the air conditioning is doing its best to combat global warming. I fiddle with the thermostat and sit down beside him. "At least this room smells like a hotel room."

There's a picture above the bed—some kind of abstract,

but as I stare at it longer, I begin to see it's supposed to represent a man riding a horse. A horse with no head.

"Kind of a reverse Ichabod Crane motif," Nix says, yawning. "Speaking of Sleepy Hollow—I could go to sleep. I could sleep right now."

I go to the sink and splash my face with water. My eyes are tired in the bright glare of the mirror, my hair tangled and stringy. There are two glasses with little paper crowns next to the sink and a blow-dryer fastened to the wall like a plastic pistol. Yep, this is definitely more what I'm used to. "What time is it?" I say.

"Just after two, if this is right."

Back in the room, the temperature is already more comfortable. Nix is watching the TV Guide channel. Divorces. Babies. Angelina Jolie. I fall over on the bed beside him. "At least we made good time."

"I should've woken you up," he says. "You should've seen the ocean—well, some kind of tidal estuary, actually. The water was majorly dark. I saw a heron—I think that's what it was—standing in some swampy-looking reeds. It must be really low around here. Let's make sure to hit the beach before we leave."

"I don't know. It almost seems—what's the word?"

"Sacrilegious?"

"I guess. That's not the word I was thinking of. Disrespectful, maybe. But yeah. Like this trip should have nothing to do with having a good time."

"Whatever you think. I'm having a good time just—" He stops.

"What?" I say.

"Nothing."

"What were you going to say?"

"I thought it might sound kind of lame."

"What?"

"Okay. I was going to say, I'm having a good time just being with you," he says.

"What's wrong with that?"

"I don't know. Sounds like a line from some stupid song or something."

I put my hand on his shoulder. "Nix—is everything okay? About last night, I mean?"

"Sure. Of course."

"No, really. Most guys would be pretty—"

"I'm not most guys."

"I'm sorry. I know you're not."

"No, it's okay, really. I mean, who are 'most guys' anyway? Whoever said most guys have to be jerks? Or playahs? Or anything in particular?"

"I don't know. Most girls?"

He laughs. "True. But if girls only knew what guys are really like—we can get pretty freaked about all kinds of stuff. It's just not too cool to show it."

I nestle into his side, feeling relieved, and kiss his arm. "You're sweet."

"Just don't tell anybody."

"Okay," I say. "Hey, did you get the number?"

"Yep." Nix pulls a yellow sticky pad out of his pocket. "Got the directions and everything. It's on the other side of town."

I can't help letting out a long sigh. "Fire Tree."

Nix nods. "Yep. You were hoping maybe it didn't exist, weren't you? That your birth father made it up."

"I guess I was. Please, let's just hang out here and rest for a while first, okay?"

He hands me the remote. "You won't get any argument from me. You think they got room service?"

Lying there, he looks so sloppily gorgeous. He's wearing a white tee and khaki shorts with little ribbons of material hanging down below his knees. I've held him so many times, kissed him over and over until we were both sore from kissing. How can I do that and not do other things?

But I'm starting to feel a little better. I arch my back until my cotton top pulls away from my jeans, exposing a little line of tummy. Did I want him to see that? Does he want to see? But Nix's eyes are closed. Pretty soon his breathing settles in, and he's gone to the world.

I try to focus on Animal Planet. Some toothless fool in Arkansas is lifting a rattlesnake into a wooden box with his bare hand. I start breathing again when he gets the lid closed. I wonder what it takes to bring yourself to that point—where you can actually touch the thing that wants to kill you.

After a while I get bored even with my own nervousness, so I call and check in with Mom, lying about our beautiful morning on the Nantahala. She makes me tell her all about the pictures.

"It's called the Blue Hole," I say. "The current got so still, and you couldn't see the bottom. They let us jump out and cool off. It was a little hard getting back in. Ann Mirette had to haul me up." Lying makes me feel like a mass murderer. "What?" I say. "Oh, just a couple of trees and a brick wall. You know what hotel views are like. I don't think so. Sure, they're around. Right on the same floor. You know kids, they want to stay up all night and party. No. No way. We might just get some pizza and watch TV. I miss you too. I've got to go. No. Sure. I promise. Okay, I will. 'Bye. 'Bye. I love you too. 'Bye."

"'Bye," Nix says.

I click the phone shut, do my best to ruffle his short hair, and kiss the tip of his nose. "How long have you been listening?"

"A while. My favorite part of sleeping is waking up enough to know you don't have to move."

"Feel better?"

"Definitely."

I lie on my back again. There's a pattern on the ceiling that looks like the sign for Pisces, two fish swirling around each other, repeated over and over again. I'm feeling misty and dreamy-eyed. Our hips are touching.

"What's going to happen, Nix?"

"With us? With life? Your mother?"

"All of it. Everything."

He thinks a long time. "I don't know. But I bet it's going to be interesting. I like interesting."

"Nothing ever bothers you, does it?"

"You're forgetting the hypnotism. Sure it does. All the time."

"I don't believe you."

He props his chin on his elbow, looking at me, and touches my arm. His fingers are hot. "Mom says there's a reason we get tangled up with certain people," he says. "Even the jerks. Even the assholes and weirdoes and crazy people."

"Okay, what's the reason?"

"Maybe you never know. Maybe you learn something from them. Maybe they have something you need."

"Even somebody like Rickey Thigpen?" I instantly realize I could say the same thing about Brandon and wish I could rip out my tongue.

"Yep. Even Rickey," Nix says. "Maybe especially Rickey. Who knows? We think he doesn't understand us. Maybe *we* don't understand *him*."

"I sure don't. I can't imagine what his parents must go through."

"Sometimes all you can do is care about somebody."

"All?"

"Oh, it's not a little thing. I don't mean that. It's the biggest thing ever. But maybe that's all you can do. You can't help them get better. You can't help them change."

"Sometimes you can't even keep them alive."

Nix wraps his arms around me, tilts my body to his. "Shit, you were seven. What could you have done?"

"I don't know. I don't know."

I close my eyes and try to flush every thought out of my brain. But the first thing I see inside my head is my mother. Sitting at that bare table, her leg shaking uncontrollably, her hair a wall of darkness hanging across her face. I open my eyes.

"I'm ready," I say.

"Are you sure?" Nix says.

"Don't make me say it again. Let's go."

fifty-four

I can feel every rotation of the tires all the way from the hotel. I can't feel them physically, but the result is physical, what it does to my stomach.

We swing through the city, gradually filtering our way through the afternoon traffic. I'm hoping to see the ocean, see anything beautiful and huge and alive, but it's hidden, maybe doesn't even exist. Instead this side of town seems to be all multiple-story houses with small yards suffocating with flowering shrubs. The trees are draped with something that reminds me of Christmas tinsel, only so brittle gray it looks as if you could blow it to dust with a single breath.

"Spanish moss," Nix says.

"God, it's everywhere. Coastal kudzu."

"Except it won't grow on anything but trees," Nix says. "I did a paper on it once in school. It's not really a true moss—more closely related to pineapples, believe it or not."

I'm glad he's talking. "But it's a parasite, right?" I say. "So it's killing the trees?"

"Nope, that's what everybody thinks, but it's something called an epiphyte. It doesn't steal any water or nutrients from the host, just takes it from the air and uses the tree for support. Indians called it tree hair. Then the French came in and called it Spanish beard to insult the Spanish. *Barbe espagnole.* Over the years they toned it down to moss. But it's still an insult."

"So what did the Spanish call it?"

"What else? *Cabello francés.* French hair."

Now we're passing a monstrous cemetery with flat marble vaults, dirty pug-faced angels, and sections where some of the headstones are knocked over, broken in half. Everything is blackened with decades of weather and city grime.

"Cremation is so much better," I say. "Look at all that wasted space. Buried husks of people who aren't even really there anymore. Caskets. Worms. God."

"I kinda like it," Nix says. "It's peaceful. Green. Nothing much ever changes, except you feed the soil. But that's New Orleans talking. Graveyards are a big part of who we are."

"Brrr."

I'm glad when we're past this place. The edges of town are weedier, the houses smaller, flat-roofed little white places with tired yards. We drive a few miles; then Nix turns onto a little road that is flecked with white and cream-colored speckles.

"Shell road," he says. "They used to have a lot of them along the coast. I guess they must've been cheaper to build. But they're slicker than owl grease when it rains."

The road narrows until it's hard to imagine two cars passing without swapping door handles. The ground looks spongy and treacherous, almost boggy. Around a bend the shell road runs out, and there it is, sitting in a grassy clearing. Fire Tree.

"Whoa," Nix says.

So this is where the monster lives. Fire Tree is a long, rectangular box made of sagging Civil War bricks. The building is two stories high, with wrought iron balconies on the second floor. The railings are oxidizing as we speak, and most of the windows are marred by toothy smears of faded white paint where somebody didn't bother to tape the trim.

There's a lot of junk up there. Folding chairs. An umbrella missing half its fabric. A white table that looks just right for kindergarten knees. A single, heart-shaped vase, but no flowers. Everything is shaded by big pin oaks and pecans and tulip poplars literally jammed against the building, shoving their branches into the walls, cracking its foundation with their roots. Nix parks the van at the far end. There are only two other cars, one of which looks as if it has been sitting here about as long as Fort Sumter. I say the first thing that comes to mind.

"It's horrifying."

"What?" Nix says. "It's just trees."

"All those leaves," I say. I'm imagining what it must smell like in there.

"You ready?" Nix says, holding open my door.

I didn't even know he had gotten out. I slide my feet around and step down carefully. "It can't be like this," I say. "We can't just walk in there and see her like this."

"But maybe we can," he says. "Maybe it will be that easy."

He doesn't understand what I'm saying. You don't just walk into the Morlock's lair the way the Eloi did. You hide from it. You watch what it does. You get away when you can.

Nix slams the door and takes my hand. Momma—what will she be thinking? How does she get through each day? Is she so doped up, she doesn't even realize what she's done? What she has to live with? Will she even still know who I am? Does she still hate me?

Does she want to finish it?

fifty-five

The woman's nameplate says WANDA GARTH. Her light blue smock has been washed so many times, it's nearly white. Some of her wispy hair has escaped its bobby pins, giving her head a misty halo.

The room is just as small and plain as the woman: a rubbery gray desk covered with scratches, a single high-backed chair, a table collapsing under the weight of a dying jade plant, its leaves like tiny yellow lightbulbs. A fan in the corner makes papers flutter each time it passes. Lights set flat in a ceiling of plastic diamonds wash the room with a sickly fluorescent pallor.

Scariest of all is what is behind Ms. Garth—a light green door with a small square window. The paint around the handle of the door is ringed with years of finger smudges. I wonder what's waiting for us on the other side.

"Do you realize what you are asking?" Ms. Garth says fussily. She's holding a white paperback book and looking up at us impatiently. I can read the title through her knotty fingers: *Chicken Soup for the Scrapbooker's Soul.* "I can't even confirm or deny if . . . the person you are talking about . . . is here. I've told you, you have to be on the approved visitors list."

"She's here," I say. "My father told me she's here."

"That's a moot point. You still have to be on the approved list." She taps a sheet of paper in front of her.

"Can I see it, please?"

Before Ms. Garth can answer, a noise starts up somewhere in the building, making me flinch. A persistent, violent hammering is coming toward us from behind the smudgy green door: *KERWUMP KERWUMP KERWUMP.* Ms. Garth looks oblivious to the sound. The thumping rises in intensity until I can't believe she isn't doing something about it. My heart comes into the base of my throat and lodges there. Then the noise stops just as quickly as it began.

Ms. Garth pulls the paper away and slips it back into the top drawer of her desk.

"It's confidential."

Nix has already tried every one of his most delectable voices; nothing has worked. It's time to bring out the big guns. I put my hands on her desk.

"But I'm her *daughter*, Ms. Garth. Francine Jelks. Isn't that good enough?"

Ms. Garth stares. There's no mistaking it: the color is draining from her face. It takes her a moment to get her composure back. "Do you—do you have any proof?"

"Yes, ma'am." I open my purse and start to dig out my driver's license, then remember my name is different. I put the license back. "After what happened, they had to change my name to protect me. But I swear I'm Francine Jelks."

"I'll vouch for her, ma'am," Nix says.

"I'm sorry, but I just can't let you in. Those are the rules. If you can bring me some sort of official proof of identification with a photo ID, we can begin the paperwork to have you added to the list."

"Aren't there any doctors here?" Nix says. "Or a manager?"

Ms. Garth takes a long strand of gray hair from her temple and pushes it behind her ear. Her voice tightens. "If you're hoping to go over my head, you'll have to wait."

"Wait?"

"The administrator's office is in Columbia. There is a doctor. She works in a hospital in Spartanburg and only comes here every other weekend. But you'll be wasting your time. She'll tell you the same thing I've just told you."

Nix and I look at each other, not knowing what to do. "But my mother asked me to come," I say, trying not to sound too desperate. "She invited me."

"Show her the letter," Nix says.

I unfold Momma's letter and lay it on the desk. Ms. Garth reads it without picking it up. "That could have been written by anyone. I can't let you in on something like that."

"Please." I startle myself by stepping forward. The desk is cold where it touches the exposed strip of my stomach. "We've come so far. All the way from Alabama. Please, I just want to see my mother, that's all. It's very important. I haven't seen her in eleven years. I just want to talk to her. Couldn't you please just let us in?"

"I told you, you have to be on the list—"

"But how long will that take?" Nix says.

"Usually about two weeks, depending on the administrator's schedule. He has final approval on all additions to the list. And then there are the wishes of your—of the patient herself to consider."

"But we don't have two weeks," I say. "We've only got today."

"You should have called ahead first. This could have all been arranged through the mail."

"But we didn't know where Ms. Jelks was living," Nix says. "We had to travel all over just to find her."

Ms. Garth stiffens. She slides her chair back with a raspy squeak and stands. She's not much taller than me. "I'm going to ask you to leave now," she says, a new layer of seriousness in her tone. "I'm here to ensure the safety of the residents. If you don't leave, I'll have to call the police and have you removed. Possibly jailed and fined."

"But—"

"Let's stop right here." Ms. Garth picks up the phone. "I've told you what you need to know. I've been polite. I've asked you to leave. Don't make me have to make this call." She waits, holding the receiver suspended in the air.

"Ms. Garth," Nix says.

"Yes?"

"Do you really want people to know you are giving Afton Jelks's daughter a hard time? After all she's been through?"

Ms. Garth waits, looking from Nix to me. Her gray hair moves in the wind from the fan. She slowly lowers the receiver to the cradle.

"You don't understand," she says. Her voice is softer now. "I feel horrible about what happened to you. I—I cried myself to sleep for a week after I heard about it on TV. So terrible. Those poor, poor babies. But you're not leaving me much choice here—you have to understand. This is my *job*. There are rules I have to follow. Regulations, some of them mandated by the state. I don't want to have you children arrested."

"No," I say, taking Nix by the arm. "You're right, Ms. Garth. Come on, let's go, Nix. We've taken up enough of her time. Thanks for being nice about it. We appreciate your help."

"Wait—" Nix says.

I tug him back toward the dark entrance, and we stop in the privacy of the airlock between the inner and outer doors. Through the glass the outside world looks like a museum.

"What are you doing?" Nix says. "We almost had her."

"You're not thinking about something," I say.

"What?"

"Nobody came running. They have no real security here." I push out into the sunlight, almost surprised at the intensity of it flooding into me.

fifty-six

Nix has driven farther up the shell road and parked the van behind a clump of weeping willows. The sun has settled into the surrounding woods, the shadows lengthening, but the day still has plenty of light. From here we can see the back side of Fire Tree. There are fewer windows on this side, and even more of the building is sunk in masses of shrubs, trees, and weeds. The boggy-looking ground is harder than I thought. The lumps are making me stumble as I hurry to keep up.

"Oh my God. It's just like *The Secret Garden*."

"Except I doubt there's neglected rosebushes on the other side," Nix says.

We're standing in front of a thick wooden door fixed into the brick wall on the back side of Fire Tree. I can feel imaginary eyes staring at us from every direction, though it's probably impossible to be seen from here—we're huddled inside a mass of beech leaves, looking for a way in. Nix examines the handle of the door. It's a metal lever anchored in a circle of rust.

"Can you open it?" I say.

"I'm almost scared to pull it too hard," Nix says. "It's so old, the handle might come off in my hand."

"You don't think—you don't think it goes straight into

anybody's room, do you? We can't do that. We can't just walk in on them. It would be too horrible."

"Don't worry," Nix says. "I don't think they'd have a door like this that just goes right into somebody's room. It feels pretty stout. I'm going to try it."

He cranks the lever and pulls hard, but nothing happens. I look around nervously through the leaves—the backyard is surrounded by a tumble-down chain-link fence. It would be easy enough for anyone to escape. I wonder if they even try.

"Could be screwed shut or deadlocked on the other side," Nix says, breathing a little harder. "Let me get my foot on it." He lifts his black sneaker and gets it against the door frame and heaves—nothing. "Damn."

"Maybe it's inward instead of outward," I say. "Doors usually open inward, don't they? Try pushing instead of pulling."

"Good gravy train," Nix says, smacking his forehead with the heel of his hand.

He puts his foot against the door and shoves, cranking the handle. Immediately there's a kind of grunting squeak, wood against wood, and the door gives a little. Nix pushes again, and it swings open, creaking like a door in *Silent Hill*. The interior of the room is completely black.

"We're going in *there?*" I say, my voice barely above a whisper.

"Let me go first."

I follow his broad back as we move slowly into the gloom, literally touching his shoulder blades. The room smells of craggy old metal and industrial grease. I don't want to let the door shut behind us. "Shouldn't we prop it open?"

"Somebody outside might notice."

"Through all that green?"

"Okay." Nix stoops, feeling around at floor level. "Here." He stands up holding half a brick and gives it to me. I kneel and slip it into the crack. My eyes are starting to adjust. We're surrounded by tall blocks of something flat and solid. I can sense that there are a lot of obstacles in our way.

"Wish we had a light," Nix says.

"God, if a spider gets anywhere near my hair—"

"Wait—look."

I see it now, a place in the room that seems a little lighter than everywhere else. Nix shuffles toward it with me following closely. Creeping around like this is nothing like the movies— it's impossible to move quickly. I have to pick my feet up and set them back down in almost the same spot. I'm terrified of stumbling or putting my hands into something nasty or dangerous.

Nix comes to a stop, and I slide up against him. "I think this is a mechanical room," he says.

"Mechanical?"

"Where they keep all the stuff that's too dangerous to put out in the open. Things like electrical panels, turbines, HVAC, etc. My dad used to work on this kind of junk."

"Oh, great. So you're saying we're about to get electrocuted or ground up into hamburger?"

"Just walk where I walk. I won't do anything stupid."

"On what kind of scale are we talking?"

I can feel him grinning. "Good one. You're braver than you know."

Sure I am. I keep shuffling my feet forward. It takes at least five minutes to navigate to the other side of the small room. I can see what looks like a second door there—a rectangle of weak light hanging in space.

"What's on the other side?" I say.

"Probably the hall that was behind the green door in Garth's office," Nix says.

"We can't just burst out in there, can we?" Something skitters across my back—I fling my hand behind me in horror to brush it away—nothing is there.

"What?" Nix says.

"Nothing. Jesus. Just keep going."

There's something undeniably mechanical pulsing menacingly on the other side. Nix levers the handle, and the door scrapes open. Instantly the air smells different. Chemicals? Cleaning fluid? Medicine? Maybe a mix of all three.

Nix eases the door open all the way while I hold my breath—but it's not the main hall, it's just another room full of machines and paint cans. It's a lot brighter in here—there's a single naked lightbulb under a little cage in the ceiling—but not much cleaner. Something nearby is throbbing and humming. I'm reminded uncomfortably of the Morlocks' underground domain.

"Air handler," Nix says, raising his voice several notches to be heard above the maddening vibration of the equipment. He points at a wall of scary-looking wiring snaking into a massive bank of metal boxes. "This is the equipment room. Those are electrical racks. Don't touch anything. Just stay close to me."

We make our way across the room until we're standing at the next door. Nix grasps the handle and pulls—the door opens a crack. I peer under his armpit at a little slice of green carpet and blue walls. We put our heads partway out. Nothing—a long, empty hall lined with identical doors receding in both directions.

"Just like in a nightmare," Nix says.

I shudder. "Garth must be down that way. What if she looks through the glass?"

Nix doesn't answer. He takes a single stride, and he's standing in the middle of the hall. No alarms, everything is still. I follow, heart jumping, and pull the door shut behind me. The carpet feels like Velcro. I don't know what I expected to smell in here—death, smoke, sickness, excrement, puke. But it's cinnamon.

We're directly across from one of the doors. The window is too high for me to see in without standing on tiptoe. The nameplate reads IVEY.

"Some of them don't have names," Nix says, starting slowly down the hall.

"Maybe those rooms are emp—"

The terrible hammering sound begins again, cutting me off. *KERWUMP KERWUMP KERWUMP.* I expect toxic leaves to sprout from the ceiling, blood to pour down the walls like rain. The sound moves rapidly toward us like a ghostly carpenter knocking above our heads. I can't scream; my soul has congealed inside my mouth.

We rush back to the equipment room door, but Nix can't open it. Something's wrong with it—oh God, something's wrong—

"It won't open from this side!" he says.

"Nix!" I say.

But he's looking in the other direction. Somebody's coming.

fifty-seven

My heart contracts—a woman is standing in the hallway not thirty feet away—for the briefest moment I think it's *her*, but she's too small to be my mother. The woman is wearing brown corduroy pants and a blousy pink shirt and blue socks. She must've stepped into the hallway while we were fumbling with the door. I don't think she's seen us yet—she's looking up the hall in the opposite direction.

I clutch at Nix's sleeve, questioning with my eyes. The only direction we can run is toward Ms. Garth. The ghostly hammering just as suddenly stops, leaving the air vibrating.

The woman turns and stares at us. She begins walking toward us in a frightening, jerky gait. Her head is cocked sharply to the left, as if she has to look at the world on a permanent slant.

"Don't run," Nix says, putting his body in front of mine.

"Did you?" the woman says. Her voice is high pitched and piercing.

Because of the tilt of her head, it's hard to tell which one of us she's looking at. I shrink behind Nix, my side against the equipment room door. The woman stops in front of Nix and waggles a bent finger, angrily.

"You have to go."

Nix lifts his arms slightly, hands open, friendly. "Hi," he says. "Um—we're here to visit Afton Jelks. Do you know which room Afton Jelks is in?"

The woman's head lurches violently to the opposite side. Her eyes are large and dry-looking, bloody-veined at the corners. Her mouth looks like a scar.

"You have to go," she says. "You have to go *now*. Mr. Carl is coming. Mr. Carl will see you. You don't want him seeing you. Don't let him in. Did you see what he did to my leg?"

Before Nix can answer, the woman unbuttons her pants and drags them down on one side; her hip is fish-belly white and covered in purple blotches.

"Does—does it hurt?" Nix says, eyes wide.

"Like a train ran over it. Three times!" the woman says. "Mr. Carl comes at night. He's coming. He always comes at night. I can barely sleep. All of you can go straight to hell."

She pulls her pants back up.

"Um. We need to be going, ma'am," Nix says. "I'm sorry about your leg."

"You'll be sorry. You'll be sorry when Mr. Carl finds you. He's coming. He's coming tonight."

My hands are on Nix's back; I can feel his muscles tighten.

"We don't know Mr. Carl," he says. "We're here to see Ms. Jelks."

"That stinking bitch. Three times. Mr. Carl will make you. He will make you. I can't let him come in. I can't. They said I can't. Three times. You sluts."

She turns away and pads painfully up the hall, head still

cocked, then picks a door on the left and steps through it. I feel myself physically sinking.

"Damn," Nix says.

"Are we okay?"

"I don't think she's going to tell anybody. But if they start popping out like that—goddamn."

"Jesus. Mr. Carl," I say. "Do you think he's real?"

"I think *she* thinks he's real. Probably a night watchman or something."

"Or a *patient*. God."

"Come on," he says.

I follow him up the hall. It feels a little better to be moving away from Ms. Garth's door. The light is dim in this section of hallway—some of the fluorescents are out. The sound of my breathing and our feet scuffing the carpeting are the only sounds I hear.

"Frances," Nix says, lifting his arm. We stop.

My heart feels loose in my chest. Nix points at the nameplate: JELKS.

fifty-eight

"You want me to look?" he says.

I grab his shirt, holding part of it bunched in my fist. "Okay."

He creeps up to the door hunched over, then slowly raises his eyes to the glass. I watch his face to see if it changes. "Shit," he says.

"What?"

He's still looking, not speaking. I can't tell anything from his expression. Momma's just on the other side of this door. The person who put a pillow over my face eleven years ago. The Morlock in her spider hole.

"Nix," I say.

He holds his hand out to me. I look at it.

He's still holding out his hand. I take two steps to him, and I'm there, standing in front of it. Her door. "Do you want to see?" he says. "I know it's her, it's got to be her. But do you want to know for sure?"

"Let me—let me breathe just a minute. I have to—stop—I have to just breathe a minute, okay?"

My eyes feel as if they are jiggling in my head. I sense the familiar numbness sliding over me.

"Hang on," Nix says, pressing my arms. "I'm right here. It's okay. You're okay. Hang on to me."

I steady myself, leaning into him, smelling the skin of his arms, drawing in long, hiccupping breaths. The breaths start to smooth out, and my eyes start to clear.

"Yes. Yes. Let's do it. Let's go in now."

"Maybe we should at least knock," Nix says. "Seems only right. We at least have to knock on her door."

I take my hand inside his hand—it's very small in his hand—and curl my fingers into my palm. "Let me do it," I say. I hold my fist up to the door and knock. We wait a long moment full of soundless screaming, and nothing happens. I knock again, harder this time. The moment stretches larger and larger and still nothing happens.

"Let me look again," Nix says. He peeks in the glass again, more boldly this time. "She's sitting by the bed," he says. "I don't think she heard you."

I knock as hard as I can. The door feels so solid, it's like the layers of another world, the whole crust and mantle and core, and I'm trying to punch my way through to her. Nix hauls me back from the door.

"She's moving, but—she's coming over," he says. "But. Goddamn." He leans away from the door. "Oh, man. I think she saw me. I think maybe she saw me."

"Oh God. What is it? Is she coming out? Is she—?"

Nix backs away from the door into the center of the hall. It takes everything I have, the blue weight of the fear, to keep me standing in front of her door. Still the handle doesn't turn.

Nix peeps through the window from a ways back. "I can't—I can't see her," he says. "She must be close to the door.

I don't know why she isn't opening it. Maybe—wait. There. She's sitting down again. I can see the top of her head; she's in the chair again. She must be waiting for us to come in."

I put my hand on the door handle—it's the coldest thing I've ever felt. I lever it down, and it moves, I can feel it moving, and—

"Francine," a voice says behind me.

I turn and a man is standing there, just behind Nix. *Oh God, one of the patients.* He's tall, wearing a dark blue suit. He could be an angel—not the kind in heaven, but the kind guarding the gates of hell.

"Ms. Jelks," the man says.

I slump against Momma's door as if hit in the chest. My breath rushes out. I pull close to Nix instinctively. The tall man is R. C. Carruthers.

fifty-nine

Everything inside me is falling, falling. I don't think there's any bottom. Carruthers waits as if enjoying the shock. Only he's not smiling. His eyes are yellow-gray and sharp. His white hair floats around his head like ghostly corn silk. Nix gets in between us, arms out in front of him, crouching like a linebacker.

"Please," Carruthers says, glaring at him. "None of that. I'm not a resident here." There's a new hard edge to his voice. Nix straightens but doesn't move away. Carruthers faces me again. "Frannie. I'm sure you will remember me. We've met once before. My name is R. C. Carruthers."

Even from here I can tell his breath is clean, almost sanitized, as if hiding some inner decay. He doesn't offer his hand this time, and I don't reach to take it. I can hear my teeth grinding together, sounding almost like saddle leather creaking in my jaw. Somehow I find enough spit in my mouth to speak.

"Um. Yes. Yes, sir. I remember," I say. "I'm sorry, but you startled us." I turn to Nix. "This is my—my friend, John—"

"We know all about Mr. Mullinix," Carruthers says coldly, still looking at me.

I don't know what to say. I'm still falling on the inside. How could he know we are here? Maybe it's a coincidence? No, he followed us. He's been following us all along. It's the only answer that makes sense. Why? We're going to be sued. Arrested. Slapped with a restraining order. My parents— God, what are they going to do?

"Did you come to see my mother?" I say.

"The authorities have been contacted," Carruthers says, as if this answers my question. "They will be here in less than fifteen minutes."

"But hey, we haven't done anything wrong," Nix says. "We were just looking for Ms. Garth and—"

Carruthers makes a dismissive motion with his hand. "Would you come with me, please? Both of you."

It's not an invitation, it's a command. I look helplessly at Nix; he shrugs his shoulders almost imperceptibly, eyes sadly anxious. *I'm sorry*, he mouths silently. Carruthers turns and starts up the hall in the direction of Ms. Garth's door. We fall in miserably behind him.

"Where are you taking us?" I say, speaking mechanically. "Wait—I want—I want to call my parents. I need to call them and let them know so they can—"

"Your parents have already been contacted," Carruthers says. "And you won't be able to get a signal inside the facility." My stomach drops. They know. They *know*.

I slip my cell phone out anyway as we walk, punching 1 for my mother and holding it down. I put the phone to my ear and get what sounds like an unnaturally rapid busy signal. I dial 3, Ann Mirette's cell. Same thing.

"I can't call them," I say to Nix. "I can't get out at all. Jesus."

"It'll be okay," he says, trying to smile and taking my hand. I let it go. I'm somehow embarrassed for him, for both of us. How quickly I need to run to my parents instead of relying on him. But there's nothing he can do to help me now. It's out of our hands.

Carruthers stops in front of a door that's indistinguishable from all the others, except that it has no nameplate. He takes something slim and black from his pocket and holds it up to the key lock. There's a click, and he swings the door open.

"In there," he says, waving his hand.

Nix looks at me, his face downcast. "I'm sorry," he says, and steps inside the room. I start to follow, but Carruthers blocks me with his arm. "Just him."

He pulls the door shut. "Hey—!" Nix's voice is chopped off.

"Wait!" I grab at the handle and turn it furiously. It's locked again. I wheel on Carruthers. "What are you doing?"

"It was requested that we place you in separate rooms until the police arrive," Carruthers says. "Come with me."

I stand in front of the door unable to move. Nix's frantic eyes appear at the little window.

"Please," I say to Carruthers. "I need to stay with him. I can't—I can't leave Nix."

"I'm sorry. You'll have to come with me."

He turns and starts back up the hall. I hang back, looking at Nix. He shakes his head, gesturing with his hands—he can't open it from his side either.

Carruthers is getting farther and farther away, seemingly unconcerned. I don't know what to do. I could try getting past him, getting out the door at Garth's end of the building. But I can't leave Nix here like this. The only thing to do is follow this thing through, whatever happens. I run to catch up.

"Please don't blame Nix for this," I say. "It was all my idea. I—I made him help me. I just wanted to see her. She invited me to come in her letter. The one you brought to me. What did you expect me to do?" I take the letter out and unfold it, try to hand it to him. Carruthers waves it away. "But I had to do this," I say. "I *had* to. Please, can't you just let us go?"

"Here we are."

Carruthers gestures at a second door. By now I've completely lost my bearings—I look down the hallway helplessly; it's so long, I have no idea which room he put Nix in. *Shit.*

"Wait," I say, backing away. "I don't want to go in there. Please. I can't. Not without Nix. I'm afraid to be alone in this place."

Carruthers sighs and opens the door. He reaches his long arm in to flip on the light switch. This room looks much bigger than the one Nix is in. It's some kind of common room, with a blank TV, stacked chairs, a coffee table, and a white leather sofa and chair.

"I will only be gone for a moment," Carruthers says. "Please just take a seat."

I turn to look at him, but he closes the door in my face without speaking. I wait for his white head to move away from the window before I try the handle, but it doesn't turn.

"Shit."

The room smells of some kind of pine disinfectant. I walk across the speckled tiles and sink into the couch. The leather is fiercely cold and so beat up and cracked it's almost fuzzy.

I can't believe it. I can't. All that we've been through, the chances we've taken, the lies we've told, the fear—we were so close to making it, so close to seeing her and getting out of this sickening place alive.

There is a digital clock on the wall, but it's flashing the time over and over. I have no idea how long it's been since Carruthers left. Will the cops come pouring in at any moment? What will happen to us? What is this, a misdemeanor? Or will they say it's worse, that we came here to threaten her? A trial—oh God, no. My mind leaps to various punishments. What do they do to eighteen-year-olds? We'll be tried as adults. Oh God. God. God. Tears track down my cheeks. I put my face in my hands.

My parents—I don't want to think about them, but I can't help it. Mom terrified, hair wild, weeping, throwing things in a bag. Dad sick, betrayed, neck bulging, face red, trying to comfort her. Their trust in me shattered.

As the numbness of the shock begins to wear off, it's replaced by a terrible, grinding depression. I'll never see my mother. I'll never see Nix again. I almost want to die.

I lift my head and look bleakly around this horrible room. It's sterile and white and old, the windows shuttered, a green expanse of Ping-Pong table peeking from around a corner—

There's a noise across the room, and I start up from the couch. The door opens and shuts. Someone has come in.

blackness

"Shine, come here," Momma says.

I pick my head up. A string of drool connects my mouth to the floor. By the size of the wet spot, I must've fallen asleep. The sound of Momma saying my name—how can I say what this feels like? I will try. I can feel it in my back. It goes up and down my back, making me feel completely cold. I can't believe it's so cold in here just because she is talking.

Why is the house so quiet? Where is everybody? Why does it feel like something is happening?

"Shine, come here."

I'm still feeling asleep, but I know I'm awake. She's calling me. Should I go to her? I want to go to her, but I also want to run and hide.

I can tell it's spring outside. That's what I want to think about, spring. Not her. This is my favorite part of the year. You can have the door open all the time, and we leave the windows open at night. I can hear all the birds and bugs and other things. It's spring, but something is different today. Even the birds are quiet. And then I can tell that all the doors and windows are shut. We're locked in, trapped. Why does it feel like that? Why do I feel trapped? What was happening before I fell asleep? I remember Momma was eating cereal

straight out of the box, and I wanted some too, but she gave
us a different kind. I don't think Momma wanted us eating
from her cereal box today.

"Shine."

She is angry, maybe, but she doesn't sound angry. She
sounds—different. I keep thinking maybe a big round cloud
has come down on the world and is sitting right on top of us,
making everything all muffled. But I look out the back window and there is no cloud; everything is clear. But nothing
is moving. The tall broom sage that can be moved with my
breathing—it's not moving. There are no butterflies or bum-
blebees or hummingbirds. I can't see the road from here.

"Shine."

I want to call Tan, but I can't hear her. And there is something that makes me not want to make a sound at all. The
floor is creaking above my head. I get up and go into another
place, and now I'm sitting in the little room where Momma
washes the clothes. I'm in a very small place between the
washer and the dryer. But it's too easy to see me here. She
can come right in the room and see me if she just looks
straight ahead.

Momma's coming down the stairs now. I hear them
creaking and popping from the sound her feet make coming
down. I don't know what to do. *Please help me. Please, somebody, come.*

"There you are."

Momma's in the doorway, looking at me. I have one sock
on and one sock off. That's what I'm looking at: my feet. So
I don't have to look at her. Because I know about her eyes,

and I don't want to see her eyes. Nobody can make me, not even her, unless she puts her face right up to my face. She's doing that now.

"I need you to come here," she says.

I look now, and her face is hanging down. Everything, her hair, it's all hanging. I don't know how to say it—her face hangs. Usually it moves so much—she has so many faces she makes when she is showing us things. Where are all the others?

"Come here."

Momma takes my hand, and her hand is very cold around mine. She pulls me up from the little place next to the washer, and I'm walking with her. She gets me to follow, and I come up the stairs wondering about my sisters, all of them. Everything is so, so quiet. We come down the hall to the bedroom.

The room. It's her bedroom. Momma has been there this morning, after she stopped eating cereal and left us downstairs to eat.

There is a smell—it's the kerosene heater. It was cold last night, and Momma forgot to turn it off again, and it ran out of kerosene. And when it goes out on its own like that, Daddy told us, it stinks up the whole house. I don't like it up here, the smell, but it crawls into my nose like a worm.

Now I come into the bedroom with Momma, and I see them, right away I see them, all lying on the bed, eyes wide open. Staring at the ceiling.

"What's wrong with the baby?" I say.

Even the baby, Suddle, her eyes are wide open. There is something on her neck, a black mark. This isn't anything I've ever seen or done or heard about before. They are there, my sisters, but they aren't there anymore. They aren't moving.

"Tan—please, what's wrong?"

Tan has never been still, not ever. She is always moving, never stopping; she even moves when she sleeps. I've seen her move and talk and kick the covers off. Please, Tan. What's wrong with her? Her eyes are wide open and she isn't looking at anything—I can tell because Tan, she always looks at everything, and I can see it in her eyes, how she looks at everything. But now—her leg is turned all wrong, and—

It all comes pushing up inside me, and I scream and scream and scream, but I don't make a sound. The scream bulges up inside me and puffs me out so big, it makes me nearly come to exploding. I look at Momma and see her eyes, and I see that there is nobody there anymore, and I try to run to the stairs. I get to the bedroom door, but she is right there, she moves so fast, and I can see the stairs down the hall through the door—I can see them, but I'll never make it, I'll never get to them. She's there, and I can't see the stairs anymore, and the scream is still puffing up inside me, feeling like throw-up.

Momma has my arm now, and still I'm not screaming, but I fight and kick and scratch at her. But she's too strong, she's twisting my arm hard, pulling me into the bedroom toward the bed. Toward the bed where they all are lying, Tan and Ninny and Suddle. When we get close to it, there is a horrible smell at the bed; someone has messed the bed, I can smell it, it's on the bed, in the covers, that smell, and she's dragging me over to it. I pull and pull, but there's nothing I can do to stop what is happening.

"Momma. Momma." I say the words, but all that's coming is the scream finally coming out, like the whole inside of me is coming out at once.

"It's time," she says. "Time to go to Fireless."

"But Momma, I don't want to go. I don't want to go."

She doesn't say anything else; her mouth is closed, her eyes are closed, and she has me almost to the bed now. I can see the pillows there, piled up in the middle of the bed. Momma pulls me very hard, and I fall on my back on the bed. Then she's taking my arms and pushing me down with both hands. Her hands are so big, her fingers are so long and big, and she's so much bigger than me and squeezing me so tightly.

Now she's pushing at me in the bed. I try to get up again, but she wants me lying down. She's pushing against my shoulders, and I'm rolling and pitching, trying to buck my legs and kick her off. I know if I stop moving, that's it. That's everything, the last of all the things there are in the world, but she fights and fights to hold me down, and all of the screams are gushing out of me now and I am throwing up, all my breakfast, everything, the cereal I had, it's spilling out around me, coming out my nose, making it burn. On my neck, around the back of my head, making it wet and warm.

I kick and shake and tear at her hands. Momma has a pillow now; she's holding it over me, then putting it down on me. She puts it down on my face, but I get my feet up against the pillow and push hard, hard as I can, but she pushes down harder and harder. Now she is lying on top of the pillow on top of me and my legs shoot out straight because I can't hold them up anymore, and the pillow goes over my face.

I can't scream now. Can't speak. The pillow is over my face and my whole world is on me in the bunches of pillow. But can't she see? Can't Momma see that I can't breathe this way? That the pillow is smothering me? Why won't she let me up? What is she doing? What is she doing? I know, but it's so bad, I can't tell myself that I know. I can't let that in, or every bad thing will come in with it.

Everything is coming out of me now, coming out warm and squishy and wet, making a big mess on the bottom of my legs. I can't breathe. I can't breathe. Oh, Momma, oh God, I can't breathe. And this is what I know—this is it, the death, here it is, this is the pillow she used to smother my sisters, and now she is smothering me.

It's the most surprising thought ever. I can't take it in. My face is not in the world anymore, it's in outer space, it's moving in outer space, but everything is crushing me, black, black, dark hot bad going down down down—it's the bad place, the dark place, I'm falling down into it—

Then the pillow is off of me. The pillow is up and it's gone, and the big huge weight of Momma's body and all her muscles, it's all gone. I feel her moving away; I'm choking, trying to breathe, feeling myself getting bigger again, coughing and trying to breathe and smelling my throw-up, but I can't see. My eyeballs are bent. They feel like they can never see again, they've been pushed too far into my head.

But they are starting to see again—there is light coming now, and I hear something moving in the room away from the bed. There is something falling and moving very close. I hear Momma making noises, and I want to scream again. But these noises are the kind of noises she makes when she needs to move something very heavy. What? What? I lift my head, and there is a man there, a man I don't know; Momma and the man are holding each other with their hands and moving and falling and pushing.

I'm crying. I can't stop crying. It seems like that's all I've ever done is cried and cried and screamed and messed myself.

My eyes are almost the right shape again, and I can see better, and the man—he's holding her. I can start to see. The man is pulling Momma away; her legs are banging the walls, leaving black marks on the blue paint. And the man has Momma's hair in one of his hands. I don't know this man. I don't know this man who is pulling Momma away from me. He is yelling something now, not cursing anymore, but yelling something at me.

"Run!" he is yelling. "Run!"

He yells it over and over. I'm trying to get up from the bed and the mess and the wet. But Tan and Ninny and Suddle won't move. They can't move, they can only watch. I think about them, what I should do, but the man is screaming at me, and I'm out of the bed now, but falling, my legs won't hold me up. I can see the man against the dresser with Momma; she is almost knocking him down, and his face is very red, teeth showing, eyes angry, mouth spitting. His arms are across Momma's chest, pulling her to him.

There's nowhere I can go, but the man is still screaming

at me. I don't know what to do. So the man keeps pulling on Momma, and I can see the door now. And I'm crawling toward the bedroom door, now getting up, starting to run, and I can see the stairs—I didn't think I would see the stairs ever again. I run down the stairs fast, stumbling, almost falling, and when I get to the bottom, the man is yelling at me to run outside, just go, keep going. And I do. I fly away into the grass and then across the grass into the fields, just running and running, until I see the trees. And when I'm through the trees, there is the creek, and I'm falling into it, dirty, filthy, running until I fall in the crawdad stream.

sixty

I see all this in an instant, with Momma in the center of that instant. My eyes focus again, bringing me back to the present. I see her standing impossibly before me.

She's at least six inches taller than me. Her arms are long, fingers long, shoulders broad. She's wearing stretchy blue pants, a short-sleeved white shirt, and white sneakers, the kind someone might wear on a boat.

At last I dare to look closely at her face. It's fuller—she has gained weight. The long tangle of bangs is gone—her hair is pulled back from her forehead and tied with a circle of white yarn. Her small eyes are brown and unblinking. I'm looking into them now.

There's a moment of suspended time where neither of us speak. I'm trying to believe she's really here—a picture rises from deep in my subconscious. A picture that has been locked in darkness ever since she put it there. A picture of me holding a gun. A completely crazy picture of me holding a gun and putting it to her chest—not her head. A picture of me putting the gun against her chest and pulling the trigger, blowing her heart out her back—

"Do you want to take my blood?" she says.

Her voice is even and steady. A little deeper than I remember. I am chewing my teeth, grinding them against one another. The image of the gun—the thought of the center of her body exploding in a huge velvety red cloud—I can feel the weight of it in my mouth, the huge red filth of the blast blurring my eyes. I'm holding my hands in fists; I spread my fingers trying to stop them trembling.

The years have evaporated. There is just me and you, Momma. There is nowhere else, and there never has been. A scream, half rage, half terror, hangs in my throat, waiting to hit the air. So this is what my life comes down to. This one last time with her. This chance to finish.

My eyes flick from Momma's hands to her face, then back to her hands. My body is morphing into a flame. My mind is sloshing in my head like heated oil. Do it to her, I think. Do it now. Do it with your bare hands. That's what she wants. That's what she needs. She needs to get loose from this. That's what I can do for her. Kill her. Set her free.

A lawn mower roars by outside the shuttered window, and the sound is so huge, it bursts the moment open, makes it feel monstrously shameful.

"Oh, Jesus," I say, the bubble of fury temporarily pricked. I'm alone. In this room. With her. Momma opens her mouth and slowly licks her thin lips.

"Do you want my blood?" she says again.

I can only think about the door, how she is blocking the door, how Nix is far up the hall locked away somewhere—

Momma's watching me, waiting for an answer. I feel her gaze like radiation on my skin. There's something about her face—a tight kind of translucence—that reminds me of a doll.

The lawn mower pushes past the room again, the growling whine getting louder and louder, commanding us to listen. Then it's gone, leaving behind the stink of gasoline exhaust and freshly cut grass. Momma's still watching me, eyes unblinking. I can see a single strand of white hair on top of her head that has lifted up from the mass and is bent in several places, like a wire.

"Are you the new doctor?" she says.

"No," I say at last, trying not to sound as terrified as I feel.

She takes a step toward me, eyes narrowing, big hands shaking slightly. Maybe—maybe I can slow her down if I keep her talking.

"I'm not—I'm not a doctor," I say quickly. I search the room with rapid glances—nothing. There's nothing here I can defend myself with. But at least she stops coming forward.

"I'm here because of your letter," I say. "The letter you sent through Mr. Carruthers."

"I don't remember," Momma says.

"You don't remember?"

"I don't remember."

I take the letter out and shake it open, holding it out so she can see it. I would hand it to her, but I can't let her get that close to me. "You invited me to come," I say. "Don't you know who I am?"

Momma frowns, head tilted down at an odd angle. "I don't remember."

"It's been eleven years," I say, struggling to sound calm.

"Look at me. Don't you remember me? You used to have four daughters. I'm one of them. I'm Francine."

I wait for her to scream, for her head to explode, but nothing happens. Is she drugged? What is wrong with her?

Then I see it. A single tear is tracking slowly down her face. I watch it all the way until it collects in a droplet on her jaw. She doesn't wipe it away. Her hands are just as still as if they have never moved. Have never held me down, have never—

"Shine," she says.

sixty-one

My legs are hollow. My arms. My whole body is hollow.

"Yes, Momma. It's me. It's . . ." I have trouble saying the name out loud in this room. "It's Shine."

"Shine is dead," Momma says. "She died."

My stomach tightens. "No. I'm not dead. I'm here. Can't you see it's me?"

"All of them are dead," she says. "They're dead. The girls—they're all dead." She bobs her head up and down slightly as if confirming this. "There was an . . . accident. A terrible accident. They died."

It's not warm in here, but I have to swipe at perspiration on my upper lip. "Please listen to me. I'm Francine. I'm Shine. This is me. Eleven years older. I didn't die. Somebody—somebody came. Somebody came in the house that day and stopped it. They saved me. Don't you remember?"

She puts a fist to her forehead, squinting her eyes shut. "Wait," she says.

Her lips begin moving soundlessly as if reciting something to herself. The lawn mower screams by again, threatening in its stench and unnatural roar. She takes her fist away and looks at me again.

"I need to sit down," she says. "Can I sit down?"

I look at the white leather chair against the far wall—at least that will take her away from the door. I point to it. "You—you can sit there," I say.

She walks to it slowly, never taking her eyes off me. I feel dizzy. I need to sit down myself, but I don't dare, with her in the room. I walk to the door instead, trying to look nonchalant. As I suspected, it's locked. I hoist myself up to the window and look out—the hall appears empty. I give the door a couple of hard bangs with my fist. "Hey! Let me out!" I call, trying not to sound panicked. Nobody comes.

Momma is still sitting in the chair, watching me. I look at her with her knees close together, arms crossed in her lap, and shudder. What is going through her mind? What can she be thinking? Does she want to—?

"I'm ready," she says.

"Ready? Ready for what?" I say.

"You."

Jesus. I have no idea how long we've been in here. Ten minutes? Thirty? An hour? The monster waits.

Okay, I think. What would Nix want me to do? I already know the answer to that question. Whatever happens, I have to go through with this—this is why I came. To find out what I need to know. I clear my throat to make my voice loud.

"Momma—do you remember—do you remember what happened? When we were a family? Do you remember what happened to my sisters?"

"They died. I told you that."

"Yes, I know, but—do you remember how they died?

Do you remember what you were doing?" I pause, looking deeply into her dark, dark eyes. I've arrived at the place I've feared most of all. The question to end all questions. "Do you remember why?" I say. "Why you did what you did?"

Momma closes her eyes and puts a fist to her forehead again. Her silent lips move almost angrily. At last she opens her eyes.

"I was watching David Letterman."

"No, I mean when—"

"I was watching David Letterman on TV," she says, eyes wet. "That was the first time."

"The first time what?"

Her left foot begins tapping the leg of the chair. "After Ninny was born I was watching David Letterman. Everything was black. It was black. He was doing that thing—that thing where he looks out the window. He was holding something out the window—he was going to let it drop on the street. And then I saw it wasn't a watermelon he was holding—he was holding *Ninny*. He was holding my baby Ninny. David Letterman was holding Ninny out the window, and he dropped her. He dropped Ninny straight down out of a high, high window, and she fell, and her head splattered on the sidewalk."

Her foot is tapping faster and faster. Her voice is quiet, but I understand every word.

"All day it was black," she says. "Everything was black. I tried to swallow a bottle of pills, and they took me to the hospital. Your father took the TV away. But the black came again after Suddle was born. I was afraid. I knew I had to protect you. I had to send you somewhere where the black couldn't get at you. I had to send you somewhere safe."

I swipe at my hot, wet eyes. "Fireless?" I say. "Is that what you thought you were doing? Sending us to Fireless?"

The violent tapping stops. Just as if she had closed a door or turned off a blasting faucet. Momma sits forward, pressing the heels of her hands into her eyes, rocking a little. The room feels unnaturally quiet.

"Fireless isn't real," she says. "It's not a real place. That was something—that was something I made up. I was *sick*. I made it up. It was all inside of me. The sickness made everything—it made it confusing. It made it black. I couldn't help it—I couldn't help you."

She cries for a little while, rubbing her hands over and over, as if washing them. Her fingernails look bitten.

"Your hands—" I say.

"They would hurt," she says. "They hurt so much I couldn't sleep. They gave me medicine to sleep, but I couldn't sleep. I could feel my hands all the time, and I couldn't sleep."

"Are you—are you okay, Momma?"

She nods and stops rubbing her hands. "I have a *capacity to distinguish*."

"Capacity to distinguish? What's that?"

"It's very important. That's why they could put me here. That's why they took me out of the other place."

"But what does it mean?"

She puts her fist to her forehead again, grimacing. But something different is happening now—she isn't speaking to herself this time. She screws her face up painfully and leans forward, hunching her back and rolling her shoulders.

"You want to watch them little gals," she says in a horrible, growling voice that I can feel in my spine. "I just might run off with them. I just might."

"Momma?"

Her eyes are half closed, lids heavy. "I ain't your goddamn momma," she says in the same growling voice.

The tiny hairs on the back of my neck lift. "Then who—who *are* you?"

"I'm the Bullard."

Shit. *The Bullard*—the Bullard was the imaginary monster Momma always warned us about that lived in the stump by the edge of the forest.

I shrink back against the door, scrabbling behind me for the handle. "But—the Bullard—the Bullard's not *real*," I say. "It's something you made up."

Momma's face immediately loosens, and she straightens up in her chair. Her eyes brighten until they are almost twinkling. "That is very good, Shine," she says in her regular voice. "You have a *capacity to distinguish* too."

Jesus. I ease back from the door, feeling myself relaxing a little. Just a little. My heart is slowing down. But I'm acutely aware of my breathing as I consider my last question. It's one I don't want to ask, but I have to ask.

"Momma, the blackness, what was it? What were you so afraid of?"

She stands up from the chair and holds herself, arms wrapped around her long torso, eyes darting back and forth as if she can see something in the room with us. The air feels like a piece of crystal about to shatter.

"I need to touch you," she says.

sixty-two

My chest floods with cold. Momma takes a step toward me—I'm cornered by the door.

"Please, I have to touch you."

"No," I say in a strangled voice. "I can't. I can't let you do that. I can't."

"But you have to," Momma says. "I need to touch you."

She reaches her arms out, palms up, slowly advancing. "Please."

"No." I say it louder. "No, stop. Go back and sit down, Momma."

She stops and stares at me, halfway across the room. Her expression is hard to read: half pleading, half menacing. I glance up; the little window in the door is empty. Where's Carruthers? I study the handle more closely—there's a hole below the handle that's too small for a key, probably something electronic. The little black object Carruthers is carrying—it must be some kind of keyless remote. If I could get it—

My head is turned a fraction of a second too long. Momma makes a noise, a kind of animal grunt—she's moving so fast, I can only recoil. There's nowhere to run—she slams into me with all her weight, pressing my back against the wall. I scream and fight to get my hands free, trying to claw her face. Momma pins my arms to my sides and squeezes me tightly, wrapping my whole body in a smothering embrace.

sixty-three

The force of the embrace crushes my face into her shirt. She's so strong—I can't get her arms off me. I want to gouge out her eyes, tear at her flesh, but I can't raise my hands, so I dig at the skin of her side through her shirt instead, trying to hurt her, rip her up. But there's nothing I can do, nothing that will make her let go. She's beyond feeling or pain or sensation. She's clutching me tighter and tighter, crushing my lungs until I can't breathe. *I can't breathe.*

Then something happens. Something completely strange and unexpected happens. It's nothing that Momma is doing—she's still holding me just as tightly. The change happens inside me. *Inside.* I realize Momma's not trying to smother me, she's only holding me, holding me as if she could absorb my molecules through her skin.

She's *hugging* me. Momma is hugging me. Hugging me as if she knows she will never get another chance to hug me ever again. Her hands, her long, cool fingers, move over my back, patting and smoothing. I don't know what to do with my own hands. Now that they are coming free, I don't know what to do with them. I can't hug her back. I just can't. But I've stopped fighting it. I can give her that. At least I can give her that.

My forehead is wet, and I realize she's weeping. Weeping over her last daughter.

sixty-four

I'm sitting on the couch, and Momma's back in her chair. Her eyes are swollen and red. We sit a long time without speaking. I guess each of us is trying to get a hold on the strange new way the world is turning. The lawn mower rushes by again, but farther away, losing strength, losing its hold over the room, over us. Momma looks at the shuttered window.

"I love fresh-cut grass," she says. "I love to smell it. I love to smell it in the morning."

"I know," I say.

"Do you remember the crawdad stream?"

"Yes. I remember the stream. Momma—you were afraid of *yourself*, weren't you? That was the blackness. That's what you were afraid of. Weren't you? You thought you were protecting us, putting us in a safe place."

She puts her hands together and looks away, doesn't say anything.

"Do you remember what it was like before?" I say. "Before all the—all the bad things happened? Do you remember the things we used to do, all the places you talked about—?"

"I remember the moon," Momma says. "I can still see it. I can see it inside my room at night. Do you know what the moon looks like in my window?"

"What? What does it look like?"

She smiles. "A bowl of potato soup."

"Oh. Yeah. I can see that. It kind of does."

"You can see it. You will see it tonight."

I look at her, trying to let her see how impossible this is in my eyes. "But I can't stay, Momma. I have to be going. I have to get out of here and find my friend."

"But you can see it the next time."

I let out a long sigh. "I don't think I can come again. This is kind of—it's a onetime thing."

"It's okay. Mr. Carl said you can come again."

"Mr. Carl? He works here?"

"Mr. Carl watches all of us. He helps us remember things. I didn't remember this is the day for the doctor."

I turn and kneel on the back of the couch, looking for a latch on the shuttered windows. I run my finger along the cold sill.

"We're locked in, Momma. We need to get out. Do you know how to open these?"

"She won't help you," a voice says.

sixty-five

The door clicks shut, and R. C. Carruthers is standing there. He's holding a manila envelope.

"Mr. Carl," Momma says.

He ignores her, watching me instead. A chill runs up my back.

"*You're* Mr. Carl?" I say. My voice is barely more than a whisper.

"My first name is actually Robert, but I've never liked it. They call me by my middle name, Carl."

"They? Who—you mean you *work* here?"

Carruther's smile is a line. His fingers tighten on the envelope. "Frannie, one of the hardest things you run into when you're dealing with other people is this: you plan and you plan, but things never go quite the way you want them to."

"I—please—I don't know what you're talking about."

Carruthers takes a small bottle of breath spray from an inside pocket and gives his mouth two squirts. He coughs into his hand and puts the bottle away again.

"I'm sorry, but I gave you a chance, and you didn't take advantage of it. You didn't finish it. That is why we are here. We have to finish."

My knees feel loose. The realization comes with so much force, I almost collapse.

"The letter. My letter—you wrote it, didn't you? You wrote it yourself. Just to get me to come here—"

I stop. The police aren't coming. My parents don't know we are here. Carruthers—God, I've let him separate me from Nix. This is something else—*it's something else.*

Carruthers takes a step toward me and begins slowly unwinding the red string that's holding the manila envelope shut. He glances at Momma. She's sitting there motionless, seemingly uninterested.

"It's almost easy, after seeing her, to start to forgive, isn't it?" Carruthers says. "She's a broken human being. You feel sorry for her. You might even want to help."

"Please, Mr. Carruthers. I won't say anything. I swear. Please, just let us go."

He takes another step toward me, still unwinding the string.

"They say we should be compassionate. They say she's not responsible. She was ill. She couldn't help herself. But we know the truth, Frannie. We know what she really is."

I feel tears beading in the corners of my eyes. "But she's not—she's *not* a monster. I used to think that. But—she *was* sick. She had a horrible sickness—"

Carruthers takes another step until he's only an arm's length away; I hear him breathing through his thin nose. He opens the flap on the manila envelope and pulls out a single sheet of paper. He lets the sheet go, and it flutters down to the coffee table.

My legs won't hold me anymore; I have to slump against the couch. The sheet of paper is a Xeroxed photograph of Suddle, my baby sister. She's lying on a blanket covered with long-eared rabbits. Her mouth is wet, eyes gleaming. Her puffy feet are raised over her diaper. Her fists are so soft, they look swollen.

I swallow. "I didn't think I would—ever see her again—where—where did you get this—?"

"Don't you ever wonder what she could have become?" Carruthers says. "What any of them could have become? We will never know, will we? Such a waste."

I look up at him; his hollow eyes are drooping.

"The world is full of throwaway people," he goes on. "You know that, don't you? Disgusting, useless, damaged, *broken* people. People who don't deserve to be here. But . . ." He lifts his arms slightly, palms up, as if to say, "Here they are."

Broken people—my mind floods with images: Rickey Thigpen, Brandon, Daddy, Momma. He could even be talking about me.

Carruthers begins wringing the empty envelope into a tube, twisting it so violently, the paper is shrieking. He drops the tube on the floor. The lizard smile turns hard.

"I had a daughter," he says, voice choking. "She was seven. The same age as you when your mother—when your mother did what she did. Threw them all away like *garbage*. My daughter—there was an accident. I had to watch her slip away—"

"Please. What do you want?" I say, starting to sob. "Please—tell me what you—"

"This *bitch*," Carruthers says. The word explodes from his mouth so hard, I feel little flecks of spit on my arms, my cheeks. He's looming over me, pointing at Momma. She's not even shifting in her chair. "I want to watch her *die*."

Everything, my blood, my skin—my soul—it all feels as if it's pulling away from me. Tears are streaming down my face. This can't be happening. I don't know what to do, what to say.

Carruthers straightens up. He takes a long, shuddering breath and brushes his hair with trembling fingers. He exhales, and I can taste his breath spray in my own mouth. He reaches into the big side pockets of his suit coat. When he withdraws his hands, he's holding a coiled red extension cord and a white plastic garbage bag. He puts them on the table in front of me.

"What is that? What is that?" I say. "Oh God, please. You want me to—you expect me to—" I can't say the word, but I have to say the word. I have to. "You want me to *kill her*. You want me to *kill her*."

The muscles in Carruthers' face tighten. "Yes," he says, speaking with a dangerous softness. "I can't do it—it can't be me who does it. That wouldn't be right. That wouldn't be *correct*. But you—anyone would understand if it were you."

"I can't," I say, sobbing harder. "I could never—I could never do that."

"I know," Carruthers says. "I know that now. It hurts me—you can't imagine how much it hurts me. How disappointed I am in you. How you have let me down. But there is another way."

Carruthers lunges at me and catches my wrists in his hands. I can feel them—the long fingernails cutting into my skin as he pins me to the couch. The scent of wintergreen surrounds my head like a shroud.

sixty-six

When I die—

I wonder who I will see first. Will it be Tan, her busy hands hunting for colored stones in the slippery creek? Ninny, with her fear of spiders and love of the rain? Will it be Suddle, coming to let me hold her again? But how could a baby guide you into the afterlife?

"Why didn't you hear me?" Tan says. "Why didn't you hear me, Shine?"

"Be quiet. I'm thinking."

"Why didn't you hear me? I was six years old. You should have heard me. I was strong. If you had heard me and come running, between the two of us—"

"You know why. I was hiding. Somehow I knew something was going on."

"But why didn't you hear Ninny? Why didn't you hear Suddle?"

"They had a pillow over their faces. So did you."

"But I would have been kicking and screaming like crazy. Why didn't you hear me? If you had come, we might have stopped her. I was strong."

"Leave me alone."

"It's not that easy, Shine. There has to be a reason."

"Are you saying I *let* it happen to you?"

"*Let* is a slippery word. I'm just asking a question. I've always wondered about it."

"So are you saying I could have done something, and I chose to not do anything?"

"Well."

"Well."

"I've just always wondered about it," Tan says. "You've got to admit, it doesn't make any sense. I was so strong."

"You've said that. About a million times."

Wherever I am, the light is fading. I watch the fading of everything around me, interested.

"I know what you're doing," Tan says. "You can't hide from me."

"Don't you think I know that? I'm just thinking. The house—it happened upstairs. I was downstairs. Maybe the washing machine was going. Maybe I thought you were just playing with her."

"Can't you tell the difference?"

"The difference what?"

"The difference between playing and getting murdered. The sound is completely different."

"Like you would know so much. Don't make fun of me. I was seven."

"I'm not making fun of you, just wondering."

"I wouldn't do that to you. I wouldn't leave you up there with that happening, I wouldn't. You know I wouldn't, Tan."

"What if you were afraid? What if you heard it all, and you were so afraid, all you could do was hide?"

"I said I wouldn't do that to you. You were my sister. I would rather—"

"You would rather what?"

"Nothing."

"You were about to say it, weren't you? You would rather die. You wish it had been you up there, and me hearing it, didn't you? I could have run away. Saved myself. That's what you're thinking, isn't it, Shine?"

"I don't know."

"I need to know."

All the light is gone now. It's black. Everything is black. When I die—

sixty-seven

I can see only blackness and starry flashes behind my eyelids. Something is over my mouth, over my eyes. Something
is holding my arms to my sides. I can't move my legs. I can't
hear anything but my own breathing and the squeaking of
shoes on a tile floor.

I can feel something looped around my neck, drawing
tighter and tighter. Cutting off my air. I can't scream. I'm
in that country that is beyond shock, that place my mother
entered that final morning.

Then—

Floating. Nothing but floating. Nothing to worry about
in the whole wide world. Everything done. Finished. Maybe
I've gone back. Maybe I've gone all the way back inside. To
the dark place in the very beginning. But I know nothing
about any of this, nothing about anything. Until the world
is suddenly in front of me, and my own little window on it
is ripped open.

I can see. I can see. For a moment everything is white,
pure gleaming white, and I'm waiting for them, whoever is
there to get me, to take me into the whiteness. But then I can
see objects—the edges of the walls, the diamonds in the ceiling, furniture, everything sharp and defined and beautiful as

anything I've ever seen. This must be the House of the World.

But then there is a movement, and large, large hands tearing at whatever is over me. I see Momma's face before me, see her biting her lip, breathing intently, concentrating, her hands pulling and ripping. And she looks so much like Tan at just that instant, I almost believe I could be wherever Tan must be.

The hole is made larger. Momma tears away more and more of the garbage bag. I can see the cheap plastic furniture, the digital clock, the coffee table, the couch, her big hands and arms working fast and hard, eyes glittering.

She pulls at the extension cord, unwinding it from my arms, my legs. I can feel the couch under my back and something warm and wet beside me. A man. The crown of his head looks dented, something spilling over the edges of the hole like the lobes of some dark new fruit. A halo of red is soaked into his white hair.

I stop looking, and Momma keeps bringing me into the room. For a while everything after I arrive in her arms feels like a kind of sightless sleep.

sixty-eight

I'm moving. Somehow I'm moving, but I'm lying down. The mattress on this bed is thin, too thin. The bed is narrow. I'm rocking in it, rocking my mind through one place of whiteness to another place of whiteness. I'm also moving in and out of myself.

"Too bright in here," I say, thick-tongued. "I'm all feeling—exposed."

"Shhh," Nix says, stroking me and kissing my forehead. "Shhh. Don't think. Sleep. Try to sleep. I love you." The siren carries us away.

sixty-nine

The house *feels*. That's the only way to say it; it *feels*—to say anything else would be saying less. Rain begins to patter against the windows. From here I can see a single black cylinder of cloud rolling across the sky like an advancing guard. The grandfather clock ticks. I'm sitting at the dining room table with my family, not speaking. Even Wiggles and the Thumb have lost their voices. I'm engulfed in their concern; I'm drowning in it.

Dad sits at the far end of the table, red-faced, hunched over his beef Stroganoff, shoulders and back pumped with compressed air. A twist of a valve, and he'll blow three thousand psi all over somebody.

I look at my mother. My *real* mother. The one who cooks my meals, washes my clothes, teaches me things about makeup I don't need to know. What this has done to her. Tonight her hair is uncharacteristically blown up, electric— you could demagnetize a credit card running it through those curls. Her eyes are worse. Dark circles, puffy from lack of sleep and crying.

Her hands are unsteady as she ladles out the sauce. She starts to speak, stops. Starts again. Looks at my father and pinches her lips together painfully. I look back at my plate.

I don't make a face so she won't know, but I can't eat this broccoli. I can't. It's overcooked, falling to pieces in my mouth. I chew and chew, trying to pretend something is there, but nothing is there; I have to swallow it in a pasty mush.

Every supper is like this now. This terrified, venomous quiet. The dead, metallic clacking of silverware—I'm slowly going insane. If I have to do this much longer, I'll lose my mind. I really will. Somebody say something. Anything is better than this corrosive silence.

"Nix," I whisper to my spoon.

For nearly a month I've spoken his name aloud each time I think of him until it has become a kind of prayer. I wonder where he is right now. Alone, somewhere in the middle of the dark continent, lost without his navigator?

I feel my throat constrict and push my plate away. "I'm sorry, Mom. I'm not very hungry."

"That's all right, honey."

They follow me up the stairs with their eyes. I feel as if I'm under house arrest. This is how it goes, night after night. They've taken my cell phone away. Nix is strictly verboten. I'm on the homebound teaching program, the program for kids with diseases, kids in full body casts from car wrecks. They're so afraid of losing me, they're killing me off themselves.

I flop on my bed and look at the stack of books on my nightstand. I pick up the one on top, flipping drearily through it. Everything I was reading before—before Fire Tree—feels as if those words passed through someone else's eyes. I can't go back. But I can't start a new one either. Like the broccoli, it's all pasty and meaningless. I can't chew it anymore.

My room is littered with greeting cards, most telling me to get well when I was never sick. The only thing I like anymore is sleeping, or trying to. Each night my bed lifts off and carries me over highways and hills and trailers and chicken farms and rift valleys. Back to the Shayland Motel. Room 16. The left side of the bed.

I can still feel every second of the time we spent there. Not being able to touch him is like being denied food, water, light—no, it's like having my air cut off. Worse. I can endure my body shriveling away to nothing, but my soul—

Then it comes to me. It comes to me just as surely as if I had gotten up in the middle of the night looking for the moon and found it right there. In my window. A bowl of potato soup.

I get up from the bed and pick up the greeting cards, one after another, and cram them in the trash. Then I stomp downstairs and plunk myself on the couch between them.

"I have to talk to you."

"What, darling, what is it?" Mom says, muting the TV. Onscreen a bubbly redhead is selecting colors from a color wheel, as if that's the final solution to everything the world throws at you—a new scheme for your walls. Dad puts down the sports section with a violent snap.

"I want to go back to school. Tomorrow. I know you don't want me to see Nix, but I have to go back. I can't stand living like this. You have to trust me. You *have* to. I can't live like this anymore, like I've got some terminal disease. I won't."

The words hang in the air between us. Mom looks at Dad, looks at me, then back at Dad again.

Dad slips into what I've always thought of as his football stance—weight forward, elbows close to his knees. "What do you want, Button?" he says. "Somebody else to find you? Someone crazy, looking to—"

"Don—" Mom says.

"Not my daughter. If that's what you think, why don't you go talk to somebody who doesn't care about his children."

"That's just it," I say. "I'm not a child anymore—I'm eighteen. I'm not your little girl anymore. I'm growing up. Don't you see that? I'm growing up, and you don't even know. You're so used to protecting me, babying me—"

"Isn't that what parents do?" he says. "We don't want to baby you; we just want to be here for you, keep you safe, help you—"

"But I feel like I'm being smothered—my whole life, that's what it feels like. I'm being *smothered*, one way or the other."

"Christ, Button. A man *died*. You nearly *died*—"

"We're as much to blame as she is," Mom says. "More. To think we let that—that *person* sit at my table, without asking any more questions than we did—"

"You think I'm going to sit still and—"

"Wait," I say, falling back against the couch. "Just *wait*. We've been through this over and over and over. Please just listen for once. *Please.* You can't understand what it was like after I got that letter. Anybody who didn't go through what I went through could never understand. It made me crazy. I just wanted to live my life. But after that I had to know. I had to know. I had to go see her."

"You're right, darling, I don't understand," Mom says. "Why? Why did you have to see her?"

I look at them both, hands clawing at the couch cushions. "I had to know if I—if it could happen—if it could happen to *me.* If I was going to grow up to be—just like her. *Just like her.*"

"You'll never be like her, Button," Dad says. "We'll make sure of that."

"No. You can't. That's the thing about it, Dad. You can't. But you know what you can do?"

"What?"

"She was isolated. She was so, so isolated. I think—I think she could have gotten some help, I really do. There were so many *good* things about her once. You don't know anything about that. You've only seen the monster. She could have been helped. If anyone had been there. If anyone could have seen it coming. My sisters—they would all be alive. Please. Please don't do the same thing to me. You have to let me go. You have to."

"But you'll always be our little Button, you know that," Dad says.

A blind fury rises inside me. "I—I don't want to be your little Button anymore. I don't want to be safe anymore. I want to do things. I want to know people. I want to go places that aren't prefab little rich person wonderland *shithouses.*"

Both of them gasp. I've never cursed in front of them before. I don't even know what I've just said. They let go. Pull back from me. I feel the tears coming, hot on my cheeks.

"I love you. I love you both so much," I say. "But I want to move on with things, that's all. I'm so tired—tired of being afraid all the time. I want experiences. I want to try things. I'm so ready for this. I really am. Don't hold on so tight."

seventy

"Breathe," Ann Mirette says.

For once the Ant Table is chattering loudly enough for us not to be heard.

"God," I say. "Is it my imagination, or is everybody looking?"

"Screw 'em. You're a celebrity."

I immediately feel sick to my stomach. "Oh no. What have you told people?"

"Only that you ran off to South Carolina with the weirdest, coolest guy in school and had to spend a month in the D-home."

"Oh. Jesus. Thanks a lot."

"No problem, girl. Betcha you have seventeen offers for the prom next year. Man, it's so good to see you. You want this?" She stabs my unbuttered roll with her knife.

"I'm not hungry," I say. "If only Nix were here. I can't believe he's gone—today of all days—"

"You never listen. I told you last night he'd be over at the armory practicing for 'Pump and Circumcision.'"

"I can't believe he's about to graduate, either. That I have a whole year of school to face without him here. I'll probably never see him again."

Ann Mirette bites the roll in half and pats my shoulder consolingly. She talks around her chewing. "No way. If Nix survived your dad, he'll survive anything. You'll figure something out. Count on it. But on to bigger and better things. I've been waiting weeks to hear the rest of the details. Spill."

I knew this was coming. "I don't really want to talk about it."

"Come on, Frances." Ann Mirette looks left and right. "You couldn't hear the Second Coming in here."

"It's not—it's not that. It's just—you don't know what it's like—coming that close—all over again. The nightmares—"

"Bad?"

"Worse."

"Maybe this is what you need then. Talking about it— you know, all that therapeutic crap."

"Like I haven't already been talking to somebody twice a week."

"Damn, girl. What do they say? The psychiatrist."

"Psychologist. She actually says I *should* talk about it. But—"

"There you go. Look. I promise, I won't bug you about it anymore. Not after today."

"Okay. Okay." I let out a big sigh. "But you already know pretty much everything. Carruthers wasn't a lawyer. He traveled around the country installing security systems. He found Momma by accident when he was working at Fire Tree. The fake letter—"

"Surface junk. Blah, blah, blah." Ann Mirette leans in closer. "Let's get down to the *meat*. I've got to know the *why*. What set him off in the first place?"

"This is all I know, really. Carruthers lost his daughter in a car crash. It was the same day Momma—well, the same day. Carruthers was at the hospital—watching his daughter *die*—and he saw the story about Momma on the news. And apparently he just completely snapped."

"So the same day he loses his kid, he sees your mom basically flush hers down the toilet," Ann Mirette says. "I'm sorry."

"Don't worry about it. Then to make things worse, she cheats the system and gets off scott free. At least that's the way he saw it."

"So how'd he find you?"

"I don't know. Just looked hard enough, I guess. They got into his apartment—the police—and there were articles and pictures of Momma and my family all over the place. And things Carruthers wrote in a little notebook. Apparently he was obsessed with the whole thing."

"No shit. Keep going."

"But that's it, really."

"Wait—tell me this—it doesn't make sense. All these years Carruthers has been getting freakier and freakier, then he runs into your Mom, and it's like a sign or something. Okay, I get that—so he's obviously the one who's supposed to finish her off since everybody else dropped the ball."

"Something like that, yeah."

"So if Carruthers was such a big hairy badass, why didn't he just do it himself? He had plenty of chances. What's the deal with that?"

"I don't know. Divine retribution? Eye for an eye? Anyhow, the way he talked, it had to be me."

"Only it didn't work out the way he figured."

"No. So I had to die instead. Then Carruthers could set it up where Momma gets the blame."

Ann Mirette taps the side of her head leaving a crumb dangling in her thick hair. "She's just finishing what she started. And since she's been declared competent—"

"Capacity to distinguish," I say, feeling a pang of guilt, as if I'm betraying a confidence.

"Right, okay," Ann Mirette says. "Whatever. So Carruthers knew this time there was a good chance your mother would be turned into a crispy critter."

I look down at the fried chicken on my tray. "Please, can't we talk about something else?"

"Hang on a second—there's just one more thing I've *got* to know. What did she use to cold cock the perv?"

"God."

I start to get up from the table; Ann Mirette jerks my arm, pulling me back, eyes apologetic. "Aw, come on, Frances. I'm sorry. Inquiring minds and all. Please chill. I've missed you too much."

"Just remember, this isn't something for your stupid blog."

"Okay. Okay. I'm *sorry*."

"Besides, I don't know what it was. Some heavy blunt object. That's all I ever heard them say. I don't know where she got it. The arm of the chair. A table leg."

"The whole table, maybe. You said she was strong."

"I don't know. Jesus."

"So it's over, then."

"I hope."

"Except?"

I stir my cooling carrots. "There's still the trial and everything. God."

"But you already gave your deposition, right? And the lawyer said he didn't think it would get past the grand jury. Self-defense."

"Not exactly."

"Well, she was defending *you*. She had to do it. It won't be too bad. If you have to go back—"

"I'll have to go back."

"Okay, so *when* you go back, I'll go with you? Okay? How about that? It'll be all right. And this time we *will* do the beach. Fort Sumter. The whole deal. You need a vacation, big-time."

"I don't know," I say, feeling listless. "I don't know what I need."

"What is it? What's wrong?"

"It's just—I don't know. I was thinking about Momma sitting there, all by herself. Probably wondering what in the world has happened to me. I almost wonder if it's a bad thing that she knows I'm alive. But I can't go back. I don't think I can ever go back."

"Can't say I blame you."

"And what's to keep somebody else from finding me? That's what terrifies my parents. When does it ever end?"

Ann Mirette touches my shoulder. "I hate to tell you, but something like this, with the 'Net? Maybe never. You'll just have to be more careful than most people. More aware the possibility is out there. Some nut with a Webcam goes up to Tennessee to your old house and—"

"Wait a minute."

"What?"

I stand, picking up my tray. "Just thinking. Let's go."

seventy-one

It's funny that I like this place. The noise of the pounding machinery. The shuffling workers moving through the various stages of production. The awful dust everything churns up, all of it reminding me this gigantic operation is devoted to feeding animals. The ubiquitous checkerboards, scratched and stained and pitted. The rumbling, smoky trucks winding endlessly beneath the drop chute. The corrugated sheet metal walls. The towers that go up and up like grain elevators. The steel catwalks over the shop floor. I'm standing on one right now, looking down at it all, my father's kingdom.

I'm thinking about him coming here every day. Seeing this same building, the same people, tasting that dust for twenty, thirty years. For some reason it makes me feel it all the more, the chance I'm about to take. I press my cell phone to my ear, talking to Nix.

"I miss you so much," I say. "Remember that."

"Crazy," Nix says.

I flatten my hand over my other ear to shut out the throbbing dog food madness.

"What?"

"I said I get the feeling you're about to do something crazy."

"Gotta go," I say. "Dad's coming. I'll call you tonight."

"What?"

"Tonight. Tonight."

I click the phone shut and put it away as Dad comes along the catwalk. He looks worried, is frowning about something.

"What is it?" I say.

"Nothing, Button. Come on up."

We make our way to his office—the metal stairs are so steep, if I slip, I would just keep on going, all the way to the production floor. But I almost run up them. The door shuts thankfully behind us. The noise is almost blocked out, but—

"It's always so cold in here," I say, taking a seat at his little conference table. "How can you stand it, Dad?"

"Huh? Oh. I'm just used to it, I guess. You should feel it in winter. The heat comes right up from the shop—you broil up here."

The phone rings three times in a row while I unwrap the food, sub sandwiches. He still isn't looking at me, is preoccupied with something.

"What's wrong?" I say when he sits down.

"Oh, nothing. Just work. You know how it goes."

"Not really."

He smiles exhaustedly. "So what's the special occasion?"

"Well." I wonder if I should just blurt it out, if it would be less painful that way, like ripping off a Band-Aid. "I was thinking about something I wanted to talk to you about."

"Yeah? What is it?" He takes a huge bite of his toasted ham and pastrami, chewing distractedly.

I look around the office, swallowing. The walls are soaked

in Alabama Crimson Tide football paraphernalia. It's like a shrine. The colors, crimson and white, work perfectly with the company color scheme. Even Bear Bryant's hat has a checkerboard on it. Here goes.

"You always said you would help me if I ever needed you. Well, I need this, Dad. I really, really need this—"

He lifts the sub sandwich to his mouth and takes another massive bite.

"I've decided to move in with Nix."

His face instantly turns crimson, the color of his team, and for just a moment I'm terrified he has stopped breathing—he coughs hard several times, getting it under control again, sputtering.

"I'm sorry," I say. "I'm kidding. I thought if maybe I joked around a little first, it would be easier for you to say yes to what I really want."

"Button—"

"Please stop calling me that. My name is *Frances*. That's what I want you to call me from now on."

"I'll try."

I put my arms around his neck, hugging him. "I love you so much, Dad. You've always been my father. The only real father I'll ever have."

He wraps his big arms around me. "I love you too. Now why do I get the feeling I'm about to be taken to the cleaners?"

I pull back from him to where I can see his eyes, and he can see mine. "There's something I need you to do for me. A very big something."

rainbows

Today is a good day in Fireless. We're sitting at the table painting Easter eggs. First we dip them in vinegar with food coloring; then we stroke them with brushes. Tan is soaking her egg in color after color until it looks like clay.

Suddle is quiet in her bassinet. I see her toes come up and go down, see her catch at them and pull them to her mouth. Ninny is painting faces on all her eggs, happy, sad, angry, surprised. I can smell grass through the open window. Tomorrow Daddy will be home, and we will hunt for the eggs. I wonder about his beard: is it any longer, will he let me brush my fingers over it, does it still look reddish on his chin? Will he bring me something? Tan says he is bringing gum, that's all. That's what he brought last time, big packages of gum, ten packs in each package. I hid mine because Ninny was getting into it. I want more than gum. Daddy has been away a long time. I want to show him my basket. I start to put some of them in the fake grass. The eggs.

"The eggs are still wet," Momma says to me. She is holding a purple egg in a spoon. The tips of her fingers are purple. "But I like them like that," she says.

She takes the purple egg out of the spoon and holds it up to her cheek and rubs it there, making a purple smear.

Momma picks up a red egg and rubs it on her other cheek. Then a blue one for her forehead and a green for under each one of her eyes. I would say she looks like an Indian, but like no Indian I have ever seen. Maybe an Indian from another world, a place that doesn't have horses and tepees and cowboys, but fountains of color in the sky.

I look at Tan. Her eyes are grinning. She is thinking the same thing I am thinking. We take the eggs and start smearing our faces with egg paint. Then our arms, our legs, giggling more and more. A breeze is coming hard through the window now, making the white curtains move. The room is cold, but it's not a bad cold. Momma is laughing at us turning our bodies into rainbows.

But she isn't getting faster. She isn't getting more and more excited, and her eyes aren't scary and loud. She's happy, that's all—happy. I'm learning that happy is a resting kind of place. It's a place where things are in control. And that's where we are this minute. This is where I have to hold you, the only place that I can. Here in my head. I love you so much right now.

seventy-two

I grew up believing there are some things in life that are so terrible, if you do one of them, your life is instantly over. Your heart can still beat, your lungs still breathe, your eyelids flutter—but from that moment on, you're dead. You can never have a real life ever again. Your soul has been canceled. Switched off. Terminated. That's what I used to believe.

"You want me to go in with you?" Nix says.

"No. Thank you."

I step up to the small porch, then turn and look at him again.

"What?" he says.

"I should say something, but I don't know what I want to say."

"Don't worry," he says. "It'll come to you."

"Here's the thing, Nix. I've cried for my sisters a million times. I've cried for myself. But I've never cried for her. Not once. Not ever."

I put my hand on the ratty wood column, feel its roughness.

"The whole time—the whole time I kept thinking maybe she would ask me to forgive her, tell me she's sorry. But it's not her who needs forgiveness. It's me. It's *me*. Do you understand? She's not a Morlock, Nix. She's not. She's one of the Eloi."

Nix touches my hand.

"What are you thinking?" I say.

"Just that . . . you're—you're the bravest person I know."

"You don't have to say that. You don't have to."

"I know. But it's true." He moves close to me without touching. "Frances."

"What?"

"If—if she—if your mother is one of the Eloi, I was wondering . . . what does that make me?"

I put my arms around his neck and hug him to me. I don't know if he can hear what I am saying, but I say it anyway. "You're not one of the Eloi. But you're not a Morlock either. You're my Time Traveler."

seventy-three

I kick a teddy bear's worm-eaten head. The head goes spinning into the shadows, leaving its moldy body behind. The evening sun slants hard through the broken windows, painting the room with bands of light and shade. The spongy wood floor creaks under my shoes.

I have to be careful where I step. The room is covered with shards of glass, chunks of brick and stone, bundles of plastic flowers tied in rotting ribbons. In some places the trash is so thick, all I can do is shuffle, pushing it in front of me with my toes. But I move through the house as best I can, sloshing kerosene on the floor. The familiar scent invades my nose like an alien atmosphere.

The wall in front of me is completely covered with writing in paint, ink, crayon, pencil, lipstick, Magic Marker, penknife. Hundreds of messages. Some big, some little, some illiterate, some not. I try not to read them.

I make a trip around the inside of each room, shaking the jug. More kerosene splashes my shoes as it comes out in pink snakes from the spout.

I save the upstairs for last. I wasn't sure I'd be able to go up there, but I find the steps and take them slowly, the jug clunking painfully against my legs. Halfway to the top I set it down to rest, breathing heavily. The floor on the landing feels soft, organic. I take up the jug again and go on.

I hesitate at the entrance to the bedroom. I haven't been in here in eleven years. I take a breath, smelling leaf mold, peeling sheetrock, musty air thick with something I can't identify. I step through.

The bed is gone, of course. I stop holding my breath and slowly let it out. The room is empty except for mounds of composting flowers—these are real, a hundred thousand petals in a snowdrift of decay.

I shake the jug, and the mounds of dead petals collapse like spitting on cotton candy. This is the last time I will ever be inside this room. I stick my head out the hole where the window used to be. Blackbirds have settled on the sagging power line, watching. The sky is low; night is coming. Across the gravel road the pig corn rattles in the field, shucks dry as crepe paper. To the east a line of pin oaks runs beside the creek. I can't see it, but I know it's there.

I take the jug to the head of the stairs and set it down again. I wonder if I should say something, leave something behind.

"Momma," I say out loud. But maybe there is nothing that can be said. I should be saying good-bye to my sisters for the last time.

I start to say their names, but I can't say their names. The landing is dark—the only light is coming from the bedroom doors. "I'm sorry," I say. "I'm sorry I didn't hear you, Tan. I'm sorry I was so afraid." My voice breaks, and I sink to my knees. The floor is soft and warm. I can smell the kerosene I have spilt here. I bow my head and knit my hands together, but I can't pray. I'm not sure how to pray about this. Anything I can think of to say doesn't seem like it's enough.

I stay like that awhile, kneeling in the stink and rot. Then I get up and brush myself off and pick up the jug again and start down the stairs. The kerosene smell circles my head— so many voices in here. My heart is a mouth inhaling.

I wonder if this is true, Momma. Life is a war, and the families are the armies. Even if you win the war, some will never see you plant the flag.

But that's the thing about life—it breaks you over and over, and you have to live with the broken places. Knowing they are there. Feeling them every time there's a change or you love someone or miss someone or feel pitifully sorry for someone.

So what do I believe now about her soul? I don't know. I don't know. It might be one of those things you have to wait until you are dead to understand. One thing I'm sure of—death is a very big place. There is room for all kinds of people.

I leave the jug in the kitchen and take the box of Blue Diamond matches out of my pocket. The first match lights with a scratchy pop; the sulfurous ignition hangs in my nose. I'm standing next to Daddy's old kerosene heater. The name on the side says FIRELESS.

The whole floor doesn't catch right away, but when it finally does, the flame rises like a growing thing, sputtery and blue. I sit on the backs of my thighs and watch it, wondering if there is something I can do to help it along. But the flame is big enough now, spreading like a blue lake across the living room floor. I breathe my sisters' names into the fire and step outside.

Nix is rocking the FOR SALE sign back and forth. When it finally comes up he knocks the clay off and lays it in the back of the Navigator. I look at Mom—her bottom lip bunches and wrinkles her chin, her eyes melting. Dad is doing his best to smile, standing there next to her. He waves.

"Thank you." I only mouth the words, but he can read my lips.

The volunteer firefighters watch the burning house from their truck. Nobody moves to pick up a hose. We watch with them until it is dark. We don't meet anybody else, don't see any other lights, until we get all the way back to town. We can see the fire from four miles away. Then five. Then none.

THE END